BLESSED TWICE

Also By Lynn Galli

BLESSED TWICE

Lynn Galli

Penikila Press

Synopsis

The problem with starting over in another state after losing your partner is that your new friends don't understand why you can't just get over it. They never saw how you were together, how much you loved her, how she was your life. They only see a number: three, as in, the number of years since she died. That's all the evidence they need to begin pressuring you to get back out there again. It doesn't matter that you've told them to back off. No, they feel it is their duty to butt into your life and ambush you with blind dates.

This wasn't a predicament Briony Gatewood anticipated when she relocated for tenure at a prestigious university. Yet after a year with her new friends, they've ceased being merely concerned and moved on to obnoxious. As if being fixed up wasn't bad enough, the dean at her college just volunteered her to teach a potentially career damaging class. Along for the experimental course is the socially challenged M Desiderius, a fellow professor who won't ever win a faculty popularity contest. But as they start working together, Briony begins to understand M's aloofness and is intrigued by the shy, brilliant, passionate woman. Enough so that she's starting to believe her friends when they say it's time to move on. And M, as complicated as her past has been and reticent as she seems now, may be the perfect person to help Briony finally heal and love again.

Chapter 1

If I hadn't been trying to make a point, I would have skipped this April wedding. Unfortunately, my new group of friends needed to know that I wasn't heartsick over the nuptials. One of the brides needed to know it, too. The other already did, but my smiling appearance at this festive event would solidify it for everyone. It was the least I could do given how I'd been the stumbling block in my relationship with Jessie.

"Hi, Briony." Quinn joined me at the reception after the short ceremony. She'd been one of the few friends who treated me no differently as Jessie's date than in my new role now that I'd been adopted by her fabulous clan. Nearly everyone else handled me with kid gloves because they thought I'd been ruthlessly dumped by Jessie. It didn't seem to matter that she'd been the one to fold me into the group.

"Hello, Quinn. You look nice." I took in her dark suit, a nice compliment to Jessie's as her best woman. She'd gotten some sun during her spring break. The new tan magnified her attractiveness and added blond highlights to her honey brown hair.

"Thanks. That's a pretty dress." She looked over the dress that had taken me three shopping trips to find, all to help with the illusion that I was thrilled to be here. "Having a good time?"

"Sure. Beautiful wedding. Lauren looked gorgeous in her dress, and her dad was cute as a button."

"Cap is a riot," she confirmed about Lauren's dad. "I'll introduce you if you haven't met."

"Met who?" Another friend, Isabel, inquired as she and Caroline joined us. Like Quinn and me, she worked on campus where we'd all run into each other on our corner of the University of Virginia compound from time to time.

"Cap," Quinn answered.

Isabel frowned, the crinkles in her mocha colored brow didn't deter from the attractiveness of her face. "Oh, I thought you were going to introduce her to someone she could date."

"Isa!" Quinn admonished as I was objecting, "Hey!"

"Oh, come on, there's no better place to meet people than at a wedding. Everyone's already romantically inclined." Her thin black eyebrows scrunched up into sleek straight bangs.

"Yeah, what do you say? There are plenty of beautiful women here today," Caroline prodded. She and Isabel had become the two in the group I was closest to other than Jessie, whom I'd gotten to know well while we were dating, and Lauren, who had made it a point to get to know me better.

"Thanks, you guys, but no." I had to shut this down before any of them ran with it. I didn't need help finding dates. Or rather, I didn't want help finding dates. In fact, I didn't really want to date. The group was a little pushy, though, something that I was still getting used to.

"You haven't had a date in a year, Bri, not since..." Caroline and Isabel exchanged a knowing look.

Crap! Here we go again. "Jess and I are much better as friends. She's not the reason I haven't had a date in a while." No, that blame could only be placed on me.

"We just worry about you, hon. You're a fantastic person and no one special has gotten the benefit of that." Caroline took on the role of head cheerleader today.

"You're not ganging up on Bri, are you, ladies?" Jessie's sultry voice still sent a tickle up my spine. She pulled me close for a hug. "Hi there."

I gripped her briefly, trying not to stare. She was easily the most beautiful woman I've seen, an opinion shared by pretty much everyone. Her long, black, curly hair, dark brown eyes, perfectly sculpted face with a wide mouth that could stun you with a smile or a kiss had captivated many a person before me. "Congratulations, Jess. I'm so happy for you."

"Thanks. I don't know what I did to deserve her, but I'll be thanking anyone who'll listen for the rest of my life."

"Aww," Isabel crooned. "We don't know what you've done with our Jessie, but keep saying embarrassing things that we can use against her if she ever comes back."

Jessie shot her a bored glance, but the obvious elation on her wedding day broke through. "Get used to me, Isa. Thanks to Lauren, I'm here to stay."

"You better be," Lauren warned in an endearing tone as she joined us, slipping her arms around her new spouse for a light kiss before turning to me. "Thanks for coming, Briony. I'm so glad you cut your trip short to join us. It wouldn't have been the same without you." She bent her long, lithe frame to hug me.

"I wouldn't have missed it," I fibbed. I would have, but I felt I shouldn't. "You did a wonderful job putting this together. Thank you for inviting me."

"Of course." Her blue eyes sparkled at me. That dazzling red hair of hers practically glowed in the sky around her. I was glad to see that any discomfort she'd shown around me in the past seemed to have dissipated. I could finally stop worrying that she might harbor some resentment.

"We'd better make the rounds, Blue," Jessie told her.

Lauren beamed and kissed Jessie again, quickly, but like she couldn't help herself. Having kissed Jessie myself, I could understand the sentiment. I felt my eyes mist and forced myself to keep from turning away. *Weddings!* But damn, they were lovely together. The couples in the group all reached for their spouses. Yeah, weddings.

An hour later, I said a quick goodbye to the brides and managed to slip away without anyone else noticing. Jessie's group of friends, who were now my group of friends, had become unbearable in a setting where single women mingled so nearby. The whole afternoon seemed too reminiscent of every picnic scene involving meddling old biddies in a Jane Austen novel. For the past year, they'd been pretty wrapped up in freaking out about two of their friends hooking up and helping to plan this wedding. Without that distraction, I seemed to be their new project. *Crap squared!* I was in for a long summer.

* * *

Stepping through my front door, I kicked off my heels and listened to the quiet, hoping. "Hi, babe, I'm home."

Ten more seconds of quiet passed before I started down the hallway and into the living room, turning slowly, taking in the neat, nearly unrecognizable room. Since I'd left my son, Caleb, with his grandparents in Vermont for the rest of his spring break to return for this wedding, I'd made it a mission to get organized and keep the house clean. I'd been letting Caleb get away with minimal chores, but seeing him at his grandparents' house let me take a step back. He could handle a little discipline again. We'd start enforcing that when he got back next week.

A movement out of the periphery had me twirling toward the kitchen. Tears shimmered in my eyes and a lump formed in my throat, making the effort to breathe more labored. I mentally scolded myself for fashioning the vision and allowing the hope. "Why can't you be here, babe?"

When no answer came, I gripped the edge of the kitchen counter. Waves of sadness rolled through me. *Breathe in through the nose, out through the mouth, in, out, in, out. The sadness will fade; you've got all the control,* my inner voice reminded me.

"God, Meg, that one was bad." Believe me, I wasn't happy with the fact that I still talked to my partner. I should have stopped years ago, three years to be exact, on the day she died. Instead, I couldn't seem to stop the words that I'd said every day for eleven years from surfacing whenever I was alone. Nor could I stop the hundred times a week I swore I caught a glimpse of her. Just a brief flash, too quick to form a clear picture of what she was wearing but long enough to make me certain it was her and for the grief to return.

I had to stop it, though. One of these days I might slip up in front of Caleb. He was getting old enough to realize that I wasn't just muttering to myself. He missed his mommy, and I didn't need to add to his sadness. Maybe it was time to reread the books on dealing with grief again. Perhaps on this pass through I'd catch some new nugget of truth that would miraculously eradicate the heaviness from my heart.

Megan's face stared at me from the many photographs up on the fireplace mantel. Pale blond hair, proud jaw, light blue eyes, and a nose that was charmingly a touch too long for her face. She'd always hated it, but I thought it made her distinctive. I considered her beautiful, but she liked handsome better. Wiry and agile, the pictures showed her actively pursuing her hobbies. All but the one that killed her. I'd taken the rock climbing photos down after the accident.

"Help me, Meg, please," I pleaded. After three years, I should be able to look at her photo without tearing up. I should be able to walk in the door and not say or even think the words I used to say. I should be able to move on.

From the closet, I pulled out the banker's box I'd placed there a year ago in my first real attempt to get on with my life. A jewelry box sat alone inside the cavernous space. I plucked it out and flipped open the lid. My wedding ring, a gold band of eternity gleamed from its nest inside. I'd taken it off a year ago on the day I'd decided to ask Jessie out to dinner. When she said yes and we began to see each other, I thought maybe I could handle more. I'd chosen Jessie for a reason, but she turned out not to be the woman everyone said she was, and I couldn't use her to jumpstart my new life. She knew before I did that I still needed time to heal. She somehow guessed that every time I kissed her, I felt like I was cheating on Meg. She'd been as wonderful to me then as she was to me now. Why most of her friends hadn't recognized the contemplative, considerate side of her, I'd never know.

As I slipped the ring on my finger, the memory of Megan placing it there at our wedding hit me like a heavyweight champ delivering a knockout blow. The extra heft on my finger felt glorious, but I couldn't keep it there. It had been my safety blanket for two years after her death. I wouldn't let it become that again. Twisting slowly, I shed the ring for the last time.

After more than a year at my new job, in this new town, with these new friends, it was time. No longer new, that starts now.

With great care, I started wrapping the framed photos of Meg in newspaper and placed them in the box. I took Caleb's two favorites and added them to the two he already had in his room. We could remember together, but I needed to break free of this sadness. Four more jewelry boxes were added to the growing pile. A few articles of clothing she'd given me, several gifts, lots of CDs, and other small trinkets I'd kept as reminders were separated into two boxes, one for charity and the other for Caleb if he ever asked for something his mommy owned. The bulk of Meg's possessions I'd donated or given to her family in the move to Virginia, but I'd thought I could keep some of the gifts, photos, and things we'd bought together. Instead, they'd only served to prolong my grief. This was the only way I could think of to start anew. It was drastic, but nothing else had worked.

The last item, the most difficult to add after my wedding ring, was the cologne she'd wear whenever we went out. I'd spritz the other pillow once a month, a crutch I'd allowed myself. Sometimes, it was the only way I could get to sleep, but I couldn't keep doing that. It wasn't fair to me. Megan was gone; it was time I realized that.

One final whiff. "I have to let you go, Meg. I can't keep living like this." Tears tracked down my face as I taped the lids onto the boxes. Setting one by the back door, I climbed the other up to the attic. "You were my life, babe. Thank you for making it so good. I love you, but it's the right time. Goodbye, Megan." I patted the box, knowing this would be the last time I'd allow myself to speak out loud to her.

As I made my way back down the stairs, the house seemed just as quiet as when I'd first walked in the door. But instead of the peaceful quiet of a temporarily empty house, it was gravely quiet, reflecting the permanence of a solitary life. The quiet settled over me. In time, I hoped I'd find it comforting.

Chapter 2

I was going to be late. I hated being late, something I'd realized over the last three years. For the eleven years before that, I never had a choice. I was almost always late. Since then, I discovered how much I disliked it now that I had complete control over my time. Starting into a sprint down the hall, I cursed the straight skirt and two inch heels.

"Whoa, Prof! Take it easy." One of my second-year students dramatically slammed himself against the wall.

"Sorry, Avery, department meeting."

"Double time it, then!" he encouraged.

As I neared the auditorium, I pulled up on the sprint. That actually felt good. I should really get back into a consistent routine at the gym or find a regular tennis partner.

"Hello, Professor Gatewood," Jonathan Wagner, one of the accounting professors, greeted as he held the door of the auditorium for me. His saccharine tone didn't fool me. He'd been angling for my chair position in the entrepreneurship program before I'd been recruited. Instead of being angry with the dean who hadn't hired him, he saved that treatment for me.

"Dr. Wagner," I managed with only minimal gritting of teeth. Trying to ignore him, I started scanning the seats for one of my favorite colleagues, Alexa, but she must have been running late as well. Only half the faculty was here. Guess I hadn't needed to rush.

"Did you enjoy your trip home, Professor," he stressed my chosen title like it was beneath him. He preferred being called Doctor as did many of the professors in the graduate business school. It was one of the few things that got on my nerves at this university.

I glanced back at him, wondering how he'd heard I'd gone back to Vermont over the break. His silver blue eyes held a malevolent glint. It bothered me that he was good looking. Call me petty, but I didn't like that his spiteful behavior toward most of his colleagues was often glossed over because he looked good. If he was an ugly little man, his ugly little comments and machinations would be seen for what they were.

"I bet that fine university there was paying you a call all week."

"I'm very happy here, Dr. Wagner. I couldn't ask for a better graduate program."

He grunted his acknowledgement of my truth and finally took the hint that I was waiting for him to go ahead of me. I spotted three empty seats in the second row and grabbed them, plopping my laptop bag into one and my jacket on the other to save them. I nodded hello to several of the faculty around my seat and shifted to watch the door and wave Alexa and my other favorite coworker, Javier, over as soon as they showed up.

First through the door was a petite, brunette woman I'd never seen before. Two other unfamiliar faces followed and practically trampled the first woman on their way past. It was as if they hadn't noticed her standing there. She, on the other hand, seemed entirely aware of them as evidenced by her large step to the side to allow them room to pass.

My friend Alexa, finance professor extraordinaire, came through the doors next, stopping beside the woman to look around the seats. I raised a hand and she headed my way. As I was tracking her progress I saw the woman take note of the course Alexa took before heading down the aisle to take a seat in the side section. Poor woman. She'd chosen a seat two over from Dr. Wagner. He turned as she sat and visibly stiffened in his seat. With a mutter of words, he stood and headed toward the exit. Curious.

"Hey, Bri, thanks for saving a seat. Full house today." Alexa pulled up my coat and sank into the seat next to me with a loud exhale. "Did we figure out what this is about?"

I smiled at the round face beside me. Her southern Virginia accent rolled smoothly across the sound waves. "Hey, you did it."

My fingertips couldn't stop themselves from folding through her newly cropped, dark brown hair. She'd been threatening to cut the long locks since I'd met her. Long grey hair, she said, wouldn't do anything for her fabulousness. Perhaps now she'd stop dyeing it to cover the patches of grey that had been plaguing her since turning forty a few years ago. "Looks wonderful, Alexa."

"Makes my face look fatter," she responded offhandedly. The observation didn't seem to bother her, nor was she fishing for a compliment. She had what most would consider an ideal body type, perfectly proportioned top and bottom. The fashion industry, men's magazines, Hollywood and, therefore, everyone else would say that her size eighteen form was large. But she moved like a gazelle on the tennis court, so I was confident that everyone else's perception of fit was out of whack.

"Now we can see your beautiful eyes." I finished ruffling through the chin length strands and tapped the bridge of her nose between her bright blue eyes.

"No wonder you haven't had a date in a year with a tired line like that," she scoffed amicably. Even my work friends liked to appoint themselves mayor of Timetogetadateville. "Is that why you cut yours? Not that we get to see your eyes when those bangs get in the way." Her comment elicited a smile. I'd recently shown her a few photos from the University of Vermont where my blond hair reached to the middle of my back. I felt I'd needed a change when I moved here. The long hair was the first thing to go, chopped to mid-neck. Getting used to bangs was also a new trick. So far I'd trained them to fall over only one eye if I dropped my head. "Don't get me wrong, the wispy long layers are hot, very becoming."

I gave an amused snort. Alexa tossed out compliments all the time, rarely conscious of it. "Where's Javier?" I turned back to look for his entrance.

The doors on the other aisle opened and in walked Dr. Wagner again. He loped up to the fourth row and inched his way toward a middle seat. I glanced back over at the section where he'd been sitting. That woman now sat alone in her row, head down, but I could swear her eyes were tracking Dr. Wagner's progress.

A body stopped in the aisle, blocking my view of the solitary woman. "*Hola, chicas.*" Short, spiky black hair greeted my gaze as Javier bent to retrieve my laptop bag before turning and plopping it onto his lap while taking a seat. He was a solid man, not too husky, not too fit, the perfect blend of the two. Half Mexican, half Spanish, his darker complexion was part bronze part olive. He had the kind of smile that could make people worship at his feet. His ethics students loved him, constantly voted him the most popular, and it only had partially to do with how engaging he was as an instructor.

"Hey, Javi, good break?" I knew he'd returned to Texas to visit his parents.

"My therapy bill is going to rival my mortgage this month," he joked. "Coffee this week? I want to hear about your trip, and you can save my therapist an hour with me."

"Sounds good. Lexi, you in?"

"I've got an extra five pounds to spare now that I've cut my hair."

"Was that a yes?" Javier stage whispered to me. He liked to make fun of her southern sayings and accent, which was funny coming from a Texan with a twangy Mexican accent. His head pitched forward from the smack Alexa issued which would have incited a slap fight if our dean hadn't stepped up to the microphone.

"Can everyone hear me?" The question finished with a high pitched electronic wail, eliciting a groan from the entire crowd. "Sorry. Okay, looks like we're all set. Welcome back from break everyone. I trust you're rested and ready to finish out the semester." Gene Goudy peered over his reading glasses at the agreeable crowd. Like anyone was going to debate that statement. "Good, now, the reason I've brought you all in today is to announce the launch of our new venture program. Five enterprising students will have their business ideas funded by the University."

Gasps of surprise rolled through the audience. "Holy hell! When did the university turn into a venture capital firm?" Javier muttered beside me.

Holy hell was right. Did they have any idea what they were getting into with this?

"There will be limitations on funding, types of businesses, scale, and location, but we believe this program will set the MBA curriculum apart from other schools." Gene proceeded to flip through a presentation outlining the qualifications, scope of the funding, and other information, all of which looked far from haphazard. Perhaps they did know what they were getting into. "This will be a graduate symposium offered during the summer session as a beta test. Obviously, we'd like the most qualified among you to run the symposium. It will mean staying on for the full summer session and a new syllabus for this unprecedented class. It will also require a minimum of two professors involved day to day." He slapped his hands together and rubbed them while waiting for his faculty to step up with equal enthusiasm.

Whispers ran through the crowd, moving to low murmurs. No one would be volunteering for this potential blazing failure of a class. Too much was still left undone and unknown. Having your name attached to something that could become a huge public relations nightmare was career suicide, tenure or no.

"Come on now," Gene continued from the podium. "A third of you are already signed up for the summer session."

"Well," Dr. Wagner's booming voice sounded from behind us. "It seems to me that this would fit right in with the entrepreneurship core of classes."

"Holy hell," Javier muttered for me. I could feel Alexa getting ready to launch herself across two rows and throttle Wagner on my behalf.

"Quite so. Briony, you've done wonders with the entrepreneurship program. You would obviously be the most qualified to lead this symposium and act as faculty advisor for the enterprising students."

Seventy faculty members of the graduate school of business waited for me to say something. I'd met almost all at least once, some I knew well. Now was the time to be eloquent. "Uhh..." *Brilliant, good start.* "I wasn't scheduled for summer session. In fact, I wasn't planning to be in the state for the summer." Plus, there were other professors in the entrepreneurship department that he could pick on.

"You're not taking a visiting professorship somewhere, are you?" Gene leaned forward on the podium, talking to me as if we were the only two people in the room.

"No," I answered truthfully. It was now too late to look into a visiting professorship, no matter how much I wished I had. The summer plan was to keep busy with Caleb, explore Virginia a bit more, then head back home to Vermont and decompress.

"Good, then we can count on you?" He didn't wait for a reply. "Who else?"

I jerked forward, but Alexa's arm shot out like we were coming to a sudden stop in a car, crushing me into the backrest of my seat. She must have recognized that I didn't have a valid argument, and even if I did, it probably wouldn't be wise to make it now that I'd been thrown onto the altar in front of the whole business school. Screwed, thy name is Briony.

"Someone from general management might be helpful." Wagner continued to scythe through the business fields he'd applied for.

"So would accounting," one of the management professors shot back.

If I weren't already tied to this project, I might find the posturing funny. Unfortunately, my new summer plans now depended on who else would be strapped in beside me.

"Marketing seems like a logical choice." Wagner just couldn't keep his mouth shut.

"They can't run the business without a solid accounting foundation, Wags, and you know it," the marketing guru on staff taunted.

"I was hoping for one from each of the core business functions," Gene persisted cluelessly. He couldn't seem to get that no one was going to stick their necks out on this project. Cue cards might help. Smoke signals would probably be too subtle.

"Since you've already got an expert on business startup, at a bare minimum, operations management would be the best support system for these young entrepreneurs." Maybe Wagner didn't know that just because he had a mouth didn't mean he always had to be using it.

When no immediate retort came back from someone in operations, general agreement noises sounded throughout the auditorium. Gene, left with grave disappointment that his staff wasn't wetting themselves to volunteer, cast about looking over his operations staff. "Dr. Desiderius? You were already scheduled for the summer session. This venture would benefit greatly from your guidance in operational matters."

I followed his line of sight toward the side aisle. No one appeared to be giving off the don't-you-dare-drag-me-into-this look, so I couldn't tell who his victim was. Then a slight movement caught my eye. That woman, the one who'd slipped inside unnoticed, who'd somehow frightened Wagner to the other side of the auditorium, gave a single nod of her head.

"Wonderful. We'll forward the memo and presentation to you both. I'll expect a syllabus and proposal ready to publish on the student intranet to invite business plans from those applying for start-up capital. Two weeks?" Once again he didn't wait for our consent. "This is exciting people. I want your full support for the success of this new project. I'm sure that our two leaders would appreciate your input. Good meeting." This was Gene's way of signaling the end of a meeting.

"You're screwed," Alexa whispered as people practically leapt out of their seats and pushed toward the exits.

Before I could skewer her with a glare, Javier added, "Royally."

Chapter 3

The ridiculous crowding at the exits made it feel like we'd missed a fire alarm. The net had been cast, and I'd been caught. What did they have to worry about? My threesome stayed in our seats, waiting out the tide of people streaming for the doors.

"How bad is this, really?" I asked their opinion, dread settling like a heavy stone in my stomach.

"Is your résumé updated?" Javier offered drolly.

"It's not that bad," Alexa put in. "But if the University of Vermont calls to ask you back again, maybe you don't immediately turn them down this time."

"Support systems are, you know, supportive. In case you didn't realize, you two are my support system. Act like it, please!" I dropped my head into my hands.

"The good news is you're capable enough to launch a business from a coma," Javier complemented. "The bad news is you've given away every spare moment you've got from now until they are launched."

"Which for you is also good news because it provides the perfect excuse for why you probably won't date all summer," Alexa offered brightly. Unlike me, she had an active social life and tried to coax me into double dates all the time. Her dating practices were a thing of envy with me and had been since her husband of fourteen years blindsided her with divorce papers over a year ago. Despite suffering a major blow to her confidence level by not knowing what had gone wrong with her marriage, she'd already managed to have a transition man and several successful dates. I suspected she relished being back out in the singles scene, also unlike me.

"I think I hate you both."

"Don't think it, sister, know it." Javier wriggled his eyebrows in a way that literally charmed the pants off of a fair share of men down at his favorite gay club in town.

I twisted in my seat to find that Gene was talking to that woman, Dr. Desiderius, keeping her in the auditorium as well. "What do you guys know about this ops prof? Is she new? I've never seen her at any of the faculty get-togethers or department meetings."

"No, she's not new." Alexa swiveled her head to make sure she wasn't being overheard.

Before I could question her wary tone, Javier spoke up. "She keeps to herself. Works hard, keeps consistent office hours, but she doesn't socialize. I'm actually surprised to see her here today."

"What were you going to say," I prompted Alexa, recognizing that she was holding something back.

"Keeps to herself? Yeah. Nobody knows anything about her. Not just anything, I mean absolutely nothing, zero, zilch. No gossip, no rumors, no clue, nothing."

"Must chap your hide, eh, Lex?" Javier goaded, receiving another swat. We both knew how much Alexa loved to keep her finger on the pulse of department news.

"I'll chap your hide, mister," she shot back at her best friend. They'd been hired together at UVA over a decade ago and knew dangerous amounts about each other.

"Seriously though," he continued, "her students love her. Her classes have the longest waiting lists. If she didn't pull her name from the voting for best professor, she'd win by a landslide every year."

Alexa snorted. "How that's even possible when she never talks to anyone, I'll never know."

"She's certainly not among the staff's most popular. In fact, most of them avoid her like she's highly contagious. So, um, good luck with that." Javier jumped to his feet before I could land a smack.

"It'll be fine. I'm sure she's just terribly misunderstood," Alexa shared in a tone that told me she didn't believe a word of it. She waved and followed Javier up to the now cleared exit.

I edged my way out to the aisle. Gene was just finishing up talking to my new cellmate, I mean, counterpart. He turned with a sheepish look. "Thanks again for leading this. I'm expecting good things out of you two. Can't wait to see the syllabus next week."

"Next week?" I croaked. Hadn't he said two weeks?

"Well, er, yes, if you need longer..." With that he turned and hustled up the aisle, leaving me with the other sucker in the crowd. Her eyes aimed briefly at mine before focusing on the retreating back of our esteemed dean.

"For that he gets paid 200 grand more than we do," I snarked to break the ice. When she didn't react, I backpedaled. "Sorry, I'm just feeling a little cornered and trying not to react like Butch and Sundance."

She glanced at me again, a flicker of recognition in her brown eyes. Either she thought she knew me or she felt the same way as I did about this.

"Any ideas off the top of your head about this symposium?" I tried to keep desperate hope from marking my tone. Two weeks wouldn't be enough time to plan a syllabus, much less put together workable text for the website. "At this point a rough outline would get us moving." I got a shake of her head and soft sigh in response. *Yeah, ditto.* "Well, I'll jot down some ideas tonight. If you've got time, maybe we could meet tomorrow?" The nod I received this time expressed the same reluctant acceptance I was feeling about this project. "I can head over to your office or we can meet in mine?"

She squinted sharply as if neither suggestion appealed then settled her gaze back on me. "Your office is fine." Her smooth, low voice startled me. I realized it was the first thing she'd said. I'd been rambling around my own mind, so hassled by this out-of-the-blue assignment that I hadn't realized she'd not yet spoken. I allowed time for her to blow off some of her own frustration, but nothing else came.

"I'm done with classes at noon tomorrow. We could get some lunch while we toss out ideas?" We might as well make use of any available time.

Her head was shaking before I'd finished. "I'm in class. Later?"

Since Caleb wasn't due back for three days, I could stay as long as I needed. "Sure, I'll be in my office. 233, come find me when your class is over."

She stood, nodding at my suggestion. What looked like a lot of relief rinsed through her expression. She grabbed a well worn leather backpack from the seat next to her and swung one arm through, ready to head out.

Shorter than me by three or four inches and slighter than me by at least one size, I didn't know how I'd managed not to notice her on campus before. Her attractive looks alone would have caught my eye, but the ping on my radar usually turned my head even when I wasn't looking for it. Studying her now, I appreciated how the symmetry of spacing between her eyes and nose matched the contour of her cheekbones and jaw line. Usually women this tiny had a pixyish look to their faces, but that adjective didn't apply here. Pretty suited better, a face in perfect equilibrium for her smaller frame. I wondered if the blond and red highlights in her short hair had been added or if she really had three different colors that made for a shade of brown that was halfway between honey and chestnut. Yes, definitely attractive.

She flicked similarly colored eyes from the ground up to me three times, presumably trying to push me out of the aisle with her gaze. I stepped back self-consciously. "I'm Briony, by the way. Sorry I didn't start with that."

"Em." That was it; she didn't offer anything else.

I held out my hand in greeting and watched her startled eyes just stare at it. For a moment it seemed like she was fighting to make this gesture seem logical. As if her brain was telling her hand to accept mine, that this was a customary form of greeting, but the synapse that linked the two body parts misfired. Normally, this kind of rebuff would annoy me. But I'd witnessed her desperate struggle, and strangely, I felt compassion for this woman who seemed incapable of even the most rudimentary forms of personal interaction. I let my hand drift back down, intrigued by the grateful look that crossed her face. "Em? Is that short for Emily or Emma?"

Her eyes flipped back up to meet mine, having monitored the fall of my hand back to my side. "No."

Okay. "What's it short for?" I persisted, intent on gaining some personal ground with this woman. We were now doomed to spend much of the summer together. It would be nice to have a friendly accomplice in this endeavor.

"My first name."

An awkward, prolonged silence passed, but she didn't relent. I backed down because it was the only option I had. "All right. You're probably feeling as ambushed by this project as I am. I get it." My hands flipped up in surrender. "Well, Em, short for some mysterious name, it was nice to meet you anyway. See you tomorrow." I started up the aisle, feeling the embarrassment of this rebuff with each step.

Her soft voice stopped me before I reached the door. "It's nothing personal. I don't, I mean, no one..."

Swiveling slowly, I didn't want to appear too eager, especially since she was having trouble finishing what she wanted to say. "It's not just me then?" I couldn't help but tease. The fact that she'd stopped me said that she was making a concerted effort. I could keep things light. In fact, that would be a necessity if we were going to survive this summer with our sanity intact.

A small twitch stretched the corners of her full mouth. Then, as quickly as it started, it stopped. "Just M, the letter. The name's old fashioned. I don't use it." Her gaze narrowed, studying my reaction. "And it was nice meeting you, too, Briony." With that she moved past me toward the door.

More than five whole words, color me impressed. "Bye," I managed before she'd opened the door and, because I couldn't help it, guessed, "Mildred? Madge? Myrtle?"

Only the hitch in her step told me she understood the quest she'd now put me on.

Chapter 4

A lone figure glided through the bustling mob at the club. Flash from the strobes provided the only light in the dark interior. Thumping base accompanied each of her sure steps. Clad in leather pants, leather vest, leather gloves that reached to her biceps, and a leather mask, she blended in with most of the crowd. At this hour she was in the minority, still being dressed. Most had shed at least their tops, but others were barely clinging to even undergarments.

Her pulse raced, a light sheen of sweat broke out under the leather. She'd be lucky to peel the pants off without a little pain tonight. But pain was good. Pain was a feeling she could handle. It didn't require contemplation. It just was. Either she handled pain or it broke her. Easy choice.

She glanced over at the bar, noting the throng of people waiting for a drink. She would go without tonight. She'd done it before. It wasn't her purpose here. Scanning the crowd, she had a decision to make. The three in the corner, one in black lace, one in black leather, one in virtually nothing. One of them might do.

"I'm yours to command," a voice breathed in her ear.

She shifted to the side to take in the owner of the voice. Layers of interlocking chain in tiny links draped across her chest. With each undulation of her body, ruby tipped nipples peeked through on too high to be real breasts. Skin tight leather shorts cupped a luscious ass and did nothing to hide the outline of her sex. Thighs to hold on to rubbed deliciously together as the woman stepped closer. A red satin mask that started below her eyes and rounded up over the top half of her head complimented the shock of black hair that ended just below her jaw.

She was drawn to the woman's plump mouth, the one that had spoken her desire so easily. So much that she almost didn't see the hand coming up. "Don't touch," she ordered, stepping out of the pathway of the darting hand.

The hand dropped in immediate obedience. "Yes, Mistress."

This one might do. The titles weren't necessary, nor was any humiliation or pain, but the submission was. A satin collar cut into the woman's long neck with tassels that hung down beneath the see-through links, stating clearly the willingness to be controlled. That was the most important factor with her choices. She didn't play into all the other games or etiquette of this particular lifestyle, but she had to be able to control. Yes, this one would do.

"You'll wait for me in the purple wing. When I unlock the door, you'll enter and take your place in the suspension harness. You're going to wear a blindfold." A shiver ran through the woman as her hazel eyes dilated with each demand. A gentle tug on the collar elicited a sharp gasp, giving away her excitement. "Go, now."

After paying for the use of a private room, she made her way into the dimly lit back hallway. Different noises met her there. The loud bumping beat of the music muffled considerably. Voices, cries, cracks, slaps, and moans emanated from behind the closed doors. The two viewing rooms up front provided a feast for the voyeurs in the hall. Men mostly, like on the other nights. Fewer women than men, a lot fewer. She didn't stop to watch the men as they sought their pleasure. The sight would only serve to put an end to her evening. She wished it weren't a mixed club, but this was too much of a niche segment to exclude one gender.

"I've got a room, kitten," a deep voice sounded from her left, causing her to falter. "You'll be my playmate tonight."

"No," she responded, not bothering to look at the man who'd issued the invitation. She hated that some men came to this club looking for something that wasn't often offered. At a gay club, this man had no right to voice his desire to her.

"You want to say yes."

"No, I don't." She turned and looked him in the eye. He was powerfully built, over a foot taller. He could hurt her if he wanted.

Several seconds passed. His eyes scraped down her length, taking in her stance, the swell of her breasts, the absence of a collar at her throat. She could tell he liked her mask and hoped it meant that she would be willing to do whatever behind the afforded anonymity. She set her expression to tell him it didn't. "Another time, kitten. I'm here every week."

"I'm not." She took a step, then another, expecting him to try to keep her from leaving. Once out of reach, she flowed into her panther gait, sure, calm, steady, ready. Turning at the end of the hall, she spotted Red Satin in the middle of the women's-only purple wing.

"Can we use a viewing room?" R.S. asked.

She shook her head. This wasn't about performing for others. "No one is going to see what we do." She led her to an unoccupied private room. Before opening the door, she said, "Your word is 'inveigle.' Say it."

Hazel eyes stared through the holes in the red satin. Those swollen lips puckered at first. "Inveigle."

She twisted the doorknob and led them inside. "Good. Strip off the shorts, leave the chains, get in the harness." When the woman hesitated, she grabbed the lead on her collar and tugged again. "You know your word?"

The hazel eyes closed briefly before opening and locking on with a nod. With a seductive motion, R.S. turned and began a slow shimmy to shed her leather shorts. The globes of her buttocks beckoned as she bent forward to step out of them. Shiny red pumps stayed on her feet, but the shorts were tossed onto the whipping board.

While she appreciated the beauty, the sight did nothing to excite her. She wasn't like the other women in this club who would flush with lust at this display. "Get in the harness."

"Touch me, please." R.S. glanced over her shoulder as she spoke.

"Later." She watched as the red pumps swiveled, allowing her a peek of the artful grooming that partially covered the woman's mound. A wax job. So, Red Satin wasn't a stranger to pain either.

R.S. slid her luscious thighs through the hanging apparatus, swaying back first, then to within reach. A silk scarf was dangled in front of her face. One last look of the hazel eyes before the scarf blinded them. Taking stock of the various toys, she chose a flogger and a set of clamps. When she returned to the swing, she looped a silk tie around the woman's right wrist, fastening it to the swing hold.

"What? No, I want to be able to touch you." R.S. folded her left wrist in against her chest before it could be secured.

"No. Grip the swing."

"Please, let me touch you." R.S. clearly knew what she preferred, what excited her, but she also knew her role here.

"No. Hand up." The order was sharp, uncompromising.

The hand moved slowly but finally went back to gripping the other swing hold. A few loops of the silk rendered it immobile. Completely unable to do anything she didn't want her to do. Boundaries set.

"Do you know your word?" she asked the bound, blindfolded woman.

A tremor began; her legs, now spread apart, twitched as a deep breath sounded. "Inveigle." Nothing more than a whisper made it through.

She picked up the clamps and moved between the tempting legs. Her leather-clad thighs easily avoided brushing against the woman's wide spread legs. Another tremor ran through the body before her. With a gloved hand, she brushed the layers of chain from one of those too perfect breasts. Yes, they were fake. Didn't matter. With care, she fastened one of the clamps on the erect ruby nipple. A loud hiss sounded, telling her how much R.S. liked it. She placed the free clamp on the other nipple then let her gloved fingers slide down the chain to the exact center and tugged.

"Oh God, yeah! Tug, Mistress." A sudden musky aroma filled the space between them. Even without the exclamation, there was no better indicator of her readiness.

Stepping back, she reached for the flogger. Softly at first, she swept the flogger to tickle its leather tendrils against the clamped breasts. The first landing of leather on skin elicited a sharp moan and unconscious arch of her body for more. Five more strokes, a little less gentle, testing her breakpoint before she moved lower. She made her wait, and whimpers turned to pleas. When the flogger's tendrils connected with the wet, plump flesh of her center, the cry of pleasure could be heard at the far end of the hallway. It only took six strokes before the woman exploded in a loud, shaking orgasm.

"Fuck, yes! I've never come that hard." Red Satin tilted her head up to where she imagined her to be standing. Her breathing was labored, body lax in the swing.

"You'll do it again." She stepped back and spun the harness swing, adjusting the pulleys to tilt the woman forward. The flogger landed on her flushed back, once, twice, again before she angled it and flipped upward.

"It's too much," the woman pleaded as the leather petals lightly swept against her swollen flesh. "Please, please too much." One word would stop this if R.S. really meant it, but that word never came.

She wished she could feel that. To be strung out from pleasure, to think she couldn't handle any more. The envy stung, but she wouldn't allow the tightness in her chest to force her arm motion harder. Now rhythmically stroking the flogger in an upward motion, she reached a hand out and forced herself to make contact with the woman's back. She slid a gloved hand up the ridges of her spine. The muscles of her back flexed under the path of her hand, counteracting the undulations of her hips toward each brush of the flogger. She moved her hand under the doubled over body to grip the chain of the nipple clamps. Alternating between tugging on the clamps and swatting her now weeping center, she guessed that the woman had no idea how much she begged for this to continue, demanding harder and faster treatment, crying for another release.

"Please, let me come. Please, let me come," Red Satin repeated over and over until her hips bucked and a flush spread over her back. Without waiting for the sought after permission, her head threw back as she roared in climax, jerking against the harness, swaying wildly in every direction. "Oh God, oh God, oh God." The repetition this time was uttered in a voice raw from overuse.

As was custom, she set the flogger to the side of the toy cabinet. A sign to the staff that it would need to be cleaned before someone else renting the room could use it. She adjusted the pulleys on the swing and brought the woman into a seated position. Heavy breaths still pumped through the trembling body.

"Please, let me touch you," those tempting lips asked.

"No."

"A kiss, please?"

"No."

"I can make you feel good."

She wished she could allow that. "You just did."

"One kiss?"

She brought her face toward those plump lips as she worked to undo the tie at her wrist. When their lips were inches apart, she whispered, "No." Swiftly she backed away, leaving the woman to get out of the other tie, blindfold, and harness by herself.

Stalking down the hallway, she entered the club, overheated and aching from want. These patrons knew just what they wanted, what made them feel good, reach ecstasy. Once, just once, she wanted what seemed so easy for them.

Passing through to step out into the open air, she felt her heart rate slow considerably and her body temperature drop. *Deep breaths, in, out, in, out. Gain control.*

She didn't want to be like this. She didn't need to be like this. But like pain, she just was.

Chapter 5

He'd been chattering for forty-five minutes straight, filling the car's silence as we made our way home from Dulles Airport. My boy. Away from me for over a week, I'd missed him more than I ever thought possible. I'd never wanted a child, never even thought about having one. But Megan had, which I'd found surprising when she finally admitted it to me. She didn't seem the type, but who was I to deny something she wanted so much? When she had our boy, Caleb, her light became my light, her desire to be a mother became my desire. Ten years into it, I was still struggling to stay afloat in this tsunami called motherhood, but it was worth every powerful stroke.

"Wow-wee!" Caleb exclaimed when we walked through the front door of our house. After a week, I'd grown used to the sight of the uncluttered, currently spotless living space. Now, I was studying it again for the first time through his eyes. "What happened, Mom? Did a reverse tornado come through here?"

I giggled with him. I wondered how long until my little boy no longer wanted to kid around and giggle with his mom. "I did my Tasmanian Devil routine."

"All by yourself?" His earnest gold-brown eyes looked up at me. Despite being his adoptive mother, he had my eyes. Megan had chosen a donor with my eye color, hoping that he'd get something that was uniquely mine. His hair had started out as pale as hers, but now the blond was beginning to darken, although not quite to my wheat blond shade. Nearly every other feature was hers, a living reminder of her beauty.

"Yep."

"You shoulda waited. I coulda helped." He set his hands on his hips. His little body was fighting with proportions right now, a longer torso than legs, feet that said he'd grow much taller than me, and sharp features on a face that would become as attractive as everyone else in Meg's family tree.

"I'm so glad you said that because it's going to take both of us to keep this place organized." I stretched an arm around his shoulders and pulled him to me. "We're making a few changes, bucko. Think you can handle it?"

He swiveled his head around to take in the orderly contents of the first floor. Not one of his toys, games, sweatshirts, balls or anything else he usually left around the house was in sight. "Mm'guess."

"That's the hip, cool, happening way of saying 'yes,' right?" I ruffled my fingers through his newly cut hair. My mother never let him leave Vermont without a trim. I wondered how many new clothes I'd find in his bag when we unpacked it. Both his grandmothers loved shopping, and since we'd celebrated his tenth birthday while on vacation, I guessed he might not have any of his old clothes left in the duffle.

"Moawmm," he whined, stepping out of my grasp.

"Let's head upstairs. I want to show you what I mean." We trudged up the staircase together, and he burst through the door marked *Welcome to Caleb's, Abandon All Hope*. We'd put up the sign as soon as he realized that having a professor for a mother would warp him for life.

"Holy moley." His room was as spotless and organized as the rest of the house. "Hey, what's this?" He raced to the new cabinet that looked like four boxy gym lockers in bright colors. His games, toys, and sports equipment were stored inside. "Cool." He rushed to his closet where all that used to be crammed in. "So much room."

"Amazing isn't it? And here's the deal, I don't expect your room to stay this clean, but clothes don't belong on the floor. If they're clean they go back in the closet or your dresser. If not, the hamper. Any food you bring up here gets eaten. Any plates or glasses get put back in the kitchen. The dishwasher from now on, not the sink."

He whipped his head around and stared wide-eyed at me. "You're back," he said softly then launched himself into my arms to hug me tightly.

When his lips grazed my cheek, I felt the weight of tears in my eyes. "Caleb, what did you mean?"

"Nuthin'," he mumbled into my neck.

I pulled his torso away and made him look at me. "Please, tell me."

"You used to make me clean my room. You used to make me help set the table and take out the trash. You never let me drop my clothes on the floor or keep my toys sitting around."

The words pressed heavily on my chest, making it a little difficult to breathe. "Mommy did," I prompted. Megan had always been too lenient with him. It was one of our few points of contention.

"Yeah, Mommy did. You always said if I had arms that worked, I should use them."

"I can't believe you remember that." I hadn't said it in three years. I hardly remembered it. I'd taken on the more indulgent role after her death because he missed her so much. He didn't need to deal with the disciplinarian in the family.

"I'm like an elephant," he boasted a comparison that Meg would always say in the middle of story time whenever he'd start mouthing the words along with her.

I tipped him back to where he almost lost balance. His arms clung to my neck as we came upright to a shriek of surprised laughter. "In a few years, you're going to be so big you'll probably weigh as much as an elephant."

"No way, Mom."

"Yes way, son." I rubbed noses with him and gave him a loud kiss on his baby soft cheek. "A horse at least. So, do we have a deal?"

"What do I get out of it?" The suspicious glint in his eye tugged another smile from me.

"Hmm, you can find your stuff quicker?" He shook his head. "Your clothes don't smell because they haven't been sitting under piles of other dirty clothes?" He giggled and shook his head. "A roof over your head and food to eat?" I started tickling his wiggly body until he grew breathless and dropped his legs to jump back to the ground. "My undying love?"

He sighed dramatically. "Ohhkaay."

"Very gracious of you, bucko." We left his room and headed out into the hallway toward the stairs.

"Hey, what's my desk doing out here?" He stood in the open loft area at the top of the stairs once filled with a treadmill that I never used and yet more bookcases with books that I hadn't looked at in years.

"Oh, yeah, I forgot to tell you this part." I smiled down at him as he tugged on my arm to get me to spill my secret plan. "You keep up your end of the deal and we'll get a TV, a coupla beanbags, a dart board, maybe even your own computer. Turn this space into your study/hangout place. Sound good?"

"Wow-wee!" he repeated. How could you not love a kid who says "wow-wee"?

"We'll start shopping at the end of the school year, 'kay?" He nodded enthusiastically, eyes already designing his loft area.

We headed back downstairs to rustle up some dinner. As we passed through the living room, he jerked to a stop in front of the mantel. *Oh no!* I'd forgotten about the pictures, having chosen to avoid this room all week.

"Mom?" His eyes darted around, noticing the other missing items, then back over the few remaining pictures of him and our extended family up on the mantel.

"Sweetie," I started but didn't know how to finish. I looped my hands around his shoulders and down onto his chest to pull him back against me. The top of his head just made it to my sternum. "I've put a few things away." I twisted him around and bent down to be on the same level. "We can talk about Mommy any time you want. We can remember her whenever you feel like it. But I need, I had to..."

"Don't be sad, Mom. You've had enough sad." He wiped his fingertips gently against my now wet cheeks.

The wisest statement I've ever heard about grief, and it was issued by my own ten-year-old. "You're right."

"I know. You should listen to me more."

I snorted a wet laugh through the diminishing tears. "I just might do that."

He glanced at the mantel once more, hugged me quickly then went to rummage through the refrigerator. With his little tush sticking out, he spoke into the fruit tray. "Does this mean you're going to go out on dates now?" He asked it casually like he was asking where he'd left his baseball mitt. When he turned around he had an apple in his hand. "I think you should."

Oh, just brilliant. Dating wisdom from a ten-year-old. Timetogetadateville, population count: one more.

Chapter 6

Walking across the Darden compound, I waved at a few familiar students on my way into the classroom building directly across from mine. It had been two weeks since the departmental meeting assigning me to the venture project. We managed to get the project pitch up on the student intranet and iron out the syllabus, but who would cover what in the symposium and how we'd handle the venture coaching still needed to be worked out.

None of these things could get done via the email exchanges we'd resorted to. I'd had to postpone our first meeting because Caleb had returned early. M took that to mean cancel, and we'd been corresponding by email ever since. When I say corresponding, I meant I'd write a succinct but friendly email with my ideas and suggestions for what we could tackle together in our next meeting. M would respond with an attachment of the project I'd been brainstorming. She'd combine my ideas with her own and work it out, down to the last detail. No text in the body of the emails, just a subject line and an attachment. She was certainly efficient. And smart. And avoiding me.

As I approached the classroom where her last class of the day was being held, I heard a rumble of laughter, several different voices, then one clear, sure voice. The tone I thought I recognized, but the rush of words, conviction, and decibel level were completely foreign.

Through the glass in the door, I watched the woman who'd somehow made herself invisible at the department meeting stalk confidently from the whiteboard to the edge of the tiered rows of desks. The room was packed with students seated on the steps of each side aisle and standing at the back of the top row, breaking all kinds of fire codes. No wonder some of the faculty were jealous. We all wanted this kind of hype generated around our classes.

Students stared raptly at whatever she wrote then interacted eagerly when she asked questions. No, that wasn't right. She didn't ask them questions like they were students and she was grading them on their participation. She involved them in the topic she was teaching. They would discuss with her their opinions and answers as if they were all in this learning process together.

Not that I didn't have a good rapport with my students, but she managed to transform the classroom setting into a vital business meeting where all of its participants would be rewarded handsomely if they worked together. Amazing. And M, taking the stairs two at a time to address a student from the back row, or hustling along the back walkway to head down the side steps, her constant motion kept the students' attention. Where was the painfully shy woman I'd witnessed at the department meeting? The one who could barely speak more than five words?

As the bell sounded, other doors in the hallway crashed open and students surged out noisily. I stepped closer to the wall to let them get by. When I glanced back through M's classroom door, not one of her students had moved. They waited until she finished her thought before they began packing up their bags and stepping down to the exit.

When the last of them trickled through the door, I slipped inside. A cluster of students bunched around their professor, continuing the discussion from the class. This was always my favorite part of class time. Sure, some of them were just kissing ass, but the ones who asked thoughtful questions loved to learn. Those students were the reason I'd become a professor.

"Hey, Prof," the ever-present Avery called out from the ring of remaining students. "What brings you over here? In need of a little operational strategizing?"

"Who isn't?" I shot back as I walked up to the start of the tiered rows of long wraparound desks and attached chairs. Like me, M placed her desk up three tiers and to the left of the classroom. It tended to throw the students off if you were among them when they walked inside. It also tended to make them choose the front row more often to stay away from the instructor's desk.

At the sound of my voice, M shifted into a gap between two students. Her eyes widened before another student demanded her attention. When it seemed like the young woman was going to ditch her question because of the now divided attention, M encouraged her with a smile, opening her stance to invite whatever thoughts or questions this timid student had. I found myself stepping toward her, the invitation so compelling.

She wore wool slacks and a sweater set similar to my own attire on this still chilly spring day. The cut and drape of her clothes camouflaged her diminutive stature and screamed refined chic. Clearly, she subscribed to the same thoughts as I had on appropriate dress code for instructors. Not only did I think dressing up showed respect for my students, I felt it was important to dress in a fashion consistent with what these students would find in the business world after graduation. So many of my colleagues dressed in khakis or even the same style of jeans that their students wore. How could they hope to command respect when their super low-rise, tight jeans afforded a peek at their thong underwear? Did students really need to know if their professors wore thong underwear?

"Hi, Professor Gatewood," Cecily, another of my second-year students, greeted as she and two of her friends made their way down toward the exit.

"Hello, Cecily." I looked back up at the third tier landing where the group was finally breaking up. They all nodded to me on their way out.

"Can I get another day on my case study analysis, Prof?" Avery angled with a sly grin as he passed by me.

"Sure."

He halted and swiveled back around, shocked by my unprecedented reply. "I can?"

"Of course you can." His jaw popped open. "You lose a half a grade point for every day it's late. Like always." I wiggled my eyebrows. They had to learn that their clients wouldn't give them an extra day, all part of the teaching process.

"You're tough," he accused. "Hey, Professor D, you'd give me an extra day, right?"

"Every leap year," she quipped back, drawing a chuckle from me.

I watched Avery's mock dejection vanish with his parting wave. Left alone, I turned back to face M. "You go by Professor not Doctor?"

"As do you."

Yes, I did, and as far as I knew, we were the only ones. "But Gene called you Dr. Desiderius." Instead of answering, she turned and shuffled some papers on her desk. When the shuffling turned to packing up her bag, I took the steps up to her platform. "Why?"

She spun around to face me and pressed back against the desk, creating more space between us. The open, inviting posture gone now, replaced by guarded steel. The momentary surprise in her expression at my proximity receded behind an impenetrable mask. "I don't control that."

Interesting choice of words. Not can't, but don't. Like she knew she could control it with extra effort and probably exasperation, but she chose not to. Or maybe she just didn't care.

"And you use an initial for your last name, too?" I remembered how Avery had addressed her. I'd checked the faculty directory, the webpage bio, and the class record. All showed only the letter M but without a period that would be commonplace with the use of an initial. Even her textbooks, both the cover and copyright page hadn't been any more informative about her full name. They did, however, tell me that she was a talented educational writer. If I were really nosy, I'd call my friend Beverly in payroll and ask her to peek at M's file, but that would cross a line. It didn't matter how engrossing the quest or captivating the photo posted on the online bio, I wouldn't go around her to get the information I wanted.

She shrugged. "Kids." Like that explained everything.

"Well, I thought I'd stop by to see if you had some time to coordinate the lecture portion of the symposium."

She narrowed her gaze. "Didn't I initial the topics I'd cover on the syllabus I emailed to you?"

"You did, but some of the topics overlap. I thought we could sit down and go through what we would cover during the lectures." A long moment passed with her gaze darting around the room, seemingly searching for a response. "If now's not a good time..."

Without glancing at the tasteful watch on her wrist, she gestured to the classroom desk behind me. I edged back behind the desktop and took a seat. As I brought up my laptop, she grabbed hers and chose to take a seat one away from mine. Resisting the urge to check my breath, I glanced down at the empty seat between us and up at her while she booted up her laptop. She seemed oblivious to her very telling choice of seat. Could I let it go for the sake of this project? No, I couldn't.

"M?" I drew her gaze from the screen and made a point of dropping mine to the empty seat between us. "We're going to have to work closely together to make this new venture a success for the university. So if you have a problem with me, I'm sure I could talk to Gene and have him volunteer someone else. As much as I disagree with Dr. Wagner usually, what he said about this course fitting within the entrepreneurship division seems right. I'm tied to this thing, but you don't have to be."

"No." She shook her head then tapped a password onto her laptop.

That's it? "You disagree about where the class fits in the catalog?" I could see how someone might think it belongs in operations or perhaps finance because of the outlay of start-up capital, but since the class was going to launch businesses, it was the very definition of entrepreneurship.

She turned from staring at her computer screen after several clicks. "No, I don't have a problem with you, and no, I don't want Dr. Goudy to volunteer someone else."

"Huh," I voiced my amazement before I could stop the reaction. That almost sounded like she was already invested in this project and that, well, she didn't *not* like me. Almost better than I could have hoped for when I'd crossed the compound earlier on my mission. "So if I took this seat right here," I pointed at the empty seat between us, "will you be playing musical chairs?"

Her response was to slide over into the seat next to me. Carefully, I noticed, making sure not to bump up against me as is so often the complaint I get from my students about the proximity of these attached chairs. "Shall we get started, Briony?" She pulled her laptop over one space and flicked a peek at me.

"Sure, M," I agreed, typing in my password. "Or is that Millicent?" My guess brought out the briefest of smiles. Maybe she really didn't have a problem with me.

Chapter 7

The lone figure moved stealthily through the corridors. Very few students occupied this stretch of tiled floor spanning out to the Entrepreneurship, Marketing, and Global Business faculty offices. It was ghostly quiet since students usually showed respect on faculty territory. It probably helped that most of the doors were closed—the opposite of what she thought office hours in an educational environment should be.

When she turned the corner onto the right hallway, she stopped dead in her tracks. Quinn Lysander, head coach of the women's basketball team, and Jessie Ximena, owner of the best health club in town, waited patiently near the end of the hallway. In their hands were flowers, champagne, cupcakes, and balloons. All very colorful, all very embarrassing.

Jessie stood out like always, that tall frame beautifully muscled and long, with black hair surrounding a face that could make anyone suck in a gasp. Yes, that was how she'd reacted the first time she saw Jessie at her gym and every time thereafter.

The one time she'd spotted her in the D/s club, she'd done everything she could to disappear within the swallowing crowd. It was the first time she'd ever seen someone from Charlottesville in the Washington, D.C. club. She couldn't help stalking her, watching what she'd do, whom she'd approach. She'd watched a lot of people at that club. None of them reacted like Jessie had, especially not on their first time. And she was positive it had been Jessie's first time. Yet the way Jessie moved so easily, interacted so confidently, garnered attention so effortlessly, there wasn't a woman in there that didn't want her. Subs pressed insistently for her affection, and Dommes offered to switch for the chance to be with her. She'd never seen anything quite as fascinating as this anthropological display of behavior surrounding the gorgeous woman.

When one of the rebuffed subs walked over to her instead, she lost focus on Jessie. For the next two minutes, the exchange told her that this sub wouldn't be right for that night.

As she was turning back toward the last place she'd seen Jessie, a voice sounded in her ear. "You're different."

Vertebra popped in her neck with the sudden twist to face this woman who'd managed to sneak up on her. Jessie stared down at her from that impressive height. Her heartbeat sped up to a rhythm that actually caused pain. This was only the second time she'd interacted with Jessie. The first was much more casual and completely innocent at Jessie's gym.

Would she be recognized? Her disguise was intact: hair slicked back in the style she only wore at this club, gel darkened it several shades, dark red painted her lips making them appear larger, and the wrap around eye mask cloaked her features. Still, she couldn't be sure of her anonymity. Her stomach clenched at the thought.

"Let's play," a sexy brunette offered herself to Jessie. Her sheer bodice covering left nothing to the imagination.

"Not tonight," Jessie brushed off the brunette, turning her attention back. "Your mask is intriguing. Enough to hide the shape of your nose, cheekbones, and eyes, not like the others in here."

No, it wasn't very similar. Breathe in.

"You wear it to disappear."

Yes, she did. Hold four seconds.

"Just enough left of your face to entice."

No, not quite. Breathe out.

"I'm enticed." Jessie's simple statement nearly knocked the wind from her. She'd noticed Jessie in town, and when she'd met her at her club, she'd given a fleeting thought as to what kind of relationship she might have with a woman like this. It would be exciting. It would be fulfilling. It would be normal. Exactly what she wished she could have. Exactly why she always found herself coming to this club. Normal was an unattainable dream and had been for a while.

When the overture didn't garner a response, Jessie scanned over her, taking in her leather tank, leather pants, and motorcycle boots. Lust flared in Jessie's eyes, bringing a wash of heat equal to stepping from frigid A/C into hot summer sunshine. Her lips, though, tightened in disappointment. "You're not a switch?"

"No." *Never.*

"Too bad," Jessie murmured seductively. "We wouldn't have to use restraints or...implements?"

Yes, they would. "No."

Jessie's enthralling brown eyes blinked slowly before taking another stroll over her body. A confident smile pulled at those kissable lips. "You sure?"

She stared up at this gorgeous woman, heartbeat clattering to the point of near dizziness. She wished she could have her. She wished she wanted to have her. If anyone could ever break through, Jessie might just be the one to do it, especially with the anonymity of this club. "I'm sure."

"Okay, doll." Jessie smiled wistfully and started to turn away but stopped. "I really like your mask." Her fingertips were suddenly sliding along the wide strap of leather at her temple and around to where it knotted in the back. Every instinct screamed to pull back or shove the hand away, but as if sensing her discomfort, Jessie dropped the fingers from their exploration. Never once did the fingertips touch her skin, not even her hair. Boundaries had been blurred but never crossed.

That had made the biggest impression, even after becoming better acquainted with her. It was often her first thought whenever she spotted Jessie, like today. Seeing their purpose at the office door, she decided to slink away before the two women noticed. Surely, they'd be gone by the time she returned later.

Footsteps clacked loudly around the corner and the tall duo spun in her direction. *Damn!* She'd been caught.

Chapter 8

H appy birthday, Briony!" Jessie and Quinn exclaimed, filling the quiet corridor with boisterous and highly embarrassing noise.

"You guys!" I admonished, rushing past the thankfully few people in the hallway to contain the humiliation. Too late. Several of my associates opened their doors to get a gander at their newly over-the-hill colleague. Thirty-nine, gadzooks! After a few more half-hearted birthday wishes, I finally reached the offending duo. They stooped to wrap me into a group hug, smiling widely, no doubt tickled that they'd managed to embarrass me.

I turned to unlock my door and minimize their exposure to my colleagues when Quinn called out, "Hi, M. How ya doing? Long time no see."

"Hello, Quinn," M spoke from her distant point at the end of the hallway. Had I passed by her without even noticing? No, she must have just arrived. I hoped even the sight of two beautiful giants with birthday treats wouldn't have districted me to the point of walking right by her. "Hi, Jessie," she greeted, advancing cautiously toward us.

"Hey there, M," Jessie offered in her usual friendly fashion.

M shifted her attention to me, glancing briefly at the balloons and other goodies in my friends' hands. "We can do this another time. I didn't realize it was your birthday."

Decked out in a tailored pantsuit, she looked both poised and ridiculously uncomfortable to be standing here with us. Unlike at the department meeting, her light brown hair was moussed or pasted into a style that perfectly complimented her beautiful triangular face. At the meeting, she'd let the three to four inch strands lie flat on her head without any product. The eyeliner and dusting of foundation had also been absent as had the small gold hoops she wore in her earlobes. I'd been too shocked by her outgoing behavior in class to notice any difference last week, but I found it interesting that she dressed and wore her hair differently in class than for department functions. Where she'd looked overtly androgynous in the meeting, her femininity was entirely present today, taunting me again with its allure. Today, however, I was no longer certain about her sexuality. She didn't seem to have the comfort level one would normally enjoy when among like-kind people.

Curiosity compelled me to find out how they all knew each other, but before I could ask, Jessie offered, "You haven't been at the gym in a while. Been busy?"

"Always." She didn't meet Jessie's gaze. So, it wasn't just me that caused her shyness. Good to know. "I'll come back tomorrow?" She directed her question to the two taped birthday cards on my door. Javier and Alexa strike again.

"No, stay, please," I implored, hoping to use her as the lever to pry these two from my office. Hastily, I reached back to grab her elbow, but it wasn't where I'd grabbed for it. She now stood two steps to the right, waiting to follow Quinn inside as soon as I opened the door. Well, at least she wasn't going to bolt on me.

"Didn't think you'd make it through the day without a birthday wish from your friends, did you?" Jessie goaded. The relaxed tone that I'd heard on the phone when I'd called to welcome her back from her honeymoon was so apparent on her face today.

"I was hoping," I muttered and slung my laptop case onto the cluttered desk where stacks of research and copies of proposals reached to nearly my height. This was the reason M and I were meeting today.

"C'mon, Bri, since this is the last birthday we'll be able to acknowledge truthfully, we couldn't let it slip by. Willa made me promise no more birthdays after thirty-nine. For the big 4-0 this year, we draped everything in black to have a somber little event. That really chapped her." Quinn spoke fondly of her partner. I'd been out of town, giving me the perfect excuse to miss the party. Now, I almost wished I'd been there.

A soft laugh turned my attention back to the open doorway. M hadn't tried to crowd into the office with us. The full smile she wore said that she also knew Willa, which made at least three of the group that she knew. Interesting that we'd never been introduced seeing as we both worked at the university.

"Thanks for giving me up." I feigned annoyance at Quinn. I didn't really care if anyone knew my age, but it might help deter them from their course.

"Oops." Quinn clapped a hand over her mouth and winked a blue eye at M. A faint tinge of pink painted M's cheekbones before she seemed to will it away.

"This is so nice of you guys." I brought their attention back to expedite their departure.

"We want to take you to dinner if you're free," Jessie said. "Lauren and Will can meet us there."

"If not, we're having a dinner party in your honor this Sunday," Quinn squelched my hope of deterring their intent. I could beg off an impulsive dinner invitation, but their Sunday dinners were a constant. If I didn't make it this Sunday, she'd do it another Sunday.

"Really, it's not necessary."

"We know, but we're doing it anyway. What kind of friends would we be if we didn't cause you at least some heartburn?" Jessie joked.

The kind that I'd want to spend my birthday with? Only I couldn't voice such a snide retort. As much time as I'd spent with them over this past year, they still didn't know I had a dark, snarky side. I found that few could actually handle it without eventually being offended. "Indeed, what kind would you be?"

"So?" Quinn persisted, fastening the balloons to my chair.

"I've got plans tonight, but thank you."

"Sunday, then. What time, Quinn, seven?" Jessie said with finality.

"Seven, my house." Quinn sealed my birthday celebration fate.

"Fine," I sighed, hoping that I just looked like I was acting bothered.

They studied me for a moment then took in M's position in the doorway. "We don't want to interrupt your workday. Happy birthday, Bri." Quinn leaned down to enfold me in a hug.

"You're different," Jessie whispered when it was her turn to hug me. "Something about you has changed."

I couldn't stop the jolt of surprise. Once again, she'd spotted a truth about me almost before I had. The last time, she'd saved us both from a catastrophic attempt at sex before I was anywhere near ready. She'd recognized it and nobly not taken advantage of my vulnerability. For that, I'd always be grateful.

"I'm glad, Briony." She nodded sagely when she pulled back. "Really glad."

I didn't have a chance to thank her before she and Quinn shuffled out the door, not that I would have been able to without tears. She recognized that I was finally ready to move on after she'd been the only one to understand when I couldn't before.

"We'd love it if you could join us Sunday, M," Quinn offered to the now unseen woman.

From somewhere in the hallway, I heard M respond, "Kind of you to include me, but I can't make it. Thank you, though." The expected response strangely disappointed me. I would have liked to see M interact with that boisterous group.

"Another time," Jessie insisted, studying the still out of view woman. "Hope to see you at the gym soon." With that, they both made their exit, having effectively done their job of embarrassing me on a day that used to be a quiet celebration for Meg, Caleb, and me.

I waited several moments for my expected visitor to resurface. When she didn't appear in the doorway, I crossed over to the opening and nearly mowed her down. As I was bringing my hands up to stop the expected impact, she jerked back as if we'd collided. "Sorry," I offered because her stance from four steps away told me I'd given her a fright.

"My fault." She glanced over at Jessie and Quinn's disappearing forms like she was expecting them to come loping back to see what happened.

"Please, come in." I stepped back into the cubicle-sized office and pointed to one of the chairs.

She cautiously entered and took the offered seat, sliding it back a bit for a better position at the L-shaped desk. Her eyes landed on every stack of work we were facing then bounced around to take in the remaining items in my office. She didn't seem as daunted as I was by the task at hand. Well, good, because I could use a calming influence to settle my own concern over the amount of work left to be done.

"Happy birthday," M said softly, her eyes taking in the champagne, cupcakes, and flowers then swinging up to look at the colorful balloons.

"Thank you." I gave a breathy laugh at the unexpected but not unpleasant surprise that my friends had managed.

"I can make it after class tomorrow instead?" She gestured at the stacks.

"Oh, no, that's okay. I don't like a fuss."

"You told them you had plans."

"Hmm?" I thought back to what I'd said. "Oh, I was trying to—" I cut myself off, realizing that M knew them and might be offended if I told her I'd blown them off. "Just my usual plans," I finished weakly.

A familiar ring on my cell phone interrupted us. Caleb didn't call when I was working unless he needed something. I hated to be rude, but it would be a couple of hours before I could call him back if I didn't take the call now. "Do you mind if I take this?"

"Please." She brushed her hand toward my bag where the cell phone issued its second ring. She shifted her chair back and started to get up.

I reached out to stop her, but once again, her arm wasn't where I'd aimed. "You don't need to leave." I grabbed my phone and flipped it open. "Hi, handsome." My greeting brought on a slight tightening of M's brow before she ignored my assurance and stepped outside.

"Hi, Mom. Happy birthday," Caleb sang through the open line.

"Thanks, but you already said that this morning at breakfast." I let a little suspicion filter through.

"I kinda called for something else, but it's your birthday."

I knew him too well. "What's up?"

"Hank invited me to Kings Dominion as soon as school lets out. Can I go?"

This was also something I was just getting used to. He was now old enough to go places when he hung out with friends instead of just sticking around their houses. An amusement park with only Hank's elderly grandmother as chaperone seemed a little precarious. "Let me talk to Lucille about it, and we'll see."

"That's the thing," he started. "Mrs. Stewart wants you to come along with us. She thinks it would be better if there were four of us."

That made me feel better about letting him go. "Sure, sounds fun."

"Way cool! Thanks, Mom, and can we go out to eat for your birthday?"

"Sure, we can. Make sure Holly remembers I'm going to be an hour later than usual this evening. We'll figure out where to eat when I get home, 'kay?"

"Yeppers," he confirmed and clicked off.

Once I'd shut off my phone and stored it, I realized that I'd lost my visitor again. "M?" When she didn't immediately reappear, I went to the doorway. She was standing on the other end of the hallway, well out of earshot of my phone call. "Ready to start?"

"Yes." She strode toward me with the same confidence I'd seen in her classroom. A door banged open and two associate professors spilled out of an office, laughing. The sudden appearance of others in the deserted hallway changed M's stride. So much so that the two men didn't even notice her as they crossed paths. Almost as if she pulled her entire energy source from her personal space and shrunk into herself to become invisible.

It wasn't until she dropped back into the open chair that she spoke again. "I hope nothing happened to your birthday plans."

"Oh, no. It was something else. I apologize for the interruption. I don't usually take calls in the middle of meetings."

"It's okay." She grabbed the pile of proposals in front of her and handed half to me, obviously eager to get to work.

"How about a birthday cupcake to fortify us?" I grabbed the plate of cupcakes I assumed Caroline had baked for me. She could do illegal things with flour, eggs, and sugar.

"Oh, I couldn't," M declined with a polite smile.

"Sure you could, Madeline," I goaded. "Melisande? Muriel?" No response. Strike three more options from the list. "I shouldn't have to eat alone on my birthday." The guilt card almost always worked, and the flash of smile told me it wouldn't fail this time either. I handed over the plate, and she plucked one of the chocolate treats for herself. "My friend Caroline is a world class baker as you're about to find out. I'll have to make sure you get your own supply of cupcakes on your birthday."

"Oh, um..." She shook her head and waved off a reply.

"C'mon, you know mine, when's yours?" I prodded.

A frown knitted her forehead, clearly perplexed by my persistence. Well, she didn't know me very well. She'd better get used to persistence. "I don't have one."

Now, that's a first. "You mean you don't celebrate yours, or you don't care for them? I was never wild about mine either, but now you know it. So, cough it up."

"I don't have one," she repeated, taking a small bite from what I knew would be a delicious cupcake.

As her word choice settled in, I backtracked, "Oh, is it a religious thing?" I seemed to remember that some religion didn't acknowledge birthdays.

She chewed pensively, the quiet building to an uproar. "No, I just don't know when it is." The soft admission stunned me. Only two reasons why came to mind. I didn't like either, not for this woman. My worried expression prompted her to offer more. "I was left on a church doorstep when I was a baby. No local birth record and no missing person's report. I know I'm thirty-seven, give or take six months, but that's all I know about where and when I was born."

"Oh my." The information snatched the breath from my lungs. I knew there were others with a similar background, but that knowledge didn't lessen the effect.

"So, no birthday," she rushed to cover the tension. Instinctively, I knew she hadn't shared that with anyone in a long time, if ever. A small grin appeared before she said, "At least I don't have to worry about people trying to embarrass me on my birthday."

A burst of laughter slipped from my mouth. Her tease felt good. Really good. Maybe she was loosening up a bit. I could get used to that.

Chapter 9

On the last day of break before summer classes began, Caleb and I headed over to his best friend's house. Today was the big amusement park day. I was almost as excited as he was. It'd been years since I'd been on a rollercoaster. I knew I'd mostly be keeping Lucille company and making sure the boys didn't run her ragged, but I expected to get on a few screamers before the end of the day.

Most of my time off this week had been spent with Caleb whose own summer break had started three days ago. Because I now had work to deal with, he'd been given a choice for his summer. He could stick around to hang out with friends and have our part-time sitter, Holly, go full-time for the summer while I worked, or he could think about summer camp. He chose the latter, spurred on by two of his cousins who would be going as well. Unfortunately, it was a sleep-away camp in Vermont, and my heart clenched at the idea of him being gone for six weeks. He was too young for that, but my parents along with Meg's parents and sisters would alternate taking him on the weekends. He'd be so busy being the treasured guest of every household and playing with his cousins at camp that he probably wouldn't even notice I wasn't around. I tried not to dwell on that.

As I shut off the engine in Lucille's driveway, the front door burst open and Hank stepped out onto the porch. His bespectacled face beneath a mishmash of brown curly hair smiled widely at us. "Hi," he boomed out as we approached. He wore the standard kid uniform of shorts and a wrinkled t-shirt. Caleb had on the same thing.

"Hi, Hank." I tapped my fist against his. Caleb told me this was the preferred greeting from now on, or until they decided on a different greeting, probably next week.

"I can't wait to get there." Caleb followed his friend inside, leaving me to shut the door.

"Hello?" I called out, not wanting to startle Lucille if she hadn't heard our car drive up.

"In here, Briony." Lucille's voice wavered uncharacteristically.

I walked through the house into the family room and found her propped up in a reclining chair. Her face looked pale, the shiny cap of white hair a bit dull. "Are you feeling all right, Lucille?" I rushed to her side.

"A touch of the flu bug, I'm afraid." She moved to get up, but I pressed my hand to her shoulder. "I don't think I'm up to an outing today."

"Of course not. I could take the boys on my own, or we can wait for a day you feel up to it." I felt disappointed that she wouldn't be there to keep me company. The boys tended to speak in abbreviations that only they could decipher.

Worry etched her face, which was understandable. Lucille had been Hank's legal guardian for four years since his mother's neglect had brought him to her. She always had a finger on where he was and what he was doing. "I had something else in mind."

Before she could tell me more, a voice called out from the mudroom beside the kitchen. "Okay, I replaced the hinge on the shed door, checked your brakes, and took down that failing limb on the dogwood near the back fence. What was the other thing you needed me to do, Luce?" Two thumps sounded as the person dropped her shoes by the back door before she proceeded into the kitchen.

My mind was just clicking the voice into place as M appeared, more relaxed than I'd ever seen in the weeks we'd been working together. When she caught sight of me, she snapped into perfect posture, a shield of armor now in place. The look on her face probably mirrored the surprise I showed on mine.

"M, dear, come meet a friend of mine." Lucille held a hand out to her. "This is Briony Gatewood."

"Yes, we've met," M stopped her as she took one cautious step toward Lucille. "Briony's the other professor assigned to the venture project with me."

"Oh, how wonderful." Lucille's eyes gleamed proudly at her visitor.

"Hello," I offered, still a little shell shocked. I spread my hands over my abdomen and down my thighs, checking that my shirt was still buttoned and my knee length shorts were fastened. Something about her penetrating gaze made me think I might have lost my clothes.

"Hi," she replied, watching my hands mark their path. "What brings you here?"

The boys burst out of Hank's room, one shooting a Nerf dart at the other before they reached us. "Hiya, M," Caleb called out, much to my dismay. He knew her?

She smiled widely at them. "Hi, Caleb." Her hands gestured effortlessly as she spoke. "You guys hanging out today?"

"Guess what we're going to do today?" Hank asked her. Three of the seven words trailed off without a hard ending. Almost every word that ended in a consonant tended to blend into the next as a result of suffering profound hearing loss when he was six. He wore hearing aids to help him discern some sound, but for the most part he was effectively deaf. His lip reading skills were exceptional, which made it almost as easy to communicate with him as it was for anyone not hearing impaired.

"Are you joining the Army?" M guessed, her hands back in motion.

"Nooo," the boys chorused together through giggles.

"Are you joining the circus?" Long fingers made deliberate gestures. Although unfamiliar, I now recognized she was signing her questions to them. Fluent in American Sign Language, too? What didn't she know how to do?

"Nooo." The boys laughed again, and I felt a smile drift across my face.

"Don't tell me you're joining the Boy Scouts?" Her lips pressed together in contemplation.

"Nuh-uhn," Caleb assured her.

"Oh, good. I never really got the Boy Scouts. Why doesn't someone just tell them to stand outside the room marked *Boys* at your school? If you wait a few seconds, the boys will come out and you won't have to scout for them." Raucous kid laughter drowned out mine and Lucille's. She had these boys completely spellbound, just like with her students. I hardly recognized her as the woman who gave such timid responses to any question I posed while hunkering over the work we'd been doing together.

"No," Hank started and continued with a blur of his hands.

"Hank." M stopped him with a kind smile and tilt of her hand. "Talk out loud, so we don't exclude others in the room."

"Oh yeah, sorry. We're going to Kings Dominion," Hank supplied then glanced at his grandmother huddled under an afghan. "Or we are if you can go with us, right, Gram?"

M whirled around and stared at Lucille. "Was this the other thing you needed me to do today?"

Lucille looked suitably guilty. "Well, I was hoping you wouldn't mind. The boys have had their little hearts set on this for weeks."

"I don't mind taking the kids by myself, really," I interrupted, knowing part of her hesitation had to do with Hank's impairment. The boys spent the majority of their time together under her watch, so I wasn't as practiced with making sure that he could understand me or knowing how to get his attention at times. For an overprotective grandmother, that prospect was a little frightening.

"How do you know Lucille?" Even though she'd asked me the question, M continued to sign for Hank's benefit.

"This is my mom." Caleb curled his fingers around my forearm.

Her eyes snapped from him to me and back again. I got this a lot because we didn't look alike, but I refused to ease people's discomfort by telling them that I was an adoptive parent. No law existed that said you had to look like your family members.

Rather than the suspicious narrowing of eyes I usually received, M honored me with a grateful smile. Her eyes shifted with a fond look to my son and his best friend. "Kings Dominion was on tap for the four of you today, huh? But Lucille got the flu and now you're down one?"

"Yep," both boys responded.

"You'd like me to go, Luce?" M posed her question to the no longer worried Lucille before turning to me. "Would it be okay if I tagged along, Briony?"

Amazed by nearly everything about her this morning, I couldn't believe that she, who always contemplated every move she made and every response she gave, could spontaneously agree to an all-day trek through an amusement park with two kids. "Of course."

The boys high-fived while shouting, "Score!" and "Cool!"

"Three conditions." M turned back to them, barely deflating their excitement. "You stick close by, no darting off without one of us." They nodded eagerly. "You bring some travel games so you don't keep asking us when we're going to get there." Hank brushed his fist through the air twice beside his face. The sign for "yes," I knew that much. "And three, you let me use you as a human shield on all the water rides."

We all laughed at that one. What a delightful way she had about herself. How was it that no one at work could recognize this about her? Well, I'd have a whole day to get to know her. I planned to use my time wisely.

Chapter 10

The day hadn't gone quite as planned. Despite insisting on the travel games, M had spent the majority of the trip getting the boys to talk about their summer plans, school, baseball and soccer teams, or whatever else she could think up. If I didn't know she was truly happy to be chatting with the boys, I'd have thought she was using them as a buffer to speaking with me.

Once we'd gotten to the park, the boys mapped out our trek so that we'd hit every ride in the most efficient manner. It was like listening to a couple of field generals. I quickly learned that I'd be the willing follower when it came to whatever was planned today.

Sometime in the late afternoon, we approached the one ride I'd been dreading: a sheer 272-foot drop. My stomach couldn't take it. As the boys ran ahead of us to the start of the long line, I stopped them. "Listen, guys, I'm going to sit this one out."

"Aww, Mom," Caleb coaxed.

"You go ahead, I'll watch from the bench over there." I pointed at one of the seating areas in the shade of the oak trees.

"Scaredy cat," Caleb taunted.

"Scaredy cat who won't risk wetting her pants by sitting out this ride," I boasted.

"Now, you've got me worried." M tilted her neck up to glare at the menacing ride. "Do you mind company?"

My head pitched back on its own, surprised by her request. "That would be nice. They'll be in line for some time."

"You guys okay to take this one solo?" she asked. They grinned like they were about to get away with something, but she stopped their hasty escape. "You stay in line. When you're done with the ride, you follow the exit right back to where it comes out over there." She pointed to the opening in the fence where dazed riders were emerging from the exit. "We'll be right here. What do you do if someone approaches you and asks you to go somewhere with them?"

"Run away and find you or a police officer," Hank responded.

"What do you do if a nice man asks for your help with finding his kids?" While the first question was pretty standard, this one had me swallowing roughly.

"Run away," Hank repeated.

"And if a nice lady in line offers you something to drink, what then?"

"Say 'no, thank you,' " Hank said.

"Does this make sense, Caleb?"

He glanced nervously at me before he answered, "Yeah."

"It's okay to talk to the people in line around you. Just don't go anywhere with them or accept anything from them, okay?" Her voice was steady and sure, trying not to frighten the kids, but I detected an undercurrent of fear in her tone. I didn't know the whole story about Hank's mother, but she was the reason he'd lost his hearing. Perhaps something more sinister than what I'd thought was her neglectful disregard of a bad fever occurred.

"M's right, kids," I offered in a lighter voice. "You're in line to go on the ride. Then you're right back here, got it?"

"Yeppers," Caleb agreed, visibly more relaxed now that I'd supported her warnings. They waved and raced away.

"I didn't mean to scare your son. Hank is used to it." M floated to the bench beside me.

"No, it's fine. I should have thought of it. Of course, I've had the 'stranger' talk with him, but reminders are obviously necessary. Thank you."

She nodded and the direct gaze she'd been using with the boys faltered. "Caleb's an extraordinary person. You must be so proud."

I caught my breath at her unusually phrased compliment. "I am, thank you. He's the light of my life."

"I've known Hank since he came to live with his grandmother." She watched the dramatic drop of the ride the kids would soon brave. "Caleb is his first friend." I faced her on the bench, shocked to hear that. "Kids don't like people who are different. Hank talks funny; he doesn't always pick up everything they say; he's hard to be around because you have to make sure you're facing him when you talk. That's not easy for adults to handle, let alone kids. They avoided him, made fun of him, were mean to him. This is his third school in four years." My eyes misted for that sweet boy. "About a year ago, Hank started talking nonstop about this new boy named Caleb. When I finally saw them together, Caleb treated him like any other kid, like nothing about Hank was different or abnormal. Because of him, Hank has made a few more friends. They aren't like Caleb, though. I'm sorry that I never made it a point to meet his mother and thank her for such a wonderfully accepting boy."

Her hands had continued to sign. I smiled and reached out to give her a break, but before I touched her, her hands dropped to her sides. She gave a sheepish look, obviously not aware she'd been signing.

"That's the best compliment I've ever received." Far better than anything anyone could say about me. "I wish I could take all the credit, but Caleb's wonderful all on his own."

"He's added decades to Lucille's life now that she doesn't constantly worry about Hank."

"How do you know her?" I brought my leg up and rested an elbow on the back of the bench to get more comfortable.

She watched my adjustment intently, waiting until I'd settled into another position before answering. "She had a flat in the grocery store parking lot and not one person stopped to help. I drove her to the tire shop for a new one then changed it for her when we got back to her car. It was the only time I've ever been late for a class."

"That was very generous of you, and you've been performing chores for her ever since?"

"It's my pleasure." She dismissed the idea that anything she did for Lucille was a chore. "She reminds me of—" I leaned forward, waiting to hear the comparison, but nothing came. When she realized I wouldn't let it go, she admitted, "The nun who took me in."

"You were raised by a nun?"

"She had to leave the Church to keep me, but she'd found me and didn't want to let me go, so she left."

"Wow. Child services didn't get involved?" That was hard to imagine, even over thirty years ago.

She looked away, her eyes flicking from person to person seeming to take a head count. "I was apparently in bad shape when she found me, some physical abuse and severe malnutrition. I had to stay in the hospital for weeks. My response rates were slow, and the doctors were convinced I'd be intellectually and developmentally disabled. In those days, the word 'retarded' made me unadoptable."

Again with the wow. Who said doctors always knew what they were doing? And looking at her now, it was amazing to imagine she'd ever had any problems intellectually or physically. "So your nun found you, got you to a hospital, and probably stayed by your side every day until she decided that you were more important than her choice of life?"

"Yeah," she agreed with an amazed laugh. "She was about Lucille's age. Being a nun was all she knew, but she gave it up for a baby who showed up late one night."

"Well, babies can have that effect on people." I spoke from experience. During Megan's pregnancy, I was scared witless that the kid would arrive and I wouldn't love it enough. The fear was one of the reasons I'd never wanted children. But like the old cliché, the second he was put in my arms, my heart melted. "Did she name you?"

The smile reached her eyes this time. I could tell she'd come to expect my guesses. "Yes."

"First and last?" A single nod to confirm. "That means there's a high likelihood that your name is Latin or a saint's name. Mary? Margaret? Mary-Margaret? Margaret-Mary?" She laughed and the sound burrowed deep inside me. "You're probably not even going to tell me if I guess right, are you?" She glanced away, but the smile remained, confirming my suspicion. "Wait a minute! A nun, an ex-nun, gave you a last name that is the first name of the man who poked fun at the Catholic Church, inciting reform while remaining a devote Catholic?"

"You know *In Praise of Folly*?" Her eyes flashed, delighted interest making them glitter in the sunshine.

I nodded and gave a breathy laugh. "Oh, I like this nun."

"Yes, she was something."

Uh-oh. "She's not with us anymore?" A slight headshake was my only reply. "I'm sorry to hear that. She sounds like a terrific lady."

She looked away suddenly. I knew that she was fighting tears. I'd made the same motion myself many times over the last three years. Normally, this would spur my own tears for Megan, but this time, my eyes misted for her sadness.

"How do you know Quinn and Jessie?" She posed the question to the start of the ride's line with a rough voice. It was meant as a diversion, but I didn't mind.

"I met Jessie at her club when I joined. Is that how you know her?"

"Yeah." She exhaled and turned back, totally composed. "Did she introduce you to Quinn or did you meet her on campus?"

"Through Jess." Since we were becoming friends, I decided to be completely truthful. "Actually, Jess and I were seeing each other for a while."

It wasn't shock that met me, but it wasn't the knowing look I'd expected either. "But Jessie is..."

"A woman?" I prompted lightly. "Yes, I'm gay." *And so are you, or at least I'm ninety percent sure. Now would be the perfect time to tell me.*

Chapter 11

The wait took longer than I expected. Park sounds filled the space between us as I waited for any telling expression to cross her face or for what I figured she'd admit. Instead, she nodded, checked her watch, then trained her eyes on the exit area of the ride.

Okay, maybe I was wrong. Or maybe I've shocked her into silence. Maybe she was now contemplating the fact that she had a few more hours stuck in a park with a big, scary lesbian. Having been raised by a nun, it wasn't outside the realm of possibility. Not that being five-five and a half is big, and I'm hardly scary, except when I've had a particularly fitful night after forgetting to take off my makeup.

"Jessie is a nice woman," she said to break the silence, a first for her. Silence didn't seem to bother M the way it bothered others.

"Yes, she is. She introduced me to her group of friends, and they've sort of adopted me."

"That's nice."

Yes, it was. I was still getting used to having a large group of friends. Some nosy, some obnoxious, some sarcastic, but all very caring.

"Mom! Mom! You missed out. That ride was so cool." Caleb raced up to us and slid himself onto my lap. The unconscious movement spurred my arms to fold around him.

Hank stood next to M looking at Caleb's position then at her. She signed something to him and stood quickly. "Did your face get stretched by the G-force on that ride?" she joked with him. He tested the stretch on his cheeks and soon Caleb was pulling at his own face. They dissolved into a fit of giggles.

"What's next?" I stood from the bench, ready to get on another coaster.

"When we were way up there," Hank pointed to the top of the ride, "we saw something we missed on the map."

"Yeah, yeah," Caleb agreed enthusiastically.

"A rock climbing wall," Hank said.

"Yeah, can we try it, Mom? Huh?"

The words slammed into me at lightning speed. Panic took hold of my heart, squeezing painfully. Swirls of hot changing to ice cold turned my gut inside out. The sudden onslaught of sensations coupled with panic shocked my system. I could feel myself start to hyperventilate. My hand shot out to grasp the back of the bench but not before floating dots of black swam before my eyes until only black remained.

Caleb's voice kept calling out to me, but I couldn't see him because my eyes were closed. After a couple of fluttering attempts, they finally opened and focused. The first thing I saw was Caleb. Those eyes so like mine showed worry, only I couldn't understand why. "Mom? Are you okay? Please, you have to be okay. You have to." He gripped my arms tightly.

I couldn't understand how I was looking up at him. It took a moment to orient, but I realized I was practically prone with my head and torso cushioned by something. "What? What happened?"

"You fainted." M's soft voice floated from somewhere above me. I couldn't see her but felt something shift behind me and realized that she was my cushion. "Are you okay?"

"Yes, I'm sorry." I propelled myself upright and twisted to look at her. The cause of the fainting spell came back suddenly and the icy chill returned.

M moved to stand from the sprawled position that must have kept me from hitting the ground. She reached a hand toward my shoulder then snapped it back to her side, her eyes glued to the appendage as if it had acted against her will. "You scared us a little, right, guys?"

Caleb climbed back into my lap. "Don't do that again, Mom." His forceful grip on my neck didn't stop the tremor that ran through his body.

"I'm okay, big guy. I'm so sorry I scared you." I kissed his cheek and tilted my face to look at Hank. "Sorry, kiddo."

"You're lucky M's quick or you mighta hit your head." Hank knelt beside us. His hand reached out to rub the back of my thanks-to-M uninjured head.

"She caught me, huh?"

"Better than a wide receiver," he confirmed.

"Well, I'm sorry I caused so much trouble. I don't know what happened," I lied confidently.

"My big mouth," Caleb mumbled. "I shoulda thought. I'm sorry, Mom. I didn't use my head."

His apology set off another bout of rapid breathing. "It's all right, sweetie. You don't have anything to be sorry about."

"What's wrong? What'd you say, Caleb?" Hank asked innocently.

"We can't go on the rock wall."

"Why not? Looks fun."

"It's dangerous. My other mom fell when she was rock climbing. She died."

Oh God, he said it. I tipped my head back, hoping the angle would help get in more air. My eyes caught the motion of M's hand to her heart and a quick intake of breath.

Hank looked curiously at his friend. "Your other mom?"

"Why don't we let Briony get comfortable up on the bench?" M interrupted. "What do you say, guys? Let's help her get up." She leaned down toward me, but the boys grasped my arms and pulled with their combined might. I resettled on the bench with a regretful look at M. She shouldn't have to deal with a mental breakdown. "Feeling better?" she whispered then reached into her pocket to hand some money to the kids. "Head over to that stand and grab Briony a bottle of water, will ya, fellas?"

Caleb hesitated only a second. "Okay." They dashed to the vender cart ten feet away.

"I'm sorry about all this." I knew it wouldn't suffice, but I had to say something. How embarrassing to pass out after having a perfectly innocent conversation with the kids. She had to think I was nuts.

"You're holding up well, I'd say. I'm sorry to hear about...Caleb's other mom."

I shook my head, helping to clear some of the haziness. "Her name was Megan, and it's been three years. I thought I'd worked through it."

"Your son wanted to try something that killed your spouse. You can't work through something like that, especially when it comes up at such an unexpected time and place."

I leaned my head back on the bench and breathed deeply. She was right. This had little to do with losing Meg and everything to do with the fear of losing Caleb. That knowledge helped ease some of the humiliation. "You're right."

"Here, Mom." A water bottle appeared in front of my face.

I twisted the cap and took a swig for appearances. "Thanks." As much as I hadn't thought it was necessary, the water helped quell some of the swirling sensations. I took two more swallows and felt much better. Maybe dehydration had helped spur this on. I pulled Caleb onto my knee and reached for Hank to bring him to my other knee. "Sorry I took a dive, guys. I know how scary that must have looked. Thanks for getting the water for me. It was exactly what I needed. Maybe we should stop for a snack before we move on to the next ride. What do you say?"

"You mean you still want to go on rides?" Caleb asked.

"We don't have to go home?" Hank looked so hopeful.

"Not unless you guys want to head home. I thought there were some more rides to hit yet?"

"Yay!" the boys cheered. Caleb turned back and kissed my cheek before catapulting off my knee. Hank gave me a one-armed squeeze around the neck and followed his friend.

"How could you have two moms?" he asked Caleb.

I froze in my effort to stand and turned to M, not wanting to take responsibility for explaining family units to a child who wasn't mine. She wore a similar expression, probably weighing how much detail to tell a ten-year-old.

Before either of us could say anything, Caleb answered, "Mom's gay, so I got two moms instead of a mom and a dad." *Well, that was easy.*

"Oh." Hank stared at his friend then shrugged. "You're lucky. Two moms would be cool." His tone was as carefree as when he talked about the latest video game. "Hey, can we get some popcorn?" He looked up at M, who shook herself slightly before handing over more money. I slipped some cash into Caleb's hand and instructed him to get some drinks to go with the popcorn. They darted off to the nearest cart to place an order.

A little dazed from their conversation, I turned a questioning glance at M. She shrugged as easily as Hank had and said, "Kids."

This time, it did explain everything.

Chapter 12

When do we get the dough?" Avery called out from his seat as I was jotting notes on the white board before the first class of summer session. A rumble of nervous laughter filtered through the room.

"Whoa, two profs for the price of one," a lanky student in the first row commented as M strode through the door.

She gave a silent chuckle and bounced her gaze around the half full room. This was probably the smallest class she'd ever been in charge of, but we'd purposely limited the class size for this symposium. Her glance landed on me last with a shy smile.

We hadn't had any time to ourselves for the rest of the day or evening last Friday. I still felt embarrassed for fainting and mortified that she'd broken my fall. When she'd dropped us back at Hank's house to pick up my car, she smiled and said goodnight then waited until we made it inside before driving off. No mention of my drama, nor did she mention whether or not she had a good time. I thought she had, but it might have become too much to handle with the talk of dead spouses, fainting spells and all.

"Good morning, Professor Gatewood," she spoke in her confident, friendly professor voice. Her linen pantsuit draped impeccably on her frame, but I couldn't help picturing the jeans and fitted polo she'd worn to the amusement park. A varied array of appearances and mannerisms, I figured even after a few years I probably wouldn't know all of them.

"Good morning, Professor Desiderius," I responded in kind, suddenly glad I went with a suit also, mine with a tan skirt and darker tan jacket.

The bell sounded and the last two students rushed inside as M took up a position beside me to address them. "Good morning, class. For those of you who haven't taken one of our courses before, I'm Professor Desiderius." She looked to me then.

"And I'm Professor Gatewood. We're going to be running this symposium together and acting as your advisory committee chairs."

"You all have a syllabus, one or the other of us will be leading the lecture two days a week," M picked up where I'd left off. "The rest of this course is self-application."

"Tag-team professoring," Avery joked, garnering laughs from the crowd. "Is that even a word?"

"No," I informed him drolly.

"We've inadvertently left a book off your syllabus. You'll want to add it to the list." M's comment sparked a groan from the crowd, but they all picked up their pens to jot down the title. "A dictionary, any edition will do. Buy it, learn it, live it."

We all laughed at her joke, but I marveled at the dry delivery. She'd just ratcheted up the ladder of my admiration. Dry humor was very hard to master. Not surprisingly, it was my favorite kind.

"Hey, Av, is your butt a little sore? 'Cause Professor D just spanked you, dude," another rangy looking guy taunted Avery good-naturedly.

"You'll be presenting your business proposals starting next week," I brought everyone back on track. "The dean and several other professors have formed a selection committee to decide on the funding elements."

"We've written up notes on each of your drafts," M informed them and began stepping up and through the tiers to hand back the proposals. "You've got two classes and the time in between to perfect these. This class has nothing to do with impressing your instructors or getting a good grade. If your idea is successful, forget about preparing for interviews and floundering until you find a job. This will be your job." The weight of M's words settled over the students. Before it had only been a class, now we'd just unleashed their competitive nature.

I waited until the excitement passed so they could focus their competitive fire. "Only five proposals will be funded. There are twenty of you in this room."

Heads twisted right and left before a loud, "Whoa!" sounded from the back row.

"Ah, a math genius," M joked, setting off a few snickers.

"Yes, that means if your proposal is not funded, you'll be working on the executive team of another funded company."

"No way!" a petite woman to my right spoke up.

"Any one of the 200 rejected proposals would love to take an open space in this class." M had finished handing out the marked up proposals and joined me back up front. "This is a decision that you'll need to make before noon tomorrow. If you can't agree to lead or work on someone else's team, send us an email. We'll produce a withdrawal slip for the registrar's office. If you move forward and find that you can't complete the requirements, you will not receive a passing grade."

"That seems harsh," Gary, one of my first-year students, commented.

"You're right. It is," I agreed. "But you're all taking up a spot that hundreds of others wanted. It wouldn't be fair to issue withdrawals when it's too late to fill the slot with another enterprising student."

Their eyes bugged a bit at the required commitment. None of my students had ever withdrawn, and I was betting that none of M's students had either; but when that was no longer a safety net, things got suddenly very serious.

They seemed to be absorbing the information as slowly as an already damp paper towel, so I made a quick decision. "Why don't you all take ten minutes to read through the notes we've provided on your proposals. When we get back, we'll start working through the best methods for tightening them up." A few of them nodded, but the rest still looked a little dazed. "Please use this time wisely."

I started toward the hallway and tipped my head at M. She looked momentarily puzzled but followed even though we hadn't planned a break for another hour. I waited to explain until we'd moved farther away from the classroom. "They needed some time to whine about the fact that three quarters of them will be working on someone else's idea rather than their own."

M started bobbing her head. "Not to mention time to deal with the permanence of the class."

"Exactly."

She smiled broadly, having forgotten to turn off her confident professor demeanor with me like she usually did. "That was effortless."

"And fun," I agreed. While we both planned to be in every class until the proposals were delivered and decided upon, we hadn't given thought to who'd talk when in those joint classes. I hadn't expected the tag-team effect, as Avery coined, but it had been effortless. Everything I thought to say next, she stepped in to add. It felt like my own safety net for this class. "I'm glad you 'volunteered' for this, M."

She smiled but her gaze turned serious as she locked eyes with me. "I'm happy to be involved, and glad to be working with you as well, Briony."

Something stirred through my abdomen. At first, I thought the dizziness from the other day might have returned, but this was an entirely pleasant feeling. Nothing at all to do with panic. "Me, too, Maria." Her lips pressed together, trying to suppress a smile. "Magdalena? Marcella? Meryl? Mirabel? C'mon, I'm running out of acceptable Latin options."

She blasted me with a radiant smile. "Let's go halt the grumble session and put these kids to work."

Chapter 13

My friends' daughter, Zalika, was in for a long night. Caleb worshipped her, followed her everywhere, and hung on her every word. Whereas Zalika, three years older, treated him like an annoying kid brother. Her parents, Isabel and Kayin, thought it was a riot and always encouraged me to bring Caleb to the Sunday night dinners whenever their daughter would be there. On the adoration scale, Zalika rated even higher than Quinn and Willa's dogs, and Caleb loved dogs.

"Zalika wants to shoot some hoops, Mom. Call when dinner's ready, 'kay?" he asked in a manner that said he was as grownup as Zalika and didn't really need permission.

"Did you ask Quinn or Willa if you could use their basketball court first?"

His whole face lit up. "Yeah, Quinn even said she'd give us some pointers later."

"Lucky you, bucko. Have fun." I resisted the urge to pat his bottom as he walked by, a reverent two steps behind Zalika.

"That's a great kid, Bri," Sam shared wistfully. She and Caroline had stopped trying to get pregnant through In Vitro and had started contemplating adoption. Something seemed to be holding them back, though. I was keeping my fingers crossed that it was simply a desire to go through a pregnancy rather than a niggling thought that adopting a baby wouldn't be the same as having Caroline's own baby. I'd never thought that way, even before I'd become an adoptive parent. Caleb was my son whether he was Megan's blood or mine or neither.

"Thanks, I like him." I bit my lip to hold back the smile.

Caroline grinned when I lost the battle. "Did you ever want more?"

"I never wanted one," I replied before I remembered that my dark humor might startle them. "I mean, it was Megan who was gung-ho on the idea, which made the decision pretty easy for me. I have to admit I've grown up with him."

"I find it hard to believe you were ever less together than you are now," Isabel complimented, or I thought it was a compliment.

"Believe me, I had a lot to learn about being a mom, but it's been worth it. Not that I need to tell you." She had three more years of experience with Zalika.

The doorbell rang and the last of the friends, Jessie and Lauren, arrived to officially start this week's Sunday night dinner. While I was invited every week, I managed to space out my attendance to once a month, sometimes longer. I really liked these women, but large groups intimidated. Ironic, seeing as I was a professor, but hey, I'm a puzzle.

"Hey, Briony," Jessie greeted when she got to my place in the circle of friends.

"Hi, Jess."

"Did you warn her?" Lauren asked, stepping up behind her partner.

"Laur!" half the group hissed at her.

My spine snapped straight, hackles raised. "Warn me about what?"

"They invited someone to dinner," Jessie responded in a regretful tone.

"An available, cute someone," another of the friends, Skye told me in her endearing Australian accent.

"We tried to stop them," Jessie insisted when she noticed my eyes growing wide and checking for the nearest exits.

"You're setting me up on a date?" I turned my most threatening stare on the group. Four of them, Willa, Quinn, Jessie, and Lauren threw their hands up as if to say, "Don't blame me." The rest looked entirely too pleased with themselves.

"She's coming to a dinner party," Isabel let me know with an innocence that wouldn't fool even the most gullible among us.

I scoffed, completely flabbergasted that they'd make this move without telling me. "Does she think she's coming here for a dinner party or a blind date?" I turned my question to Jessie, knowing she'd tell me the truth.

Unfortunately, Des, a.k.a. the loudmouth, responded first. "We might have mentioned that our beautiful, single, very available, desperately in need of a date friend would be joining us at the dinner party."

"You guys, I can't believe you did this!" I exclaimed and took several steps backward. "I can't believe you did this on a night when my son is here. What were you thinking?"

Most had the decency to look suitably chastised. It suddenly dawned on them that it might be difficult for a boy to watch his mother be on what he thought was the first date after his other mother had died. I'd never told him about my dating attempts with Jessie. Something deep inside told me that it wouldn't work out, so I never had to ease him into the idea.

"Oh," one of them managed.

"Yeah, 'oh.' I've got to get out of here." I started toward the door.

"No, don't leave!" three of them exclaimed until Isabel took over. "We'll pull her aside, give her the skinny."

"What are you going to tell her? 'Gee, I know we invited you to meet our loser friend who can't get her own date, which is why we're butting into her life; but, hey, her kid's here, and he might be a little upset to see his mom showing romantic interest in someone who isn't his other mommy?' " I knew my biting retort sounded harsh, but damn, they'd ticked me off.

While I apparently had Caleb's go-ahead to start dating, having a date in front of him might be testing that consent. When I was ready to start dating, I knew I'd have to tread carefully. Tell him only after I'd been on several successful dates, arrange a brief first meeting, then an innocent outing with no displays of affection, then ease him into the affection bit by bit.

A long silence ensued with guilty glances bouncing from couple to couple. "I'll show you to the back drive. It comes out next to our house a street away," Jessie offered. She didn't sound guilty. Like every other surprising moment with her, she just understood.

"No, don't go," Caroline pleaded. "We're sorry, Briony. We only want you to be happy. It's true we weren't thinking when we invited Erin on a night that you brought Caleb, but this doesn't have to be a date. Just meet her."

The doorbell rang, and I went completely rigid. I hated being cornered. I threw a desperate look at Jessie, the only one who seemed to understand my panic, but it was Lauren who reached for my hand. "C'mon, we'll go get Caleb and walk around the other side of the house to collect your car. I'll show you the way to the back drive."

Willa was already rushing to the French doors that led to her back patio and the path that would take us to her basketball court. The protests began, but Quinn silenced them all. "Enough," she said firmly before slowly heading toward the front door to let in her guest.

"I'll kick their asses for you," Jessie informed me as Lauren slid her hand into mine.

"Sorry about this," Willa apologized as we reached the back door, but it sounded more like, "Sorry about them." From what I knew, Willa and Quinn were the most recent additions to this tight-knit group, arriving four years before me, and her private nature often put her at odds with the group's actions and intentions.

"I'm sorry I snapped," I offered to the co-host of tonight's dinner party. I knew I was overreacting, but I still felt justified.

"Are you kidding? You're now my hero," Willa confided in a low voice with a smile before shuttling us out the door.

"That went as badly as I thought it would," Lauren told me as we passed by the pool. "Caroline called me on my way home from the office, and I told Jessie as soon as I walked in the door. She almost sprinted up here without me."

"Thank you. I wish I hadn't reacted that way, but…"

She stopped me after we'd cleared the view from the house. The sound of a bouncing ball from the sport court a hundred feet away wafted over us. "Don't be sorry for that. I've known most of them for nine years, and there's a reason that my best friends in the group are the two I'd made on my own back in college. The group can be overbearing and inappropriate. They were both to you tonight."

I let a relieved smile touch my face as I stared up at her. "Thanks for understanding."

"Jess and I think of you as a good friend. And I owe you for helping Jessie become the love of my life." She must have recognized the confusion in my expression because she explained, "Jessie was already on her way to making some changes in her life, but she told me that dating you made her understand just how much she'd been missing. I consider myself very lucky that the timing was wrong for you two."

I sucked in a deep breath. "That's…I don't know what to say." I really didn't. The partner of the woman I'd dated briefly was thanking me for preparing said woman for marriage? I couldn't take credit for that. "I hope you know that even if the timing had been perfect, we weren't right for each other. I suspected that even before I'd seen her interact with you; then I knew it for sure."

She beamed at a wattage level that only hopelessly-in-love people are capable of reaching. "Well, it only took me eleven years of friendship to figure it out," she poked fun at herself as we started toward the sport court. "None of them think you're incapable of getting a date, by the way. They just think a little push now and then isn't such a bad thing." Before we stepped onto the court, she turned toward me again. "Is it? Jess told me she thought you might be ready to start dating again. We'd be happy to introduce you to some women we know. Just introduce, not a blind date."

"Thanks, Lauren, I'll think about it." I squeezed the hand that was still gripping mine. Turning to the kids, I called out, "Caleb? Hey, bucko, I'm sorry, but I forgot about some papers I need to grade before class tomorrow morning. We'll have to beat feet out of here without staying for dinner. We can grab something on the way home." Not entirely a lie since I did have some work to do.

"Oh." He shot a disappointed look at Zalika, but because the sit down dinner was his least favorite part, he didn't stay disappointed too long. "Can we get burgers?"

"Sure." It was the least I could do, since I was cutting his "date" short and all.

* * *

After four groveling phone calls, I relented and headed down to Caroline's café for lunch and to clear the air. I hadn't handled the situation well. I could have been more cordial in my expression of worry over a blind date with my son as a tag along. But that they'd put me in the position where I reacted poorly still trumped any bad behavior on my part. Either way, three of the offending members had called, Caroline twice, and the least I could do was hand in an empty apology just to move past it.

I wasn't stupid enough to go alone, though. Javier rode shotgun as we found parking near the café. He was hoping to get a ringside seat to my humiliation and a free lunch. I just needed the buffer.

The café crowd bustled loudly. Javier grabbed a table while I went up to place our orders. Thankfully, it was busy enough that Caroline would be preoccupied at best. Someone at the counter took my order, and I was turning back to the table when Caroline came through from the kitchen.

"I'm so glad you're here." She came around the counter and hugged me. "I'm really sorry about last night. We weren't thinking, obviously."

"I'm sorry I snapped at you all. It's just I need to be careful with Caleb, handle it on our time." We smiled apologetically at each other, the tension vanishing. I could still be ticked that they'd tried to ambush me, but I couldn't be angry with friends who didn't understand my situation or how Caleb might react.

"But you could handle getting back out there when Caleb has a sitter?"

She looked so hopeful I had to throw her a bone. "I'm thinking about it."

She broke into a brilliant smile, the scar on her lip stretched wide. She'd gotten a little careless with her knifes in culinary school and had nicked the edge of her top lip. With her mouth resting, the scar was more visible than when she smiled or talked. "I'm so glad you said that." Something in her tone had me canting my head in suspicion. "Hey, Javier," she greeted him after walking me back to the table. "Done with classes for the day?"

I wanted to get back to her shifty tone, but Javier persisted in being the chatty Cathy he could be. I dropped into the seat facing him and looked up at my friend. I didn't think I was imagining her impish look. "What did you do?" I unleashed all the misgiving I was feeling.

She turned her best innocent face in my direction. "Nothing. I'm just glad to hear you're open to being set up."

"Do tell." Javier waggled his eyebrows at us.

"Hold up, I did not say anything about being set up."

"Just a meeting, not a blind date," Caroline assured. "If you had enough warning that you'd be meeting someone and Caleb was squared away, you'd be open to that, right?"

"I'd rather choose my own dates, but thanks for thinking of me." I tried for the brush off, but I didn't hold a candle to her persistence.

"C'mon, you can meet someone if I tell you in advance. We know a lot of great women."

"I can get my own dates," I grumbled, but they weren't listening.

"That's settled then." Caroline checked her watch presumably to note how far gone the lunch rush might be. When she didn't head to the counter right away, I went back on alert. "Would ten minutes be enough of an advance notice?"

Javier burst out laughing, causing Caroline to giggle along with him. Nothing like having friends who laugh at your misery.

"You did not!" I stated emphatically.

"Hey, you rushed out last night. Erin didn't get a chance to meet you. We had to give her some lame excuse for you not being there. I told her that I'd try to get you in for lunch today. Y'all could meet now instead."

"Car!" I shrieked and glared at the hysterical fit Javier was having. "Help?"

"Are you nuts? This is priceless. I'm only moving far enough away to get a good view of your little date."

"The pain will be physical and long lasting," I threatened him. "You'll no longer have use of certain muscles."

"It'll be worth it." He looked unfazed.

"I'm not doing this, Caroline. Call her and tell her that I didn't show."

"Nope, she's already on her way. C'mon, I know y'all will hit it off."

"No, no, no. This is not happening. You've got to give me fair warning. Tell her I blew you off, had a class, needed emergency acupuncture, got committed to an asylum, anything."

"A quick meet, please, Bri?" She batted her eyelashes at me.

"No. Sorry. Can't," I said with absolute finality.

Which was how ten minutes later, I found myself on a date.

The woman, Erin, was a bartender who liked action flicks, playing golf, fat Elvis better than young Elvis, old-fashioned arcade games, five card draw, and, you guessed it, long walks on the beach. Oh, and piercings, gauging by the number of holes in her face, ears, belly button—yes, she showed me—and the telltale loops at the peak of her breasts under her glued on tank top. And what ambush blind date meant to drive me to sign my own commitment papers would be complete without knowing her favorite sexual position? Woman on top, in case you were wondering, because I hadn't been. Her fit of giggles told me she thought that was a keen play on words. All this information within five minutes of plunking her bony frame into the seat my traitorous, one-time friend, Javier, had occupied. *Gaawwd!*

Aside from the woman being way too young for me both in age, ten years, and attitude, twenty years, I had to wonder what my friends were thinking. This setup was as bad as any that my straight friends might attempt when they'd suggest I meet the only other lesbian they knew, thinking, hey, they're both lesbians; they'll be perfect for each other. Honestly, someone help me.

The high maintenance, pale blond hair, lanky form, plump lips, and narrow nose were attractive enough, but I suddenly wondered if my friends thought I had a type. Not that Erin looked like Megan, but Meg wore her pale blond hair the same length and had a fit frame, too. Healthy, not bone thin like this one. Perhaps this was the best they could do on short notice? I shuddered to think about how many pale blondies they'd shove my way.

Sorry, Meg, I had nothing to do with this. I felt like I needed to at least think that in case she'd just heard me drag her into this fiasco. I caught Caroline bussing a table behind Erin, taking her sweet time picking up the one coffee cup left behind. I made a mental note to ask Lauren, the lawyer in the group, if juries took into account the people that you kill in a murder trial. As in, if they deserved it, maybe the sentence wouldn't be so endless. She stopped by Javier's new table, and they proceeded to have a quiet yet enthusiastic conversation that involved a ton of furtive glances in my direction.

Erin came up for a breath to take an audible gulp—pet peeve number one—of her cappuccino and bite into her carrot cake. "Of course," she started, talking with her mouth full—pet peeve number two along with any disregard of table manners—and continued, "everyone's dying to know how you managed to stay friends with Jessie after going out with her?"

Huh? How did we go from discussing the restrained jealousy her sisters had for her freewheeling lifestyle—her words not mine—to verifying a rumor about me? Thinking she'd just continue to mow down any attempt at a response on my part, I sat silent, waiting for the next shift in topics.

Perfect. On this, she was waiting for an answer. "Why wouldn't we stay friends?" Basic psychology: echo the question you don't want to answer.

"Because Jessie never stays friends with the women she fuc—" Her blue eyes snapped away then back to me. "Um, dates. I mean, she'd always stay friendly in case she wanted to go back for more, but somehow you managed to break into the inner sanctum of her group of friends. What's your secret?"

So Jessie hadn't told anyone other than Lauren and maybe Quinn that we hadn't slept together? I doubted it had anything to do with wanting to maintain a reputation and more to do with the fact that she was a lot more private than most people realized. She certainly wouldn't invade my privacy by sharing intimate, albeit G-rated, details of our relationship.

"Don't know." I wasn't about to offer anything more to one of the bartenders at the only gay and lesbian club in town.

"So," she began, leaning in too close. "Is she as good as everyone says?"

Please, she did not just ask that. What would make this woman think I'd talk about my sex life—or nonexistent sex life, rather—with a stranger?

She carried on, "I've heard all types of stuff about her. Like whatever you ask for, any fantasy, she'll deliver. Is it true? C'mon, you won't shock me."

Somehow I had the sneaking suspicion I could. Rather than attempt it, I made a big show of looking at my watch. "Oh, wow, I've got a class to teach in fifteen minutes. I'll just make it to north campus if I leave now. It's been nice," I knew I stumbled over that word, "to meet you, Erin."

"Okay?" She stared up at me, startled by my sudden change in elevation. "When can we do this again?"

She must have been on a different date than I'd been on because she couldn't think my not saying anything for twenty minutes straight and her clear envy slash unhealthy interest in Jessie, a recently married woman, was worth repeating.

"You know," I began, "Caroline didn't really tell me she'd arranged this meeting between us. If I'd known, I would have told her that my summer class schedule is going to take up all my free time. I tried to get her to call you, but you were only minutes away. It's been so nice getting to know you, though. I'm sure we'll see each other around town."

She stood, seemingly understanding that the dating version of awkward TMI was coming to a close. "I understand busy. The bar gets slammed during the summer. So, um, I'd be all right with a casual...buddy understanding." She hunched closer, using air quotes around the word "buddy" before finishing with, "Help blow off a little tension from the busy days. You down?"

Like I'd agree to a NSA arrangement with a total stranger who said things like "you down?" Even my ten-year-old son thought that phrase was out of style. Was this what dating was going to be like?

To do list: purchase gun, brandish in front of friends for fair warning, keep handy to put me out of my misery.

Chapter 14

Even though it wasn't my day teaching the symposium, I headed over to the classroom to see if M would take my advisory committee meetings next week so that I could take Caleb to the airport a couple days earlier than planned. One of his aunts was going on vacation with her family and wanted to see him before my parents packed him off to camp.

Two steps from the door, I heard a booming voice from inside. "That hardly seems efficient, Dr. Desiderius." M's reply was too soft to overhear before the voice sounded again. "Really? Is any of this relevant to launching a business? I was hoping that the university's resources had been placed in the proper hands."

Goddamn bastard! I recognized Dr. Wagner's voice as the one intentionally giving M a hard time in front of our students. The lowest form of low. Without trying to be quiet, I yanked open the classroom door. M stood behind the never before used podium. Her hands gripped the edges; if not I would bet they'd be clenched in anger. Mine sure were.

"Excuse me, Professor," I addressed M formally. "Class, sorry for the interruption. Dr. Wagner, I didn't realize you'd be auditing our symposium today. May I have a word, please?"

"After class, Professor," he nearly choked on the title.

"Now, please. I'm meeting with Dr. Goudy soon. I'd hate to keep him waiting because you couldn't pry yourself away from our engaging symposium." I smiled conspiratorially with the class.

He looked like he wanted to object again but knew I'd probably blame him for my delay in meeting with the dean. With a pointed stare of disdain at M, he stalked down the steps and brushed past me to the door.

I waved at the class in parting and glanced at my colleague in silent support. What I saw kept me from immediately following the Big Ass out the door. Rather than look relieved to have that menace leave her classroom, she looked visibly shaken. In a show of forgetting something, I headed back toward the center of the room. "One last interruption if you don't mind, Professor." She nodded as shyly as she had during our first few weeks of knowing one another. "We've got a change to the lineup of entrepreneurs for Thursday's class. I think you'll all be impressed by the guest speakers."

"Who'd you get, Prof?" Avery prompted.

"You want to spoil the surprise for the rest of the class, young man?" I bluffed, hoping the extra time would help wipe away Dr. Wagner's comments. "Have some questions prepared on something that isn't the cocktail napkin from the bar you go to tonight." They laughed at my warning, and I gestured for M to continue with the class. She looked a damn sight more sure of herself than when I'd first entered the room.

Dr. Wagner barely waited for the door to close behind us before demanding, "What's this about, Briony?"

I continued down the hallway to get us out of earshot. "Do not ever do that again."

He huffed at my menacing tone. "What are you talking about?"

"Your little power play in M's class. How would you like it if we slinked into your class and started questioning your expertise?"

"I did no such thing!" he proclaimed like he'd suddenly become a member of the royal family.

"You were purposefully trying to undermine her authority and question the validity of this program. Dr. Goudy won't be happy to hear that one of his faculty members was trying to stir up disquiet among the student body."

"You're exaggerating." Blotches of red appeared on his neck and face. "Besides, you weren't even there."

"I heard enough to know that you crossed the boundaries of professional decorum in an effort to make a colleague look foolish. That's unacceptable."

"You don't know what you're talking about. I asked a valid question, and she had no answer. I've heard how your little symposium is going." He sneered pompously. "You're letting the students take over. This project isn't a student club; it's serious money to fund serious businesses."

I resisted the urge to grab his lapels and shake him. "Don't talk to me about this project. You couldn't wait to throw your colleagues in front of the firing line for this class."

"I don't have to take this from you," he sulked.

"Not since I'll be reporting your behavior to Dr. Goudy, no, you don't. You'll have to take it from him." I smiled sweetly, watching as perspiration beads glistened on the red blotches.

"Screw you," he spat and stormed off.

So much for his Ivy League degree. Clearly, vocabulary lessons weren't included in the price of tuition. "Goddamn bastard!" I hissed loudly as he disappeared around the corner.

"I think that's his legal name." M's soft voice sounded from behind me. I twirled in surprise to see her standing alone in the hallway. Before I could ask about the students, she offered, "I gave them ten minutes to jot down some questions for these mysterious new guest speakers on Thursday."

Oops. She'd seen right through my ruse. "Hey, I could be planning a field trip to the flea market where they can talk to all sorts of enterprising individuals."

"That might work." She glanced back at the path that Dr. Wagner had followed. "He must really want to be involved now."

"Goddamn bastard!" I didn't like that she seemed so willing to forget what an asshole he'd been in her class.

"Bit of a long first name, but fitting," she mused.

I laughed at that wonderful dry humor. "I wonder if he shortens it to G.B." My tease elicited a burst of laughter from her. She looked almost as surprised by it as I was. "I came by to see if you'd switch advisory committee dates with me next week?"

"Sure," she responded without hesitation.

"Thanks, I appreciate it."

The playful glint in her eye looked like she wanted to say something. I realized if we'd been flirting, she might ask something like, "Hot date?" And if I remembered how to flirt back, I'd respond with, "That depends on your availability." Only I hadn't flirted in over a year, and with Jessie, I'd been rusty. Why was I thinking I could flirt with her when I'd been a disaster on my arranged date? And more importantly, I didn't know if she was gay, so flirting would probably lead nowhere.

When she did speak, it was a polite farewell. "I'd better get back."

"If I leave them alone for even a couple of minutes, they start planning a mutiny. With you, they're probably planning a party."

"Doubtful." A flush hit her cheeks, and I felt the same kind of heat bloom inside me. "I'm sure it would take at least fifteen minutes to plan a mutiny."

I had the sudden urge to nudge my shoulder against her, but she stood too far away. "What do you know about planning mutinies, Mathilda?"

Her teeth bit into her lower lip, trying to contain a smile. "That no one named Mathilda could pull off a mutiny. See you Thursday, Briony." She started back toward the classroom but stopped a few steps away. With her back still turned, she offered softly, "Thank you for dealing with Dr. Wagner."

Her quick escape kept me from being able to hug away the grateful yet defeatist tone. I now wanted to track down Dr. Wagner and deliberately taunt him throughout his own daily activities just so he could feel as awful as she had. I'd known he was the typical academic pompous ass, but he'd been downright underhanded in her class. If I found him now, would he be in the middle of tying some damsel to the train tracks? It honestly wouldn't surprise me.

* * *

Back from the lunch break for the afternoon session and I'd already run out of visiting entrepreneurs. Any minute the class would figure out I'd been bluffing about my promise of new speakers. I should have invited local executives to help fill the time.

Just as I was about to admit my defeat, the door opened and in walked my friend Willa followed closely by M. "Hi, Briony. This is the right time, isn't it?" Willa gave me an innocent look. "I wasn't supposed to be with the morning group, was I?"

M made a show of pressing her fingertips to the bottom of her chin and nudging her mouth closed. My gaping mouth took her hint and clamped shut. "Of course, yes. Class, our last guest speaker is Willa Lacey, founder and CEO of Jucundus Software, number twenty-three on *Fortune's* small business enterprises. I promised you someone who could walk you through every stage of getting funding and establishing a business. She's also the only one of our speakers who's launched an IPO. We're extremely lucky to have her with us today."

"Thank you for the gracious introduction, Briony." She smiled modestly and turned to the class. "I remember being exactly where you are right now, and I'd be happy to impart whatever advice I can to get you through each start-up stage."

Hands shot up from every student in the class. Unfortunately, she called on Avery, a.k.a. the smart-ass, first. "I saw you on CNBC when your IPO hit. Wasn't it one of the top ten highest single-day IPO gains?"

"That was quite a day, yes. I didn't expect the stock to go hot, but it's every entrepreneur's dream. I also didn't expect to be called for an interview. I nearly turned them down, but my co-founder threatened to kill me slowly if I did."

Avery slipped in another question while the class was laughing. "Aren't you Coach Lysander's...?" He seemed to be searching for the right word.

"Avery," I warned, embarrassed that he was resorting to gossip.

Willa smiled and squeezed my shoulder. "Yes, to all those words, but I'm here as a business owner today. If you want to talk basketball, come visit me at the next game."

A proud smile surfaced on my face at her easy response to a subject that usually made her clam up. I turned the smile on M, who'd managed to do that disappearing while still visible thing again. I just had to know how she'd gotten the elusive Willa to come to campus. Making a motion to Willa that I'd be right back, I gestured for M to follow me out.

Once the door closed us into the silent hallway, I asked, "How?"

She looked back through the glass in the door. "I asked."

"I've asked her plenty of times. She always turns me down. She says the campus is Quinn's domain. She'll invite my class down to her company, but I need my students to focus on the start-up stage or they might be tempted to take shortcuts."

M tilted back, her eyes flipping up and to the left in contemplation. "That makes sense from an entrepreneurial standpoint. For my ops students, it's crucial to see how all types of businesses function operationally. Jucundus is always fun and informational to visit."

"Is that how you became friends with her, Quinn, and Jessie?"

"With Willa, yes, and to some extent Quinn. I only know Jessie through the gym."

That explained why the group had never introduced us. "But how did you manage to get her on campus?"

The slow smile that inched across her face drew me in. "I know something about Willa that most don't." I flipped my fingers back toward my upraised palm twice to get her to give it up. "She never says no for favors for friends, so I told her I considered this a favor."

"And you asked her here because I overcommitted on Tuesday?"

Her sheepish glance away told me I got it right. "I wanted to prevent a mutiny as you'd feared."

I trained my eyes on my savior for the day. "You're something special, Minerva." My tease caused her cheeks to color, but more noticeably, it caused my heart to flutter.

Chapter 15

How's it possible that a smoking babe like you is still available? Is something wrong with you?" Yet another blonde, Rachel, asked with a smirk that she probably considered sexy.

"Yes," I answered honestly. Everyone had something wrong with them. Of course my biggest problem right now was that I was on a date with her. And that Caroline seemed to think that she could continue to do this to me.

"I've only recently been back on the market myself."

Wait, hadn't she heard me? If someone told you there's something wrong with her, didn't you follow that up?

"The bitch, I mean, my ex, left me two months ago. I've only had the guts to get back out there this past month. It took me a while to get over her, even if she was a bitch. We were together for a whole year, longer than I've ever been with anyone else."

Was Caroline playing a joke on me? I glanced around the restaurant, envious of the other diners. None of them were on a blind date, or if they were, theirs was a good one. I'd be willing to put money on the fact that no other blind date was admitting to having only had short-term relationships in the past. Nor were they saying that it only took them a month to get over the year-long relationship.

"What's your favorite movie?"

Yet another topic change. This woman's mind was like a maze. "*Vertigo.*" It wasn't, but I was testing her.

"Is that a Quentin Tarantino movie? I thought I'd seen everything he's done. He's one of my favorites. Did you see *Reservoir Dogs*?"

Test over. She probably hadn't seen a movie made before *Die Hard*. And who confuses Hitchcock with Tarantino? "Yes."

"Didn't you just love it? Most people like *Pulp Fiction* better, but I think *Reservoir Dogs* rocked. *Pulp Fiction* is so much worser."

Just plain worse. There's bad, worse, and worst, no worser, but I kept the correction to myself. As much as I wasn't enjoying this date, I wouldn't forget my manners. "I didn't really care for either." I thought they were fine, but as favorites? Not for me.

"How's that possible?"

Let's see, the same way a "smoking babe" like me is still available? I wanted to retort. Lots of things seemed impossible to this woman. And what was I, eighteen? Smoking babe? Please, someone give me strength. "A matter of taste, I guess." I should have said "tastes", but I doubted she'd get the distinction.

"You just haven't seen them with the right person. Not everyone gets all the nuances."

Yeah, because I'm a moron who couldn't possibly understand all the intricacies of a pop culture film plot. Gee, thanks. I wondered if letting my inner snide free would get her to give up on this date.

"We'll cuddle up on my couch and watch some Tarantino films for our next date. Guaranteed you'll love them this time." She winked and nodded her head with a confident smile. "So, why are you single, again?"

Seriously? Someone must be recording this. No one could actually be this self-involved, especially not on a date when you're trying to impress someone. If I looked around, would I spot Caroline and Isabel with a camcorder documenting this disaster to show at the next Sunday dinner?

"You've got commitment issues, right? Hey, that was me before the bitch, but that eight months changed my mind."

Eight months? What happened to a "whole" year?

"If she hadn't cheated on me, I'd still be with her," she continued.

"I'm sorry to hear about her infidelity." Best just to focus on her and soon the date would be over. They closed the restaurant at some point, didn't they? Note to self: never pick an all-night restaurant for a date.

"Yeah, well, she said it was to get back at me for sleeping with an ex."

"What?" I let slip but managed to keep the burst of amazed laughter to myself.

"Well," she pronounced the word like she was talking about a sheep's coat, "she was my high school sweetheart. That's totally on the laminated list. A one-time thing, so worth it."

Now torn between wanting to dig deeper into her twisted mindset and getting the hell away from someone who admits to cheating on her "longtime" lover to a potential new lover, I cast about for any way to end this evening early.

Her phone rang. Again. Without a word or gesture to me, she snapped it open. "Hey…Yup…Nope…Hell, yeah…Will do." She snapped the phone closed then looked at me. "Can I get a picture of you? I told my friend you were a hottie, and she wants proof."

Truly, someone was pulling my leg with this woman, right? "Please don't." My tone left no room for argument, but she raised her phone to take a picture anyway. "Do you mind?"

"Why not?" She stared incredulously at me but finally lowered the phone. "Camera shy? Trust me, baby, you've got no reason to be."

"I would rather you not take my photograph."

"Whatever. I'll just invite her and her wife out with us for our next date."

Would we all cuddle up on the couch together to watch Tarantino's latest wannabe mafia-slasher-snuff-romantic flick? Caroline must be punished. As badly as I was being punished right now.

Before I could form any sort of reply, her phone rang yet again. "Talk to me," she said after flipping it open.

Was I really the only human on earth who considered this behavior rude? Just because the phone rang didn't mean you had to pick it up. Of course, there were exceptions—kids, an illness, a personal crisis—but none of those accounted for the six phone calls she'd already taken. Not to mention the numerous text messages. I was also probably the only person who considered text messaging to be the modern day equivalent of passing notes in homeroom. But could I really be it when I blamed cell phones for the loss of manners in society?

When the phone snapped closed this time, she narrowed her gaze at me. Perhaps my expression told her that she was being rude and childish. My own phone rang, but I ignored it. I'd turned on the ringer during her third call to prove a point. I didn't think anyone would actually call, but I'd hoped for the chance.

Her eyes snapped to my bag. After the next ring, she got antsy. "Aren't you gonna answer that?"

"No. We're having dinner."

"But it's your phone."

"What's going to happen if I don't get it? I'm not a doctor, police officer, or drug dealer, so it's unlikely to be something that needs immediate attention."

The disbelieving look I got told me she didn't get my attempt at sarcasm. "How do you stand it? It could be important."

"I can get to whatever it is after dinner," I stressed. "If it were my son, then I would excuse myself to take the call, but that's not his ring."

"Just take the ca—hold on a sec. You've got a kid?"

"Yes, his name's Caleb. He's ten." I knew my face beamed at the mere mention of him.

She started to rise from the table, a hand waving at me. "Caroline didn't say a word about a kid. No way. I don't do women with kids. That's not my deal." My mouth gaped as I watched her snap her phone into its belt holster, ready for a quick draw in case someone called at high noon, I guess. "This isn't going to work out. Kids don't like me."

Convenient, 'cause neither do I, was the retort that came to mind.

She shoved her wallet into her pocket and twirled her keys around a finger. "Doesn't matter that you're hotter than any of my exes. Take care, Briony. It's a damn shame we couldn't hook up."

Speechless, I watched her walk out of the restaurant, leaving me with the check, and well, a hell of a lot of relief. I really had to get Caroline to back off before someone decided to put up hazard cones around me for being so horrible at dating. After that, I'd be buying Caleb a huge present.

* * *

A hand came up to stop my narration before I heard anything. "No way!" Isabel said, not bothering to hold in her laughter.

"Come on, you're exaggerating, Bri," Caroline insisted, joining Isabel's giggle fit.

"I'm not, and thanks, by the way, for not warning her that I have a kid. I could have saved myself an hour and eighty bucks."

"We figured it would come up in conversation. You're always mentioning him around us," Isabel said matter-of-factly.

I shot forward in my uncomfortable food court seat. "Do I talk about Caleb too much?" Had I turned into one of those moms? I so didn't want to have to hate myself.

"Not at all, cutie," she assured me. "I just thought you'd say something in the first few minutes."

"It's not like you're so chatty about anything else. At least Caleb's a personal topic you're willing to talk about." Caroline picked at the salad she insisted would be a better option than the rest of what she called plastic food at the mall.

I knew my jaw had nudged open, but I couldn't hide the stupid look. Was she saying I kept things from them? True, I'd only recently decided that they were more than just my "Virginia" friends. Maybe I'd subconsciously been treating them as acquaintances rather than actual friends. "You know, neither of you have been on a first date in a while. How do you know what people talk about?"

Caroline, she of the eight-year relationship, pursed her lips and stabbed a tomato. "We talk to people all the time in our jobs. It's not that different. Besides, we used to hear about Lauren, Austy, and Jessie's dates all the time." She couldn't hide the wince as soon as she remembered that I used to be one of Jessie's dates.

"Well, they're all married now, so clearly they're better at dating than I am. I'm not going to pour out my whole life story over dinner."

"Saying you've got a son isn't exactly your life story." Isabel, she of the five-year relationship, said before shoving a fry into her mouth. She had one of those metabolisms that could wipe out a fast food menu without gaining an ounce. I, on the other hand, hadn't had a French fry in three years.

"She wasn't exactly versed in conversation, Isa. I felt like I was conducting an interrogation, and she was more than happy to continue talking without any duress."

They both laughed again. I wanted to grab a handful of Isabel's fries just to keep from having to talk anymore. Shopping with them was excruciating enough since they both believed that you had to try on every single thing before rejecting it and moving on to the next store regardless of what kind of store it was. But they were my friends, and I needed to get out more, especially since I only had one class and no Caleb this summer. Even if I'd rather be with their partners who were at the electronics store playing video games. Shopping wasn't my thing.

"I can't believe she said that she doesn't do women with kids, though." Caroline frowned at Isabel. Years of friendship allowed them to communicate without words.

"I should've guessed something would be off about her when Kayin suggested her." Isabel took a huge bite of her hamburger and wiped the corner of her mouth with a napkin.

"Wait, she wasn't even your friend?" My hand dropped to the table from the perch it provided my chin. "I thought these were your friends. You told me these were your friends."

"She is a friend, well, I'm friendly with her." Caroline didn't bother to look guilty. "Besides, the purpose is to set you up with dates. We can't possibly know everything about them. Rachel's gorgeous, nice, successful; we thought she'd be a great match."

"How do you know she's successful?" Suspicion leaked into my tone.

"Kayin's her CPA," Isabel reported.

I let out a burst of laughter. "I'm not sure you're supposed to be sharing that kind of information, Isa. Kayin might get upset."

"Upset about what?" Kayin appeared at our table with Sam in tow.

Originally, it was supposed to have been Caroline and me on this shopping trip. Then Isabel got invited because she was Caroline's best friend and they never went shopping without each other. Later it snowballed into having their partners along. Not only did I prefer smaller groups, but once again, I found myself as the fifth wheel. Something I'd never minded with my friends in Vermont after Megan had died now became uncomfortable with this group. They seemed to think I wasn't a complete person unless I had someone in my life.

"I told Bri that Rachel is successful."

"She is," Kayin confirmed, shattering my view of acceptable client confidentiality. Although, Rachel had done it herself when she'd listed several well known clients that her advertising agency handled.

"Did you know that she has a problem with kids?" I asked.

"What kind of problem?" Kayin's dark brow furrowed.

"She ditched me at dinner as soon as she found out about Caleb. And I mean ditched, as in, she got up from the table and left the second I mentioned him."

"Jesus!" Sam swore softly. She was a quiet woman, more action than words, but her soft southern accent was a surprise to hear coming from such a solid frame. Practical and to the point was her motto. Even when it was just her and Caroline at my house or theirs, she didn't talk a whole lot. Of course, Caroline talked enough for the both of them.

"Bitch," Kayin hissed. "Sorry about that, Bri. We'll make sure the next one isn't such a bitch."

"Yeah, about that," I cut in, "no more next ones. I can get my own dates."

"Oh, come on. Between the ten of us, we know everyone in this town. You never go out to the bar with us, so how are you going to know who are the available lesbians in town? You'll like the next one, I promise." Caroline tilted her head and batted her eyes at me.

"I haven't liked the three you've shoved down my throat so far."

"Bri," Isabel started in a suffering tone. "You want to be with someone, you have to date. Not everyone is going to be Jessie."

"Whoa!" I brought a hand up. This idea of theirs that I was hung up on Jessie was getting tiring. "I'm not looking for anyone to be Jessie. That's not my measurement. Let's be clear on that. And I'm not looking for someone to be Megan either because I know that's impossible." I made sure to make eye contact with each of them, but I wasn't sure if they believed me. "I knew dating wouldn't be easy. Not even with Jessie. She was wonderful, but we never would have worked out."

"Obviously. She was the biggest sl—"

"Kayin!" I cringed, barely stopping the epithet before she finished.

"What? I'm just saying." Her hands flipped off the table in a careless fashion. "You're a sweet, sophisticated woman. We all thought Jessie was way out of her league with you."

This wasn't the first time Kayin's bluntness had rubbed me the wrong way. I was starting to pick up that it did the same for Isabel, which would account for some of the strain I sensed between them. At least Des wasn't here. I could only imagine what she'd have to say about Jessie and my non relationship.

"That's an unkind thing to say about one of your best friends," I scolded. "Not to mention how insulting it is to Lauren."

"Hey, I'm not saying she hasn't changed, but when she started dating you, she was still the same old date-and-ditch Jessie."

I blew out a frustrated breath. "You guys really don't know her at all, do you?"

"Don't get upset, Bri." Caroline squeezed my forearm.

"I can't help it. My friends, and I do appreciate that you're my friends, are talking about another friend in a way that I wouldn't let anyone talk about one of my friends."

They all shifted restlessly in their chairs, remorseful glances bouncing about. "You're right." Sam was the first to speak up. "We know that Jessie's changed, but you weren't living here when she was the way we've mostly known her."

"Okay, I can accept that, but you need to accept that she was never anything but decent to me. She wasn't the woman that I've heard described by you or anyone else. And she didn't dump me. I wasn't over Megan, and Jessie was smart enough to see that. Oh, and *she* never had a problem with the fact that I had a child." In fact, Jessie and Caleb got on so well now that Lauren and I were often forgotten whenever we all got together. "Not exactly a winning trait of Rachel's."

"That does suck," Isabel agreed.

"Vicki's not like that. She's got two of her own. You'll like her," Caroline said.

They had another all lined up? Was Caroline a madam on the side? "No more setups, please."

"You had one bad experience, but Vicki's great. She brings her kids into the café all the time. They're a cute bunch. I just know you'll hit if off." Caroline squeezed my arm again, pleading in her eyes.

I so wanted to say no, but dating seemed like a healthy step for me. Certainly better than what I'd been doing for the past three plus years. How could one more date hurt?

Chapter 16

Nothing about this was enjoyable or satisfying. It didn't matter how often she had to remind herself that she should be getting something pleasurable from it. That any person who liked this kind of thing would be having fun.

"That was fantastic, baby," the naked woman bound in a human X against the velvet wall complimented. Her back was slick with sweat, making the black skin glisten. Tremors still rolled along her spine. Her mouth had begged for rough but screamed frantically with the softest touch of the feathers used. "If you let me loose, I guarantee I can make you come in thirty seconds."

No, you can't, she thought. It bothered her that she'd come back to the club so soon after her last visit. Two times a year, three max, was all she'd ever allowed since she began visiting this club three years ago. But something in recent events, maybe someone, made her get suited up and drive into the city, thinking that being here might bring back her equilibrium. "Not interested."

"Stone, huh? That's just fine, baby. You can tie me up any time." The woman twisted in an effort to establish eye contact. Her white elaborately tasseled mask was slightly askew from the thrashing of her head while she'd been "tortured" with the feathers. "Gimme a kiss."

"No."

"You can't not, baby, not after that fucking. My body's going to ache tomorrow. A kiss would make it all better." The woman managed to rotate her hips against the wall so she was half turned while still bound.

"No." And they hadn't fucked. Touch, sharing, reciprocation, none of that had occurred, and most especially not tenderness nor intimacy. She couldn't image fucking this woman or any person this way.

"Really stone, that's rarely fun, but you made an impression. I'll let you slide for tonight." Brown-black eyes tracked her movement as she set the feather flick aside and advanced toward her to release a wrist. When the hand came out of the shackle, it shot forward to grasp the back of her neck.

"Don't touch," she warned, jerking out of reach.

The smug look dropped the woman's attractiveness down several notches. "Can't blame me for trying."

Yes, she could. "Goodbye."

"Wait! Let me out of these things." Her eyes blazed in alarm.

"Your hand is free; use it." She stayed just long enough for the miffed woman to turn back to the wall and easily reach up to release her other wrist. It would take another couple of minutes for her to release her ankles and get her leather skirt and bra back on. Enough time to clear out without the woman trying to touch her again.

Tonight she headed straight for the exit from the back rooms. She didn't want to go back through the club, didn't want to see how all the other patrons seemed to be enjoying themselves. Have their arousal, lust, and ecstasy scorch a brand of abnormal on her. This wasn't working. It never had. She didn't care what the advice had been to help her past this hurdle. She couldn't keep convincing herself that the next time might be the one to make her normal.

In the dark alley, she found it hard to breathe through her anxiety with the pungent stench. She strode quickly toward the side street where she'd parked her car. Busy beating herself up for going to the club, she didn't feel the usual energy shift she always got when someone snuck up on her.

"You're mine now, kitten." The man who'd propositioned her last time declared from the darkness behind her. Before she could feint left out of the reach of what she guessed was a right handed man, he'd grabbed her forearm and spun her against him. "You're going to beg me to fuck you."

"No." She used the same even tone she'd used before despite the spurt of fear and revulsion at being squashed against his tall, muscular form. "Let go."

"You'll like having someone take control." His hands moved up her leather clad arms toward the bare skin at her shoulders.

"Wrong. I'm not the type. Do you hear me?" she told him flatly. Protesting vehemently or showing any emotion usually made Doms like him think a woman was playing the role of the reluctant sub.

"You'll change your mind," he insisted. "Surrender to me."

"No. Hands off." Her pulse pounded in the wake his hands left on the material of her long gloves. When his fingers infringed on her bare skin, she felt scalding pain race through her arms and into her shoulders. Instantly, she retreated to that safe place she'd created for herself so long ago. She hadn't known it still existed inside her. She'd nearly forgotten about the glorious blend of colors and how they'd whip past her in a blur as she ran and ran, thinking there had to be a place where things like this didn't happen to girls and women. Where pain wasn't an everyday feeling. Where someone might touch her with care again.

It would be so easy to stay in this beautiful dream state, completely disconnected from reality, but she wasn't that person anymore. Forcing herself to focus on the burn of her skin where he touched her, she snapped back to attention. Her arms moved straight up against her chest before she ripped them apart, throwing his off. Following the fall of his hands, she grabbed one and twisted it around until he was forced to turn and kneel on the ground. A standard martial arts move meant to incapacitate within three seconds ended with his arm now painfully braced up against the middle of his back.

"Argh, fuck! Let up!" his yell turned into a strangled scream of pain.

"Why should I listen to you when you didn't listen to me? Your control is gone. How much do you like it?" Her heart pounded explosively in her chest. Nervous sweat broke out everywhere. She could break several bones in his arm and hand easily. She wanted to break them all. That realization scared her more than anything he could have done to her. She didn't like losing the grip on her control. Nothing good ever came from her losing it. "Don't ever assume that taking someone's control is a good thing."

"I get it, bitch, okay?" His tiresome posturing only served to make her want to hurt him more.

"No, I don't think you do. This club is for people who like to control and or be controlled. When someone tells you she is in control, you will listen to her. It's about consent. If you ever touch me or another woman against her wishes again, I will snap both of your thumbs. Tell me you understand." She twisted his thumb against the socket in demonstration.

"Yeah, I get it!" he wailed. That maneuver always reduced the biggest of men to tears.

Shoving with all her might, she watched as he toppled forward, barely getting his free arm down to break the fall. Like a shot, he came up from his knees, hand cocked back in fury. But she was quicker. She now gripped a collapsible baton against her thigh. His eyes grew wide at the sight of the police issue weapon that she always kept in a hidden pocket against her calf. Those eyes should be worried; she'd had to take a certification class to carry it. This wasn't the first time she'd brandished it, but it might be the first time she used it on someone. "You don't want me to lose control. Next time I see you, I will."

He weighed her resolve, watching her fingers re-grip the baton. "Too bad, kitten. You would have liked what I was going to do to you." He walked backward until he was out of the radius of the baton swing. Only then did he turn and fearlessly saunter to the back entrance of the club.

Breathe in, hold four seconds, breath out. Again. And again. She tried to focus on the spot where he'd touched her shoulders because it still burned. The ache was the only tangible evidence that she was still in control. Without the pain, she knew she would have followed him to show what losing control for someone like her meant to his overall health.

Chapter 17

As I walked into Gilmer Hall for a colleague's retirement party, I wondered if I'd still be a professor after forty years. Thirteen often seemed like it was enough, but then I'd have a class like the one this summer, and I'd get reenergized.

"Hey, Bri." Alexa stood with some colleagues beside the overflowing buffet. "We've decided we're jealous of the psych department. Their food is so much better than ours."

"Not a bottled cheese spread in sight, pretty fancy," I agreed, tongue in cheek. "Looks like the entire staff at the university is here."

"Just about." The comment came from our best accounting professor, Olivia. "Trying to get an audience with Dr. Jackson is nearly impossible, too."

"I'll say," Paula, a finance professor, seconded.

"Yeah, I'm glad we got here early," added Fred, better known as Flick Fred because of his penchant for showing films to make his educational point.

While I was contemplating heading over, I caught sight of M slicing through the crowd, invisibility cloak intact. Her petite stature allowed her to squeeze through partygoers seemingly without notice. She approached Dr. Jackson slowly, looking reluctant to join them but had a warm smile for the retiree. What irked me the most was that within thirty seconds, every other person in the group had stepped away. It was possible that they'd all been monopolizing Dr. Jackson's time, but that seemed unlikely.

"How's it going with her?" Olivia asked.

"Yeah, heard you pulled the low card on that." Paula commented.

"Especially since you're stuck with anti-social woman. Is she as freaky in class as she is around the faculty offices?" Fred jabbed his elbow into Paula's side.

Flash anger started somewhere in my belly and pulsed out to my extremities. "Stop it! She's an amazing teacher and a wonderful person."

"Jeez, sorry, but you don't have an office beside her. I have to deal with her cold shoulder all the time." Fred stepped closer to Paula.

"Have you ever tried to get to know her?" I pressed.

"We've talked to her, but she never says anything other than hello. She'll talk forever to her students, but she doesn't have time for us," Paula said.

"Does she slam the door in your faces?"

"Well, no."

"Does she tell you to get out of her office or she'll call security?"

"Of course not."

"So, your problem is that she actually uses her office for office hours with students and doesn't gossip with you or listen to your rants about the way the department is run?" I purposely picked the worst of Fred's traits. It was mean, I'll own that, but after insulting M like that, I thought he deserved it.

"I don't rant, and everyone but her socializes on our floor. It's just weird."

"Well, she's never been anything but nice to me." They shifted uneasily at the finality in my tone.

"We're glad it's working out, aren't we?" Alexa insisted and received reluctant nods from the other three. "Why don't I walk you over to chat with Dr. Jackson?" She grabbed my elbow to get us moving. "Yeah, that wasn't awkward at all."

I let go of an amused snort, appreciating Alexa's sarcasm. "I'm getting a little tired of these petty games. This isn't what I signed on for here, and I certainly don't need it during a summer session that I was volunteered for."

Alexa turned to me, stopping our progress. "I know what vicious, snipey children they can be, but you don't usually concern yourself with department politics. Is something bothering you? Are you missing Caleb?"

"Sorry, I really didn't mean to come off as a royal bitch. This whole summer isn't what I'd thought it would be. I guess it's affecting me more than I thought. Please, stay my friend? I couldn't survive this place without you."

She beamed and pulled me in for a brief hug. "I'll stay true, hon, don't you worry. It was kinda fun to hear you tell Fred off. I've been wanting to for years."

"I don't know how you've refrained." I turned toward Dr. Jackson to see M taking her leave. She froze in place when she spotted us and another visible struggle took place.

"Briony, Alexa," Dr. Jackson greeted us. "So good of you to come."

"Congratulations on the retirement." I hugged her.

"And congratulations on the wonderful job you and M are doing on the venture fund project. You both must be so proud."

I smiled at M, who looked like she wanted the floor to open up and drop her through. "It's been a delight to work on, I have to admit." I kept my eyes on Dr. Jackson, rather than look at the main reason the project was such a delight.

"We're proud of our girl," Alexa chimed in, then thankfully remembered her manners and corrected, "our girls. We'll be the talk of the academic world before these two are through with this first round of ventures."

"I should say," Dr. Jackson agreed. Her fond look at M told me she was acquainted with M's shy mannerisms.

"I've got to run," M said, much to my disappointment. "I just wanted to stop by and wish you well in retirement."

"Thank you. I plan to live it well." Dr. Jackson reached to squeeze M's forearm.

She stiffened like Dr. Jackson had grasped a sore muscle, but she didn't pull away. Instead, she forced a smile then turned to us. "Nice seeing you again, Alexa. See you in class tomorrow, Briony."

"That's an extraordinary one," Dr. Jackson commented as we watched M's smooth traverse toward the exit.

"After only a few weeks in class together, I know how right you are," I agreed wistfully. Not that I hadn't recognized it before, but with each shared class or advisory committee, I knew that M Desiderius was rare indeed.

* * *

There were about a million other things I could be doing right now. Playing tennis with Alexa, reading a mystery, working out, talking to Caleb at camp, whitewater rafting, banging my head against a low hanging beam, and all would be more pleasant than my sixth blind date. Cripes, Caroline knew a lot of women. A lot of women who were so wrong for me.

This one's name was Polly, and she worked as a court clerk. After her third cup of coffee—I'd learned never to commit to anything that might take more than one course to complete—I could sum up Polly's personality with one word: drama. Or issues. Or get me the hell out of here, please!

"And then I was, like, 'what do you think you're doing with my stuff, bitch?' I mean, can you believe she was, like, walking out on me and expected to take the one and only gift she, like, bought me in the entire three months we'd been together? I was, like, 'you didn't even pay me rent for three months, you're not taking my Maroon 5 with you.'" Her pretty green eyes stared expectantly at me, asking me to agree.

Still stuck on some of the other intimate details she'd shared prior to talking about a massive blowout over a piece of plastic that costs twelve dollars, I merely nodded then shook my head. I didn't know if she expected me to say, "Yes, I completely agree, even though you're a loon," or "No, that's just awful, especially since there's no way you could ever replace such a priceless item.

Unless, of course, you walked into any music store, or better yet, downloaded the songs so no one could walk out of your life with her love and your CDs."

"You're so easy to talk to," she jabbered on after I'd apparently given the appropriate response. "I can't believe Caroline never introduced us before. I'm having so much fun."

Yeah, because drinking coffee was a riot a minute. I really had to come up with some way to make Caroline stop.

"So, like, what's your story?" She paused long enough to make me think she actually wanted an answer.

Well, I've never used the word "like" as a verbal pause; I've never moved in with someone after only one night together; and I've never considered a CD worth the effort of an argument. Oh, and I now deem dating a soul draining experience.

"Wait, let me guess. I'm, like, really good at this." She pressed her lips into a thin line and jutted her chin. "Your last girlfriend wasn't smart enough for you, so you, like, tossed her aside for one of the grad student honeys?"

The sip of coffee I'd just taken fought to break free. I concentrated on breathing through my nose and finishing the swallow. Grad student? Puh-leeze!

"What happened? Get caught having a 'study break' in your office?" She winked and nudged my forearm. "Doesn't matter, I'm just glad you're, like, available now."

Why was that again? Oh yes, I'd stupidly allowed my friend to get away with thinking she could do this to me. Then again, it was my dim-witted idea to imagine dating would go anything like it had with Megan or Jessie. The fact that I'd met Meg during an intern program at a company where she worked as the receptionist and had gotten acquainted with Jessie at her club before our first date probably had something to do with it. Well, several dates down and the only thing that didn't annoy me was that I now had the answer to the question I'd posed before. Yes, dating really was like this now.

"Briony?"

I looked up and felt my stomach plunge as swiftly as if I'd been pushed out of an airplane. M stood beside my table, iced coffee in hand on her way out. She was in casual clothes, showing a hint of midriff at the hem of her shirt, the start of envious calves under her capri pants, and just the barest promise of cleavage beneath the v-neck collar.

"Hi there, M." I hoped she caught the relief in my tone. Wow, she looked good. No makeup today and her hair was a little more chaotically styled but wickedly attractive. Beyond, actually, more like hot. Yes, hot suited her just fine. Why wasn't I on a date with her? *Oh, crap, Polly.* "This is Polly. Polly, my friend and colleague, M."

"Nice to meet you." Polly narrowed her eyes.

"Pleasure," M responded, glancing at the door but returning her gaze to me. My heart started thumping when I realized she didn't want to leave right away.

Polly must have picked up on it, too, because the next thing I knew, she was telling M, "We'd invite you to join us, but we're on a date." She reached out to squeeze my hand like the contact would prove we were on a date.

I wasn't sure who cringed more, me at the idea that this could really be counted as a date or M at the rude dismissal she'd been issued. My eyes snapped up to M's in apology. Before I realized what I was doing, I made the ASL sign for "help" which I'd learned from Hank along with several other words that might come in handy for when the boys spent time together. This was the first time I'd ever used it, and I never imagined I'd be using it for evil instead of good.

"Pardon the intrusion, but I thought we said three o'clock?" M asked with the perfect amount of urgency and innocence. "I grabbed a table up by the windows and left all the lecture notes and draft business plans there. It's a few hours of work and I've got plans tonight, but if you need a little more time, I understand."

"Is it three o'clock already?" I tilted my wrist to check the time on my watch. "Gosh, I'm sorry, Polly. I didn't mention this work thing because I never thought we'd still be here. You just made the time fly by." Two hours that I'll never, ever get back.

She beamed at my compliment but disappointment peeked through. She shifted her gaze between M's nonthreatening stance and me. "I understand if it's a work thing. Caroline said you were a bit of a workaholic, but we can fix that."

I stood, irked that Caroline characterized me that way to a blind date but relieved to find this over with. "This was nice," I lied.

Polly started around to my side of the table. "I had a great time. Let's do this again soon." She made a move to hug me as I was holding up my hand to shake. We did that awkward hug, shake, hug, shake thing that seemed to never end but finally did. When her mouth descended toward mine, I turned away at the last moment, pretending to reach for a cheek kiss of my own. It was either that or let her kiss me, and I couldn't do that. Not only because I didn't want to, but M was still standing there. Farther away since Polly had stood up but still there.

Finally, the sixth date on my path through hell was over. Polly banged through the coffee house doors with all the drama she'd expressed during her diatribe. I let the tension I'd been feeling for the last two hours drain away. "Thank you for saving me."

"Not a good date?" M asked, reluctance drifting into her tone.

"Not a good setup. I'm starting to wonder if the friend who keeps doing this to me knows me at all."

A smile cut across her face. "Well, I'm glad I could help."

"That's twice now that you've been my savior. I'll have to return the favor some time."

"Think nothing of it." She said it like she believed it when I was considering erecting a lifelike shrine of her and lighting a candle every night. Her eyes darted to the exit as her customary introversion returned. "It was nice running into you."

"Tell me about those plans you mentioned," I blurted, but only because I knew how quickly she could scram.

"I lied," she admitted with a shy smile. "I figured if I didn't give a limited window of time, she might think she could get us to postpone our work meeting."

Strangely, I felt more relief hearing this than getting out of my date with Polly. "So, you've got nothing going?"

"No."

"You do now." I stepped toward her with a smile.

Chapter 18

Now, this was how you spent a Saturday. Like our day at the amusement park, it flew by effortlessly. She was game for anything, a true adventurous spirit, my favorite kind. We'd started walking around town at first, hitting an art festival, then contemplated joining a volleyball game at the park, going up in one of the festival's hot air balloons, taking our bikes out for a ride, or rollerblading. Instead, we ended up continuing our walk, taking our time with each art display, watching the volleyball game, then making plans for a bike ride and rollerblading some other time. We finished the day having dinner together out on a bistro terrace, watching the waning summer sunset.

"Thanks again for saving me from that catastrophe," I said as we walked back to the scene of the crime, or crime of a date, I should say.

Her gaze flickered downward before meeting mine. "It didn't look like you were having that bad of a time."

"I've learned to grin and bear it. My friend, well, friends, seem to think it's time for me to start dating again."

A long moment passed before she inquired, "After?"

"After a year, which is actually three plus years," I admitted and watched her brow knit at my cryptic response. "A year ago, I decided it was time to get over Megan, or try, at least. I'd met Jessie at her club and got to know her a bit. She's a great person in addition to being gorgeous, and I figured if anyone could make me want...well, she'd be the one."

"Did she?"

Somehow I knew she wasn't asking if we'd slept together. She was asking if dating Jessie had gotten me to stop considering myself a married woman and stop thinking about what Meg and I would do over the upcoming weekend. "No, which is why I've been pestered relentlessly ever since. They think that I'm still hung up on Jessie, so they're encouraging me elsewhere. I get the impression that they've had some practice with that in the past."

She studied me, understanding making her gaze sharper. "None of them figured out what was really going on?"

"Jessie did. She told her partner and, I think, Quinn, but the rest of the group just thinks I'm odd or busy or too involved with Caleb to start dating again. They lifted the moratorium recently, though, so..."

"Pleasant time with Polly?" M joked, a sly smile enlivening her expression.

"So pleasant," I agreed dryly. "What about you?" I watched her step back and wave a hand through the air, shaking her head. Apparently, she thought that was a response. I could tell she didn't want to answer, but I was too curious and it was suddenly vital to know. I waited her out as we came to a stop on the sidewalk.

"Well, this is me." She gestured at the building behind her.

"You live here?"

"Yeah, it's nice enough." She shrugged like she was embarrassed.

"Beautiful building. Is it as authentic inside as it is out here?" It was the same style as so many others in the historic district, probably Colonial or Federal if I remembered what I'd learned on the tour when I first arrived in town.

"It's truly grand." Her eyes lit up. From our discussions earlier today, I knew architecture was a passion of hers. "It has features only found in buildings from the eighteen hundreds. It's one of the reasons I chose the apartment." She turned and looked up at the façade and back to me. "You could come up and take a look if you have time—if, if you wanted."

"Yes, I'd love to see inside." I wanted to quell her sudden insecurity.

On our way up to her apartment, she confirmed for me that it was a Colonial Revival then pointed out some of the unusual details in molding, arches, and on the banister of the wide stairwell. Course marble from over a century of foot treads exaggerated the sound of our footsteps.

Once we'd reached her floor, we passed two men coming out of an apartment. They smiled in an obvious manner and checked us out as we crossed paths. While I did nothing to encourage their leers, M acted as if she had no idea they were paying attention to us. Not until we reached her door where she hesitated before unlocking it. Tilting her head just enough to watch the men out of her periphery, she waited until they finally turned and headed to the elevator. Only then did she unlock the door.

"This is amazing. Are all the apartments like this?" I tried to take in all the details at once while she stopped to disarm the security system. Two marble columns reached up to the ornate tin tiles on the high ceilings, marking the separation from her living room to the kitchen. A wrap around counter delineated the kitchen from a dining area that was eclipsed by the large twelve-pane windows overlooking historic downtown Charlottesville. Original oak planks, not the snap together kind from the modern home improvement stores, butted up against elaborate floor molding. The building could be a museum on its own.

"I've only been in the manager's apartment. It wasn't laid out the same, but it had a lot of the same details. It was once a mansion that they've turned into apartments." She'd turned back from the security panel but hadn't moved farther inside.

As I waited for her to warm up to the idea of joining me, I started noticing her furniture and art. Where I'd been taken with the architectural details before, the complete absence of color now overwhelmed me. Antique white to match the marble columns washed every wall and a few pieces of furniture. The rest was black. The artwork consisted of black and white landscapes or architectural photographs, stunning in their starkness.

Sparsely furnished throughout, only the bookcases partially covering two walls were cluttered. Books of all types and shapes lined the shelves, stacked both ways not for artistic style but because she had so many. I couldn't help but smile looking at them. My own would look the same if Megan hadn't set a limit. I couldn't blame her, but I'd always hated those two Saturdays a year when she would make me go through the shelves and donate those books I wouldn't reread or reference later.

"M?" I spoke to the bookcases in front of me. "I can leave if you want." I looked over to take in her stance by the door. She hadn't moved, clearly reconsidering her invitation. "I'll leave. The place is great, thanks for showing it to me." I started back toward the door.

A hand shot up in front of her body, trying to hold me in place from five feet away. "I apologize. I'm not used to having guests. Would you like some coffee?" She moved past me and into the kitchen. "Please, have a seat."

Relieved to find that she now felt comfortable enough to enter her own apartment, I headed over to the leather couch and plunked down on the comfy cushions. Directly in front, I noticed that the fireplace mantle was bare. I thought about the family photos on mine and twisted my head to see if I could spot them someplace else. Nope, not a single one, no college friends raising drinks after finals, no work friends huddled around a cubicle, no young M clutching a too fat cat, nothing personal at all.

"Where did you go to high school?"

M stopped on her way back from the kitchen with two mugs of coffee. She furrowed her brow at the seemingly off the wall question. "Are you asking if I'm from here?"

"Okay." I hadn't been, but whatever she wanted to give me. Our conversations thus far had been rather lopsided. She was very adept at pulling info from me while avoiding adding anything too personal of her own.

"I'm not." She set my mug on a coaster, and rather than take a seat next to me on the couch, she sat in one of the chairs perpendicular to it.

"And you're from?"

"A few different places." The clipped response was so different from how she'd spoken all day, not to mention how well we'd interacted while working together. We were back to the tug of war over getting anything out of her. Before I could respond, she continued, "Caleb told me he moved here from Vermont, is that where you're from originally?"

"Born and raised, but I went away to college and my first teaching positions were at UConn then Harvard." I let a few beats pass before I speared her with my gaze. "Which different places?"

"Around Illinois."

"Your nun," I paused before asking the question I wanted to ask. "What's her name?"

"Kathryn." The admission sounded reverent, giving me the impression that she'd called Kathryn by her name rather than Mom. I wondered whose choice that was but wouldn't ask. Yet.

Getting back to my original hope of finding out why she'd grown up in more than one place, I asked, "Kathryn had to move a few times for her job or something?"

M turned an impassive face toward the fireplace. "She passed away when I was nine."

"I'm so sorry." I felt my heart clench for her. She hadn't been much older than Caleb when he lost Megan. "Did you move in with one of her relatives afterward?"

"No, she didn't have anyone."

"Foster care?" I prodded when she didn't continue.

"For a while."

"After that?"

She looked back at me, a mixture of frustration, apprehension, and sadness tainting her expression. "Youth detention."

"Oh, M." I inched forward on the couch, but she pulled into the corner of her chair.

"I hurt someone when he tried to hurt someone else."

"You were sentenced to Juvie for that?" I couldn't get my brain to process that. As far as I knew, self-defense of others was a legitimate legal defense.

"No, but the foster system wasn't set up for violent wards of the state. Only one place is."

"You're not violent." I didn't have any personal knowledge to make my declaration, only the certain belief that this woman could never hurt anyone unless she was protecting herself or someone she cared about.

She stared at me like I was crazy. "You can't know that. I dislocated someone's shoulder then broke his wrist and nose, easily and without conscious thought or regret."

As startling as that was to imagine, I knew there had to be a reason. "What was he doing?"

Again, she turned back to the fireplace. "He was trying to rape the girl who shared the room with me."

Jesus! "You stopped him?"

"Yes."

"You're not violent, M." I wanted to reach out and pull on her chin to get her to face me, but she was too far away. "Whenever Kathryn asked you what you wanted to do for the day, what did you say?"

Her head whipped back around as I'd intended with my non sequitur. A flicker of emotions glistened in her eyes. Surprise and gratitude added to the others I'd seen before. "Ice skating."

"Really? We'll have to go this winter with Caleb and Hank." My suggestion prompted a raised eyebrow, telling me she'd like that. I was beginning to realize why it was easy for her to be so quiet. She had such an expressive face. For someone who got to know her, words were almost unnecessary. "You're probably going to leave me in the dust when we bring out the rollerblades, aren't you?"

She smiled tentatively. I'd stay just long enough to make sure she knew that I was okay with what she'd shared, but not long enough to make her regret asking me inside. I felt confident that we'd just crossed over from being friendly colleagues to genuine friends.

Chapter 19

How's the dating going?" Jessie stopped by the bicep curl machine where I was trying to keep from growling out loud.

I suppressed the urge to glare at her for buying this machine and putting it in her health club, but I couldn't hold it against her. I'd chosen to use it, and she was my friend. "It's like a train wreck, and although I may have the best car on the train, it doesn't make the wreck any more enjoyable."

She laughed, causing others nearby to turn and stare. Jessie always posed quite a sight, drawing stares whether she was laughing or not. Especially since she was no longer in her workout clothes but dressed for a night out. Her long wavy mane was wrapped in a casual updo with tendrils framing her lightly made up face. It really should be illegal to be that gorgeous, not that I'd turn her in. "That bad, huh?"

"Does Caroline hate me or something?" I quipped.

"Maybe a little bit." She held up two fingers spaced an inch apart. "They won't tell me who they're setting you up with." She seemed saddened by this, probably because she might have firsthand knowledge of the women I'd dated.

"Erin, Cindy, Rachel, Vicki, Linda, and Polly," I listed with as much enthusiasm as I gave to counting the reps on this machine.

"Goodnight nurse! Polly?" Lauren exclaimed incredulously as she snuck up on us. Equally dressed to kill, she slipped into her partner's arms for a hello kiss then turned back to me. "Don't tell me they set you up with Polly?"

"Last Saturday, two hours of my life that felt like two years." My comment drew chuckles from both as they stole a glance that said how glad they were to be off the dating market. I knew just how they felt.

"I'm surprised it only lasted two hours. I can barely shake her loose after an hour at the courthouse. What is Caroline thinking?" Lauren looked the question at Jessie.

"They're thinking they finally have another victim who's too polite to do anything to stop them." Jessie grinned. "Our friend Austy used to let them wrangle her into dates."

"Actually," Lauren started with a raised brow, "I found out that she only let them set her up. She'd cancel then tell Car, Isa, and Des that the date didn't work out. Sly girl."

"Genius girl," I muttered.

"We can talk to them for you." Jessie offered to run interference. "You don't have to let them set you up."

"Yes, let us introduce you to some people. If you like them, you can take it from there. No pressure." Lauren looked eager but without the devious glint of my two current pimps, Caroline and Isabel. "Jess, who would be good for Briony? What about Penelope?" She indicated the pretty trainer who was in the process of torturing some man with abdominal lifts.

"She's nice, great work ethic, considerate of the members. You might like her," Jessie confirmed rather unenthusiastically.

"Or Kylie's sweet and Jenna, you've always been friendly with her, Jess," Lauren continued. "Nicole or Olympia, c'mon, help me think." As each name rolled by, Jessie started looking a little pale. Lauren paused when she noticed and slipped her arms around Jessie's waist. "Darling, I told you that the person these women think they know is not the woman I married. They can think they know you, but they don't. Only I do."

Jessie's smile brightened our little area. She leaned in and whispered something in her spouse's ear, causing a matching smile to erupt on Lauren's face. She tilted back and gave me a sheepish look. "Pardon me, Bri. Sometimes I can't believe how lucky I am, and I just have to make sure she knows it."

"I'd say you're both pretty lucky." I watched them with warm envy, not the jealous kind, just the wistful wish to have that again.

But I'd had it once, and that was one more time than a lot of people get.

"So, what do you think? Would you like us to introduce you around?" Lauren offered without making it sound like I was deficient for not having a girlfriend.

"Maybe. I don't know. I'm ready to date, but God, it's tedious. Why can't you just meet someone and click? Get to know each other, become friends, and if something happens, it happens?" I mused not allowing myself to admit what I knew was becoming true for me.

Lauren bent her five-eleven frame to look me in the eye. "Do you have someone specific in mind?" Her blue eyes danced in delight before tapping a hand against her partner's shoulder. "Jessie, torture her. I want a name."

We laughed at her demand. "No, it's just, there's this woman at work. She's unusual, the really good kind, you know? I enjoy spending time with her. I enjoy her, but I don't know if she's gay, and we work together, and she hasn't sent any signals that she's interested in me, so it's nothing."

"Briony, that's wonderful!" Lauren bounced excitedly, the silk of her green dress rippling with movement.

"Did you not hear what I said?" I kidded. "I don't know her sexual preference, and even if I did, she's shown nothing but professional courtesy while at work and guarded friendship away from work."

"That's only half a problem. We're bound to figure out her preference. This isn't that big of a lesbian community. Someone we know has got to have confirmation. As far as the guarded part, well, maybe she just takes a little while to warm up to people." Lauren's sunny outlook was almost catching. "Who is it? Maybe we already know."

I didn't immediately respond. It felt like I was giving up someone's secret, but of the friends, these two could keep it to themselves. "Her name is M Desiderius."

Lauren frowned in thought, but Jessie's frown looked more like worry. "Hmm, no, sorry, I don't know her. Darling?" She looked at her partner.

"She's a member here," I supplied when Jessie didn't. "She's also friends with Willa. Pretty good friends, I think."

"Oh, well, Willa probably won't know. She's annoyingly respectful of people's privacy," Lauren scoffed humorously. "Is she just a member or do you know her, Jess?"

Again, Jessie seemed to hesitate. "She's quiet, dedicated, thoughtful but takes things pretty hard. I used to train her at the old gym She doesn't like small talk, and she doesn't answer personal questions, which made our training sessions pretty quiet. But I always liked her and still do."

"Is she gay?" Lauren asked the pertinent question for me.

"I don't know for sure." Her response was a relief. Nothing like finding out the woman you're interested in has already been with the most gorgeous woman in town.

"But you have an inkling?" I asked, fighting the impulse to cross my fingers.

She glanced away, checking the position of everyone in the room. Either she was concerned that her trainers weren't doing their jobs correctly or she didn't want anyone to overhear what she was about to say. "I thought I saw her once."

"Where?" Lauren and I asked together.

"A club. If it was M, she's gay." Her brown eyes flipped back to mine with a hint of apology and concern. "But I didn't get a good enough look to be sure, and the M I know doesn't seem outgoing enough to enjoy the club scene."

While fleeting, it was still hope. I wasn't sure if I was interpreting the caution in Jessie's eyes correctly, but at least I had something to hang my hopes on.

* * *

My best and most annoying student, Avery, would be the death of me. He was currently leading the class down a path that had nothing to do with the topic I'd introduced. Several of the students groaned when he started on one of his rants and I wanted to join them. Instead, I glanced up at the third row and caught the curve of M's lips as she reined in a smile. We shared a withering look, appreciating the student's enthusiasm but knowing we couldn't let it continue.

"Good point, Avery," I cut him off. "But it's not something that can be proven absolute during class. So, why don't we get back on topic and discuss exit strategies? Anyone?"

"Leveraged buyout," Cecily, the only female team leader—much to our chagrin—piped up from the second row.

"Did we see that on your plan?" I shot a worried glance at M, who shook her head. For Cecily's type of business, it would be the least appropriate exit strategy.

"No, but I'm thinking about it. Janice brought up some good points in our last meeting and Eric and Andy agreed."

M leaned forward on the desk, ready to jump in if necessary. We'd started coming to each other's lectures after Willa appeared as a guest speaker. It wasn't anything we'd discussed, but with the advisory meetings now overlapping with lecture topics, it seemed crucial that we not miss anything that might shape these fledgling ventures.

"It is an option, Dynasthai," I addressed Cecily's team by its business name. "However, there are others, which is why we spend time going through the options before deciding on your individual plans. So, pros and cons of each exit strategy?"

That set off a rousing group discussion where I became only a minor participant to encourage students around the topic. I stepped up the stairs and sat in the seat next to M, smiling conspiratorially at her. She was the master at getting her students to interact and come to conclusions on their own with only gentle coaching from her. We both inserted comments throughout the discussion, and like every Tuesday or Thursday, the time passed in a blur. Soon the students wound down, sensing the bell before it rang.

Walking back up front, I gave my closing remarks for the class. "Great input, everyone. Dynasthai, I'm meeting with you tomorrow at ten, and, Selesia, at one o'clock. I want the five-year pro forma financials completed so we can focus on the marketing strategy. And remember, next week we start looking at commercial real estate. Start thinking about whatever requirements you'll need for your business space."

Dramatic sighs sounded from the eight students involved, but they grinned to let me know they didn't see it as a problem. When the bell peeled, they all shuffled their laptops and books together, called out goodbyes, and funneled through the exit door.

"That went really well," M spoke from her seat.

"Thanks to a little coaching from you, Mavis." Her only reaction was to stand and move around the desk to collect her notes. "Moira? Margaux? Myrna?"

She ignored my playful taunts. "Do you think we need to worry about team Dynasthai?"

"I'll know more after tomorrow. You're welcome to sit in on the planning session with me." Only partly because of how much better our lectures were when she did.

"I just might."

"We could squeeze in lunch together before the one o'clock?" Her hesitation brought on another tease. "C'mon, Mertice, you gotta eat."

She laughed out loud at that guess. "Mertice? Really? You're just making up names now, aren't you?"

"Well, if you'd tell me your name, I wouldn't be stopping by my friend's bookstore once a week to collect more guesses from a baby names book." I stepped up to the ledge beside her desk.

"I told you my name already. I can even show you my license to prove that I had it legally changed. What's so wrong with M?" she asked, suddenly serious.

"It's beautiful," I responded immediately because of that serious tone and, before I could stop myself, added, "Like you."

Her eyes flared, and I felt my stomach react as if I were walking a high wire. I scolded myself for letting that slip while we were at work. It might have been easier to toss off as a mere compliment if we'd been outside of work.

"It's just a name." She turned away, rushing to collect her stuff.

Uh-oh. I had crossed the line. "Wait." I reached to grasp her shoulder, but before I made contact, she swung around and stepped back out of reach. "Please." She reluctantly met my eyes, but her hand reached for her backpack, ready to run off. "Did I make you uncomfortable?" Her expression remained inscrutable. "I did. I'm sorry. I like your name, M. I'll stop guessing if it makes you uncomfortable."

She shook her head, a long moment passed where she seemed to be having a debate with herself. "It's not that, I mean, it is, sort of. No one's ever stayed this curious, but it wasn't that."

"What then? Tell me, please." I edged closer, needing her to be open with me.

"You, you called me, no one's ever called me..." She looked away without finishing.

"Beautiful?" How was that possible? Even if she wasn't extremely attractive, she had the kind of tender, caring soul that defined beauty. "Oh, M, you're very beautiful." I reached out to touch her cheek. When my fingers first grazed her soft skin, I realized it was the first time we'd touched. Not even a nudge or an inadvertent arm brush. As I was marveling at that lack of contact and mapping the texture of her supple skin, I kept my eyes on my fingers. When I finally looked back up at hers, I saw fear. Actual fear, not the kind that might happen if I were making an unwelcome pass. This kind of fear forced my hand back to my side in a flash. "I keep doing the wrong thing. I'm sorry. I would never hurt you."

"I believe you," she whispered. Those guarded eyes still followed the movement of my offending hand. For a second, it looked like she wanted my hand back, but then her eyes snapped back to mine. They blinked until the expression showed tentative courage.

"Do you believe that you're beautiful?" I insisted because no one had told this remarkable woman that she was beautiful. I didn't care that this was a professional setting. She needed to hear it and know it.

"I'm not." She twisted back to her desk and snatched the backpack up against her chest. "You're the one who's beautiful." Her head jerked into a shake, eyes blinking in shock, obviously surprised she'd said that out loud. That made two of us. "I should go."

My heart started thumping so fast I felt woozy from the rush of blood. "I won't stop you, but thank you. And you are beautiful, M. If there's one thing I plan to do as your friend, it's to make sure you know that."

She shook her head, trying to negate my words, but before she fled the room, she nodded once. It could have been a parting gesture, but I thought it might be her way of acknowledging my pronouncement that we were friends. At the very least, I hoped.

Chapter 20

The club was packed tonight. Saturdays in the summer appealed to the D/s crowd, especially since it was sweltering outside. She liked how she'd spent the Saturday before last better, but that wasn't likely to happen again. Since that attempt at humanity hadn't gone swimmingly, she was back here. Trying again, because she didn't want to fail at this, too.

The trio of lace, leather, and skin loitered near the bar again. She might try one of them; Leather looked good. In the same line of sight, Red Satin stood talking to a tall, excited looking woman. Their conversation stopped as soon as R.S. caught her gaze and started over without a backward glance. A death glare came her way from Tall, Stocky, and Eager, but she knew nothing would come of it.

"I've been waiting for you. Want another round?" R.S. asked, raising a hand to cup her face.

"Don't touch," she reminded. The offending hand slammed back to her side in obedience.

"Yes, Mistress." Her eyelids lowered briefly before stepping closer. "I'm dripping. I need you. Please, command me."

She hesitated because she didn't repeat, but R.S. was a known commodity. Maybe that was what she needed tonight. "Wait in back. You'll strip completely. We're using the bench."

A wide smile was the only reply she received. Tonight's mask covered only her eye sockets and the bridge of her nose, allowing a better look at her round face and the halo of black hair styled like that of a 40's screen goddess. She watched Red Satin disappear through the crowd and went to arrange for a private room.

"What do you have that I don't?" the stocky woman who'd issued the death glare asked. Her stance threatened, bulk leaning forward trying to intimidate.

"Nothing," she responded truthfully.

"Damn right you don't." The woman rubbed a hand over her sheer short buzz cut. "Let me at her." A folded bill came out of her pocket and slid across the bar to pay for the room as a gesture to share. "You strap her down, do your thing, then let me have some fun with her."

"No."

"Blindfold her, she doesn't have to know. I want her. She was supposed to be mine tonight." She sneered in a way that made her look ugly rather than menacing.

"No."

"Don't mess with me, chickie. I'm horny as hell, and you just blocked me. I'm trying to be decent about this and share her with you."

"Everyone who comes in here has a choice. I won't take that from her even without her knowing." She held her ground. Nothing about the tall, bulky form frightened her. The worst that could happen was pain, and pain, she could handle.

"You'll do what I want." A thick finger stabbed at her chest.

"No, I won't." Her mind deadened the exaggerated twinge the finger jab caused. When she didn't back down, the woman eased off with a huff. Bluster must have been her thing. Collecting the key from the bartender, she headed to the back.

"I was wondering if you'd ditched me," R.S. said from outside one of the rooms. The insecure look didn't suit her, nor did it add to her appeal. "I've been waiting for you for months. I didn't want to think I'd missed out on another chance with you."

"Inside," she ordered after unlocking a private room. She didn't like that she'd made an impression on this woman. She didn't like anyone thinking of her that way. "Strip and get up on the bench, face down. Your word is 'inveigle.' "

Lightning quick, R.S. stripped off the one-piece red satin teddy. Pink nipples beaded atop those perky breasts. The grooming had gone too far this time. A heart shaped nest of black hair covered her mound. Ridiculous, but not an issue. When R.S. turned, it was a slow spectacle meant to torture. Little did she know, it had no effect. Her climb onto the apparatus was practiced. R.S. settled onto her stomach, stretching her arms up and spreading her legs to the corners.

As she was fixing the Velcro straps to her wrists and ankles, she wondered why she was here. She didn't want to be here. It was no better than last time, no better than any other time. She wished she'd never discovered this club, this way to experience an act that everyone else could do so easily. Even if she was only a cursory participant, she forced herself to endure for a sample of something that everyone else seemed to crave.

Once completely bound, R.S. pleaded, "Use the whip. Hurt me."

"No."

"I like it. I want it."

"Pain isn't part of this. Not with me."

"But it's so good. Please, hurt me." Muscles strained against the straps as R.S. whimpered her plea.

She thinks I'm beautiful. The thought zipped through her, forcing a step backward. What was she doing here? An intelligent, gorgeous, kind woman thought she was beautiful, and she was here, forcing herself to engage in this. She didn't want this. She wanted that gorgeous woman. She could never have her, but she wanted her.

Reaching out, she undid a wrist strap. "What?" R.S. looked over, confused.

"We're done."

"No!" she pleaded. "I'll do anything you want."

"Not tonight."

"Please, don't leave me hanging. I'm gonna burst any second."

She reached for the woman's left leg strap but hesitated with the plea. She'd essentially teased her and had no intention of following through. That was cruel on its own. "Do you want the woman you were talking to earlier?"

"I want you. I've waited for you."

"I'm done for tonight. I can release you or I can send the other woman back or both." She knew what the answer would be, but she couldn't control this woman's mind.

"Send her in," R.S. requested predictably with a loud sigh. "Will you be back soon?"

"No."

"Will you ever be back?" Her eyes pleaded.

"No." Unlike the other times she made the promise that she wouldn't force herself to come back, this time she knew it was true.

Chapter 21

A hand slid around my waist and onto my stomach just before a familiar body smashed up against me from behind. The added body weight gently propelled me into the balcony railing.

"Damn, babe, you're wearing that sexy garter, aren't you?" Megan's husky voice licked at my ear. "Under that tight skirt, are you trying to make me crazy?"

I smiled out at the lights reflecting off the dark Charles River. Megan was in the mood, guess the garter wouldn't go to waste. I'd worn it because, like with Meg, good things usually happened when I did. I'd had my final interviews with the University of Vermont earlier today then flew back to Boston after receiving a job offer for a tenure track position. Most would call me insane for not pursing tenure at Harvard where I currently taught. But the University of Vermont was my ideal placement, where both Meg and I wanted to return, where we could raise our son together with his grandparents, aunts, and cousins nearby.

"Hi, babe, I'm home," I finally got to say because she'd been busy breastfeeding Caleb and trying to get him to sleep when I got back to our apartment fifteen minutes ago. I knew better than to interrupt his nighttime ritual or we'd be looking at another hour of trying to settle him down.

"Yes, you are, and we'll soon talk about your magnificence in getting tenure, and the fact that, even with our flourishing little business, I'm now going to be a kept woman, and how you're responsible for finally getting us back home. But right now, we're focusing on this garter." Her hand slipped from my stomach down my thigh and curled up under my skirt. "Tell me you're not wearing panties, and I'll pass out right here."

I chuckled and turned in her arms to face her. My spouse, my wife, my lover, my partner. She looked a little tired from taking one of our adventure company groups out sculling on the river earlier and caring for Caleb on her own tonight, but her face still short circuited my brain. "You'll have to find out."

"Don't do this to my heart, babe." She brushed her lips against my ear.

My face turned into the path of her lips, catching them with my own. That familiar burst of passion jolted me back against the railing. It had been a while. Caleb was eighteen months old and exhausting, even with both of us. She hadn't been in the mood in months, and I hadn't been much more motivated either. But this felt great.

"I'm supposed to be exploring the status of your undies," she moaned as my fingers slid up to flick over her erect nipples.

"Find out later. I have to touch you now." My hand shot to the waistband of her sweats and slid underneath to cup her sex. "Oh God, who's not wearing any underwear?"

"We had a bath earlier," she managed as her lips dropped to my throat. "Didn't think the rush to get dressed before Caleb started squawking would come in handy."

"Very handy," I murmured, my fingers slipping into the plump, wet folds.

She groaned then bit my neck when I grazed her clitoris. Thankfully, I'd had my interviews already; that bite was going to leave a mark. She started to unbutton my silk blouse, and I used my free hand to shove her t-shirt up over her naked breasts. Larger since she'd been breastfeeding our son, but still the same shape I'd known for years. I cupped one then the other, delighting in her throaty groans. The hand touching her fiery hot center grew more insistent.

"You're making me nuts."

"I can't believe how long it's been." I pushed back to look at her. "Let's not let that happen again."

"Completely with you," she moaned, her hips tilting into my hand, asking for what she loved best. "Ahh, jeez, not gonna make it."

"Yeah?" I teased, thrilled that she was this close to the edge already. It meant she'd missed this as much as I had. "Give me what I want, Meg."

I slipped inside her slick, hot sheath. She twitched around my fingers as I added my thumb to her clit. She bucked against me, letting go of those familiar half moan half groan pants until the thrusting and rubbing forced her climax.

"God, so good, Bri." She tilted toward me, using my body to help keep her taller frame standing. Her hot breath blew against my temple as she recovered from her orgasm. "I needed that." When she managed to bring her head upright, she gave me a determined stare. "Time for my fun, babe."

With an almost feral look, she spun me to face the river again. Her body crushed up against mine, hands roaming to find bare skin under the loosened shirt. I felt her drop to her knees behind me. Her hands slid up the back of my legs and under my skirt. When she found my underwear, she teased, "You'd win at strip poker." Slowly she brought the panties down my legs and with each gliding inch, I felt myself get wetter. "Step," she ordered to free them from my legs. When her hands moved north again, she took my skirt upwards until it bunched at my waist. Exposed to the night air, I could feel the chill caressing me and mixing with the searing heat swirling through my body. "These are so sexy." Her hands traced the lace of my garter down the straps to my thigh-high stockings. "You're so sexy, Bri, with or without the garter."

"You make me feel sexy, Meg."

She stood and brushed up against me. Her mouth began to suck softly on my earlobe. "I have to take you, right here, right now." No foreshadowing touch at all, she just plunged inside me, filling me completely.

"God, yes, good," I groaned, bracing forward over the balcony railing to give her better access. The feel of her inside of me flared lances of fire everywhere. I moved against her thrusts, trying to stay quiet so we wouldn't wake Caleb or our neighbors next door. In no time, I recognized the churning in my abdomen. "Close."

"Yeah, do it, babe." Meg's other hand slipped around my front and took my clit between two fingers. Alternating between sliding and pinching, with one more rough thrust, I was done. A gruff whispered shout escaped before I could contain it. My body trembled and twitched through the best climax I'd had in years.

Boneless, I could barely turn around and open my eyes to look at the woman who'd done this to me. As they fluttered open, Megan's voice, slightly deeper and with a different cadence said, "You're the one who's beautiful." My eyes focused, and it was M's face that stared back at me.

I bolted upright in bed, suddenly awake, heart beating so fast I could see the rhythm under my t-shirt. Perspiration flushed my body hot, tight and strung out from the unfulfilled climax that my dream had escalated. My muscles ached, but my heart ached more. I'd relived that night on the balcony more times than I cared to admit over the past three years, but this was the only time I'd turned it into a fantasy. This was the first time I'd ever fantasized about someone else. I'd had more than just a sex dream about M. I'd taken one of my favorite true life moments and attached her to it. A psychologist would have a field day with me.

I sprang out of bed, ignoring my aching muscles and stumbled into the bathroom. I flipped on the shower and stripped off my sleep shorts and shirt. Gripping the counter, my head bent to avoid looking at my reflection before I gained control. When I stepped under the hot spray of water, I felt my muscles relax a little. Only one thing would make me lose the tension completely, but I wouldn't do it, not even if it would only take two swipes of my fingers.

The soap felt slick on my hypersensitive skin, but I didn't permit a second of pleasure. I went about washing my hair and shaving my legs. When I turned to face the spray, the water splashed against my throbbing center. I slammed my hands against the shower tile and gave up, tilting my hips so that the spray would hit right where I needed it most. Ten seconds of pulsating water and I came in a charge of pent up frustration and sorrow.

It was a dream, just a dream, I tried reassuring myself. The fact that the frustration overpowered the sorrow got me to abandon the shame. I had some hope that I was finally past the grief of losing my spouse and open to someone new. That left only frustration. If a spontaneous climax didn't relieve the frustration, only one thing remained.

Unfortunately, too many people had the same idea. Jessie's health club teemed with people this early, adding to my irritation. If I had to wait in line for one machine, I might lose it. Thankfully, an upright bike beckoned and, with a little maneuvering, I hopped onto it. Plugging in the required data to get the machine to clock my heart rate and calorie burn, I started the mindless spinning of the pedals.

From my bike seat, I watched the early morning townsfolk go about their daily routines through the window in front of me. After twenty minutes, I shifted to check out the rest of the gym's patrons in the mirrored wall to my left. I caught sight of Willa in front of one of the free weight bench presses. She was laughing with the person she was spotting. So this is when she worked out. Of all the times I'd been in here, I'd never seen her even though she claimed she used the gym three times a week.

I almost stopped pedaling to go over and say hello, but the sight of her workout buddy kept me glued to my bike seat. M popped up off the bench after replacing the bar, smiled, and said something to Willa while getting into spotting position. A sleeveless exercise top showed off chiseled arms and hugged a fit torso. Her nylon shorts highlighted powerfully feminine thighs and calves. My weakness: perfect legs. I should have known she'd have perfect legs. I felt my throat tighten and fought to keep the dream from resurfacing in my head.

Keeping an eye trained on the duo, I heard the bike issue a series of sporadic beeps indicating my increased heart rate. For two fairly staid people, they seemed to be chatting effortlessly.

When they moved to another machine, I couldn't help noticing how closely they walked and stood together. We'd become friends, good friends I thought, yet M still kept a few steps between us whenever we were together. An unfamiliar flicker of jealousy ran through me. Why could she drop her guard around Willa but not around me?

"Morning, Bri." Quinn stepped into my eye line in the mirror, startling me. "Didn't know you worked out this early."

"I don't normally." I smiled up at her, taking in her running shorts and UVA athletic department t-shirt. Yet another sickeningly fit specimen of woman, the group was filled with them. There should really be a limit imposed. "Don't you usually exercise in the basketball facility on campus?"

"Usually." She waved at a man who called out to her from a machine in the next row. I found it amazing how well she dealt with her admiring public when they had no problem telling her how to do her job. "Jess and I took a run this morning and ended up here rather than doubling back toward our houses. I'll get a ride back with Will." She turned and sought out her partner among the club's members. "Doesn't look like she's done yet."

Because she was here and I might as well use every resource I could, I asked, "How well do you know M?"

"Hmm?" She turned her attention back to me. "Oh, not that well, actually. She and Willa hang out mostly when I'm on road trips with the team, and, as you can see, they like to work out together. She's taken care of our dogs a few times when we're both out of town, and she's been to dinner at our house once. I think she said ten words to me the whole night."

That made me laugh, at least M wasn't more forthcoming with Quinn than she was with me. "They look like they're pretty close friends."

Quinn narrowed her gaze at me before a knowing smile stretched her lips wide. *Splendid.* Since when had I become such an open book? "They are, but for Willa that means she's comfortable calling her spontaneously." She glanced into the mirror at my reflection and pointed her gaze in the same direction as mine. We watched the friends laugh at something while huddled together. "Or were you talking about their proximity?" She did a lousy job of hiding the teasing expression on her face. Almost as lousy as I was at hiding the blush I now wore. "According to Willa, two people who have large personal bubbles don't need to worry about the other invading her space."

"I've never noticed that about Willa," I commented, trying to make sense of what she'd just said.

"That's because she's gotten comfortable with our friends. She won't bite their hands if they try to hug her anymore." She grinned and winked.

I thought back to M's reaction when I'd touched her face, and it hit me. *Oh, crap.* She hadn't been fearful that I was coming onto her. No, she hadn't wanted to be touched; she didn't like being touched. Well, that would make having a relationship a little difficult, wouldn't it?

Chapter 22

This time when I approached her door, I didn't bother to look at the architectural details. I was too excited to see her. My inline skates hung over my shoulder, but I barely noticed their weight. I knocked twice and waited.

"I'm not late, am I?" I asked when M opened the door. "Gene stopped by my office before I left. I wasn't sure I'd get out of there in time."

She smiled, familiar with how our dean's drop bys killed thirty minutes more than was ever necessary. "You're right on time. Ready?"

"Mind if I use your bathroom? I didn't get a chance before Gene cornered me, and I had to leave to get here."

She hesitated briefly but stepped back to let me inside. "Sure, second door on your left at the end of the hall."

"Thanks, I'll just be a minute." My bladder rushed me through the living room and into the hallway. I caught a glimpse of her home office on the left as I walked past the first open door. As pristine as her living room and kitchen, a black and white workspace where I guessed she spent a good deal of her apartment time.

When I resurfaced from the immaculate bathroom—clearly, she didn't have kids—I made my way back at a much slower pace. As I passed the next door, what I saw brought me to a standstill. Her bedroom, smaller than her office, was awash in color. Two tones of yellow on two walls butted up against the other two walls with burnt orange blending up into cinnamon. I was immediately reminded of the fall season in Vermont. Color must represent some sort of comfortable place for her. To see it everywhere would strip it of its meaning. That it was in her bedroom told me she needed the security it brought to help her sleep. Along with the clustered furniture in the small area, it made for a cozy, sheltered space.

Not wanting to get caught, I hurried back out into the living room. M was just grabbing her skates from the front closet. I studied her again, piecing together what I knew about her. She'd had a hard childhood. She didn't make friends easily. She was painfully shy. She didn't like people violating her personal space. She needed a security blanket. And she was slowly stealing my heart after years of being locked in limbo.

"All set?" she asked when she turned back.

More than you know. "Yep. Do you have a specific trail in mind?"

"We can get to the park pretty easily from two streets over." She opened her door and waited for me to head out in front of her.

I resisted the urge to brush up against her on my way by. After Quinn told me about Willa's personal space theory, I realized that I needed to get M to trust that I wouldn't infringe on her space without her permission so that she could drop her guard around me. As much as I was starting to feel for her, I knew it would be one of the hardest things I'd ever do.

"M?" I started before my brain could issue the signal to stop. "Are you gay?"

She stepped backward until her body banged against the open door. Wide eyes screamed at me as loudly as my own head did. How could I have asked such a private question? I'd just done the exact opposite of what I promised myself I wouldn't do. It didn't matter that I hadn't touched her. I'd just violated her personal space, especially for someone not used to answering personal questions. My own wish to know that I wasn't developing feelings for a straight woman should never have been put ahead of her comfort level. *Stupid, stupid, stupid.*

"Don't answer that. Sorry, I've lost my mind. It's none of my business. Forgive me, and please forget I said anything." I stepped out into the hallway to give her more space. "I keep making you

uncomfortable. Believe me, I don't like it any more than you do."
I chanced a glance at her. She clutched the doorknob, a stunned
look on her fact. "I'll understand if you want to call this off. Maybe
another time." Like when I had some duct tape for my mouth.

I was turning to leave when she shook her head and joined me
in the hallway. After locking the door, she adjusted the laces on
her skates so they'd fall more comfortably over her shoulder and
started off down the hallway. At least I hadn't frightened her back
into her shell.

While we strapped on our skates on the street, we didn't
attempt to speak because of the continuous stream of cars on the
street. That and the fact that apparently my brain could only
contain me physically or verbally but not both at the same time. I
didn't want to chance saying something that would make her
permanently rethink our friendship.

We threw our shoes into my car and started south until we hit
the park entrance. She was incredibly good on skates, as sure as
she was standing in front of her classroom. Her lean muscles
worked effortlessly to make her glide like a professional skater on
the blacktop. As often as Megan and I had done this, I had to
struggle to keep up with M's pace.

When the path turned from pavement to cobblestones, she
pulled up at one of the benches that edged around a flower garden.
I wanted to shout in triumph that she was giving us a break after
what felt like hours of blading but was maybe forty-five minutes.
She floated down into one corner of the bench, watching me as I
took a seat close to the other side. We were the only ones in the
area. In fact, we hadn't passed anyone for over a mile.

"Whew!" I exclaimed, catching my breath. "That was fun. It's
been a while for me, and you're better than good. You must do this
a lot?"

She stared out at an unusually shaped dogwood tree for a
moment then spoke for the first time since we'd left her
apartment. "I don't know."

"Take it from me, I know. You're a very good skater. Are you
better on the ice or with rollerblades?"

"No, that's the answer to your question. I don't know."

My question? Oh, that question. She didn't know? "That's usually something someone knows," I offered tentatively, having never heard that response.

"I realize that." She still wouldn't face me.

"But you don't know?" I repeated, and then it dawned on me. "I see. You've only been with men, so you wouldn't know if it's a curiosity thing or not." The realization made my heart sick. "Well, if you ever have any questions..." I trailed off in a dejected voice. "Although, if you still date men, you probably don't have any questions." *Lame, stupid, idiot.*

"I don't." She turned her gaze on me.

"Of course not," I agreed readily, embarrassed to have brought up a subject that she clearly had no way of relating to.

"I meant that I don't date men. I never have."

"What?" I used a stall tactic while I tried to make sense of what she said. "You've never dated a man?" She shook her head. "Have you ever dated a woman?" Another shake of her head. "Are you saying you've never been with anyone?"

She turned away, blinking harshly to hide a film of moisture. The knuckles on one hand grew white from the strain of gripping an armrest. "Not by consent."

She hadn't chosen the person? Had it been—wait, that wasn't what she'd said. She used the word "consent". *Oh, no! Please, no.* "Tell me, please?"

When she spoke, her voice was raw from straining to keep her tears at bay. "The boy I hurt was the much adored son of the third foster family I lived with. When he came into our room, I was awake. I waited for him to come to me like he had before, but when I heard SueElla's muffled scream, I bolted out of bed and took him off her. She was only twelve. I couldn't let him do to her what he'd done to me. He was almost eighteen and so much bigger than me. I honestly don't know how I'd managed to hurt him when I couldn't stop him before."

"Jesus!" I wanted to hold her and let her know how much I cared that she was safe now and that her past couldn't touch her anymore. But I knew that was the last thing she'd want. "That's an unspeakable thing to have happen to you. I'm so sorry. I wish that hadn't been part of your life."

She nodded once, continuing to look out over the brightly colored flower garden. "This isn't how I expected today to go."

"Have you ever told anyone?"

She shook her head, and I felt a physical pain bloom inside my stomach. "It's not a subject I like to dwell on, which is why I don't have an answer for you. I'm pretty messed up."

"No, you're not. You're wonderful, M. An amazing teacher, an inspiring mentor, and an incredible friend. You're remarkable."

She shook her head, sighing. "I don't get you. Everyone else at work avoids me. Even the people I consider my acquaintances don't press for anything from me, but you never give up. You've made sharing our class so easy for me. You've made working together fun. You've made getting to know someone simple."

"You meant to say 'you've made becoming friends simple,' right? Because we're friends, please know that."

"I do," she admitted softly, shyly darting her eyes away then back again. "Thank you."

She just thanked me for being her friend. This extraordinary woman could make me fall deeply for a second time in my life when she'd never known it once. That hardly seemed fair.

Chapter 23

She moved from the rowing machine to the treadmill, the one in the corner, away from the televisions and other treadmills. Almost no one used it, but it was her favorite. She'd run for thirty minutes until her friend arrived. Her friend. She liked thinking that. She'd not had many friends in life, and now she seemed to have an abundance.

Setting off at a rapid pace, she glanced around to make sure she was alone in her little corner. Only then did she zone out. *She thinks I'm beautiful. I've never been beautiful before.*

"How's it going?" Jessie was suddenly at her side. Like that time in the D/s club, she'd managed to appear dangerously close without her sensing it.

She stumbled when her left foot didn't stride as far as the right. It took some concentration before she got back into rhythm. "Fine, Jess. You?"

"Couldn't be better. How's the class going?"

She wiped her brow unnecessarily, wondering why Jessie was asking about her work. "Really well, thanks. It looks like it's going to be a huge success. Of course, I'm not responsible for that."

"I don't believe that," Jessie pointed out kindly. "Plus, I've heard otherwise."

"She's too quick to give away credit."

"Now, that, I believe." Jessie gripped the bar of her treadmill and casually glanced around the room. Only half full on this late morning with the closest patron working out about twenty feet away on the free weights. "You're becoming friends?"

She smiled fondly, unable to stop herself. "Yes."

Jessie matched her smile. "Good friends?"

"I hope so."

Jessie nodded, seemingly in approval. "Maybe something more?"

The heart rate monitor on the machine betrayed the clattering in her chest. She pulled off the finger clip before Jessie noticed. Jessie never pried; she could count on that. In all the time they'd known each other, Jessie never pried. Why was she starting now?

"She's very special," Jessie commented softly.

With a press of a button, she increased the grade of the treadmill, somehow hoping the harder she ran the farther she'd get from this conversation. The part of her mind in charge of counting began ticking off each step while the part responsible for feeling irritation flared up at how easily she'd slipped back into the protective habit. Neither the habit nor the irritation helped her situation, so she dropped the irritation but kept up the running count. When Jessie didn't move away after a prolonged silence, something that usually got to everyone else, she had no choice but to agree. "Yes, she is."

Jessie glanced behind her and on each side again to make sure no one had come closer. "Listen, I've got no right to say this, but I can't help looking out for my friends."

The comment caused her brow to furrow. "That's what good friends do."

Jessie nodded and trained her gaze on the treadmill readout. "If you tell me you don't need it, she doesn't ever have to know."

She squinted in confusion. "Need what?"

Dark brown eyes flicked back to hers with worried concern. This conversation was making Jessie uncomfortable, too. "The D/s club."

Oh, God! Jessie had known all this time and never said anything. A dread she hadn't felt in years returned with enough force that she forgot about the counting and gripped the handrails to steady herself.

"I'm not judging you. I don't have any room to judge. I was there, too, if you'll recall." Jessie's voice was even, not judgmental or filled with shame.

But it was your first time, and you never returned. It was something you wanted to try once, she thought.

"I'm just going to say this," Jessie plowed on in a tight voice. "If you still need that, then I'm going to ask you as a person who very much wants to be your friend, please tell her before anything happens between you two. I don't know for sure, but she didn't seem the type to have those...proclivities. I wouldn't want her to become involved only to find out later that she couldn't handle that kind of scene. She's had enough heartbreak."

"Nothing's going to happen," she admitted against the protest of her heart.

Jessie studied her with sad eyes. "Because you don't want it to?"

She pressed the cool down button and slowed to a walk. "Because it can't."

The sadness in Jessie's eyes deepened. "I know all about desiring certain things and then not. About being thought of a certain way but not being that way."

Walking through her cool down, she waited for Jessie to tell her that her fledgling friendship had no chance of getting off the ground because Jessie had to protect her friend. She wanted to tell Jessie that this wasn't any of her business, but she'd do the same thing if a friend of hers had the potential to become involved with an abnormal freak. From what she knew, Jessie was too good a friend not to warn her off.

"If that's not you anymore, I get it. My marriage proves that someone can be one way and then not be that way anymore. Not miss it, not desire it, not even think about it. Lauren did that for me, and I thank every higher power for giving me the chance to become who I am with her." Jessie tilted her head wistfully. The fingers of her right hand absently twisted the shiny platinum and rose gold wedding ring on her left. Joy from her new life was so apparent on her face and in her relaxed stance. "If you don't want something different, or if you've already moved on to something else, then ignore me. I'll just be a nosy friend who overstepped and begs your forgiveness." She bared a timid smile. "But if you're like me at all, I'm certain that Briony is the kind of person who can do for you what Lauren did for me."

Her fingers tightened around the rails. She knew how true Jessie's statement was. Too bad she couldn't find out just how true. As much as she longed to be something more with Briony, it wasn't possible. Recently, just staring at Briony's beautiful face with its exquisite cheekbones, fine nose, golden eyes that darkened to ginger when she spoke passionately, and delicate pink mouth caused pain. Every time Briony dipped her head, she ached to brush the blond bangs from her right eye and tuck the strands behind her lovely ear. Or finger the elusive dimple that only appeared when Briony was trying to fight back a smile. She wondered often what it would be like to bury her face in the hair that almost reached to the bend in her neck. To brush her lips over the silky skin there. To feel Briony's reaction to her mouth sliding along her neck. Would the touch be welcome? Would Briony shiver or tremble or moan? She wished she could find out. But she couldn't do any of those things. Normal people did things like that. Normal people didn't have issues with touch, didn't have issues with intimacy, didn't have issues with sex.

She came to the end of the cool down and stepped off the treadmill. With a quick glance up at the towering figure of Jessie, she nodded but said nothing. There wasn't anything she could say.

Chapter 24

Usually, when a woman blushes in your presence, it's a flattering thing. But after the fourth flush on M's face, I was starting to worry. It wasn't a shy blush of romantic interest, nor was it a self-conscious flush of temporary embarrassment. No, this looked like she was uncomfortable in my presence. I really thought we'd moved past this.

"Everything all right, M?" I asked without looking at her because that seemed to increase the redness.

"Sure," she responded, but I caught the quick flick of her eyes to check if I was looking at her.

We sat side by side in my office, going through the finalized business plans. Our class was coming to a close tomorrow. Far more successful than anyone imagined, and I sat next to the reason why. The symposium would turn into an independent study course to keep the businesses up and running. M would take on the two manufacturing heavy businesses, while my three were in the service industries.

"What do you have planned for the break?" I'd tried asking her this several times over the last few weeks but never got an answer. I wanted to know what she'd be doing, but mostly I wanted to know if she'd miss seeing me as much as I would miss her.

She tilted back in her chair and gave me that hand brush off again, her way of saying she didn't think her answer was interesting enough to share or that she didn't want to share. "What about you?"

Since I'd already answered this before when she tried the same deflection, I slowly turned and pegged her with a glance that said I knew exactly what she was doing. Her tempting neck grew pink as the flush made it up to her cheeks. I would have insisted on an answer right then if my cell phone hadn't started the familiar ring that my son had programmed in for me. "Excuse me, that's Caleb. Do you mind?"

"Please." She gestured toward my messenger bag and pushed back to stand.

I reached out to keep her in place but took my hand back, remembering. "You don't have to leave." Her eyes widened at the movement of my hand, but she didn't leave. "Hi, handsome," I spoke into the phone as soon as I'd dug it out.

"Hiya, Mom. Camp's so great. I wish I could stay forever."

I laughed at his simple declaration. "I'm that horrible of a mother, huh?"

"No!" he exclaimed. "I just meant I wish I didn't have to leave here to go back to school."

"You want to become a mountain man, do ya?" I teased.

"I can't wait to show you everything we made up here. When are you coming?"

"Next week. We'll hang out with Grandma and Grandpa for a bit, visit Grams and Papa, too."

"I wish Hank could come with you."

The mention of his friend prompted a glance at mine. She was busying herself by looking through my library of textbooks. "You'll see him in a few weeks. I think he's still at camp, too."

"Are we going be home before school so I can hang out with him?"

"A few days before, plenty of time for sleepovers and all-night chat sessions. You'll be all caught up on your summers in no time."

"Can't wait. Oh, gotta go, Mom. It's swim time at the lake. I'll see you next week. I love you."

"I love you, too, Caleb. Be good." I closed the phone, giddy as usual from talking to my son, who sounded more and more grownup every time we chatted.

"How is he enjoying camp?" M turned back from the bookshelves.

"They gave the kids bows and arrows to use; he's beside himself."

She laughed and the unexpected sound made me a little lightheaded. "Hank's having a great time at his camp, too. They've come up with an entirely new form of ASL to fool the camp counselors daily. The kids love it, but I'm guessing their parents will be exasperated when they get back and try using it at home."

"How did you learn? Was it because of Hank?"

She shook her head and slipped cautiously back into her seat. "Kathryn would volunteer on weekends at a school for the deaf in Chicago. She worked with the special needs kids who were also hearing impaired. I tagged along and picked it up."

Remarkable. Everything about M was remarkable. "She seems like an amazing woman."

"Very much so." She picked up the business plan we'd been working on, obviously ready to get back to work. I bit back the groan of disappointment. "Actually, that's where I'm headed for the break. They're having a fundraiser and need some extra help."

"See, now, why couldn't you just say that before, Miranda?" I teased, stopping myself from nudging her with my shoulder.

"Not this again," she sighed dramatically, but her tone and expression didn't seem at all bothered. "I thought you'd given that up."

"Not a chance, this is better than reading a good mystery." I wiggled my eyebrows at her. "Hmm, let's see, M names that I haven't guessed yet. Michelle? No, not old fashioned enough. Marilyn? Old fashioned but still quite prevalent. Medussa? No, no one would do that to a child. Mae, Marianne, Marnie, Maude, Melanie, Medea, Melissa, Meg—" My heart jumped into my throat as my stomach twisted tightly. *No! Please, don't let it be.* I gripped the armrest of her chair. She flinched, but her eyes showed concern for what must have been a much paler version of me facing her. "I know you're not giving me your name, but please tell me it isn't—"

"My name isn't Megan," she cut in, returning the placement of my heart and uncoiling my stomach.

"Thank you for telling me." I faced forward slowly. A tremor shook my hands as I placed them in my lap. "That's what I get for teasing you."

She gave a soft laugh, allowing me the dignity of trying to play off my near meltdown. "How long were you together? You don't have to answer if you don't want to talk about it."

"Eleven years married, a year seeing each other before that."

"What was she like?"

I let out a puff of air. Never an easy question to answer, but with M, I didn't mind attempting. "A little audacious, a lot compassionate. Meg could convince anyone of anything if she truly believed in it. And kids were her weakness. Whatever they wanted, she couldn't deny them. Caleb always knew which mom to ask when he needed permission. Her nieces and nephews got away with murder whenever they stayed with us." I laughed as I remembered a particular sleepover where kids were up puking all night because Megan had let them skip dinner for three courses of desserts. "Mostly, she was easygoing. Nothing seemed to faze her or surprise her, which I thought was a fabulous trait when I was a stressed out twenty-four-year-old dealing with a dissertation committee, but it got a little irksome as I got older." Especially when I'd put a lot of effort into surprising her or wanted to get her riled up about something that I felt was vital.

M's smile told me she understood why that tendency might be frustrating. "What did she do for a living?"

"She was a receptionist when we met, but after I got my Ph.D. and we'd gotten a handle on finances, we started an adventure company together. During the school year, I'd take care of the behind the scenes business stuff while she led the vacation tours. In the summer, I'd be out there with her." I'd always loved that. Summers hiking, rafting, hand gliding, kayaking, wind surfing, and any other activities that Meg had planned for our clients on their week-long adventure. I'd always thought that teaching summer session couldn't compare to the trips we'd take, even with some of the more whiny clients. No way teaching a class could beat that. Not until this summer.

"Sounds exciting."

"A little too, in my opinion. It was mostly fun for me, but she absolutely loved it." Miraculously, I didn't feel the usual sadness whenever I talked about Megan with people. Further proof that I was healing. I glanced at M and recognized she wanted to ask *the* question but wouldn't. "Rock climbing was her favorite. I enjoyed it, too. I remember being annoyed that she'd chosen to schedule a rock climbing trip a few weeks before spring term was done. She hadn't done it to keep me from going. She just couldn't wait to get in the first climb of the season." While my heart beat a little faster, I wasn't experiencing the usual need to hyperventilate when I thought about that trip I'd missed. "Someone in the group went off line, a hotshot, thought he knew what he was doing but got stuck without a way out. Meg unclipped and free climbed over to help guide him to the best holds. She got him safely back to the line and was on her way when a hand and foothold gave way."

M sat quietly absorbing. I liked that she didn't try to placate me with empty words. "She saved a man's life."

Succinctly put. "Yes, she did."

"That was very brave of her." She slid the business plan back between us on the desk. "Thank you for sharing that with me."

"You're the first person I've told here." I felt it was important to let her know that she was special to me.

She did a double-take. "Not Jessie?"

"No." It was one of the reasons I knew Jessie and I weren't right for each other. I could tell her now, but while we were dating, I didn't feel like I could have.

"Oh," she acknowledged softly. The flush returned unexpectedly, and she turned to study a framed photo of Caleb on my bookcase. "Have you seen Jessie recently?"

"Yesterday, why?"

"Nothing." She shook her head and a tremor rolled through her body.

The tremor worried me. What if Jessie told her about the conversation we'd had? Jessie wouldn't betray a confidence like that, would she? "Did she say something to you?"

She studied me for a long moment. "No, I don't get much chance to speak with her at the gym."

I wanted to blow out the breath I'd been holding but knew it would look obvious. "Well, you could come to dinner with me on Sunday up at Willa and Quinn's and have a whole evening to talk to her if you wanted." Mentally crossing my fingers, I fought to keep her gaze. Her eyes widened. For a second, it looked like she'd agree to come along, but the look was replaced by the same type of panic I'd been feeling. I decided to let her off the hook. "Of course, if you did, my friend Caroline would probably start trying to fix you up, so maybe not."

"Definitely not," she agreed quickly then added, "but thank you for the invitation."

"You're welcome." I was almost as relieved as she was, but only because I knew what my friends would be like with her. If any of them found out I was harboring these feelings for her, she'd never escape and my humiliation would be turned into an after dinner game.

Chapter 25

The department meeting would go differently this time. I was sure of it. As I entered the auditorium on the last day of the summer session, I scanned the seats for M. She'd sit with me today.

"Lucked out with those students. Could have been a disaster if they hadn't had such well prepared plans," Dr. Wagner grumbled bitterly as he stepped past me down the aisle.

Only because M and I helped them make the plans stellar, I wanted to shout back, but I kept my snarky retort to myself. I was a professional even if he wasn't. Plus, my flash annoyance dissipated when I spotted M sitting in the side section alone.

"Is this seat taken?" My question caused her to jolt forward and swing her head over to me in the aisle.

"Don't you want to sit with your friends?" She pointed up to where Javier and Alexa sat first row center.

"I will be." I gave her a pointed stare and indicated the vacant chair next to her.

She smiled widely and looked away, but not before I caught the blush. God, she was beautiful. "Please." She tipped her chin at the open seat.

"Glad to be done with summer session?" I swiveled in my seat to face her. "Three classes, one you didn't even sign up for?" I'd only had the one class, and I was wiped out.

"I enjoyed every minute." She locked eyes with me and a lance of heat shot through me. This time I felt my own face flush. It was getting harder and harder to fight this attraction to her.

"Well done, everyone," Gene called out from the podium, snapping my attention back. "Another successful summer session.

This one landed us on the front page of the *Wall Street Journal*, by the way." He held up the evidence of his statement. "Thanks to our brilliant venture program, we now have one of the top five entrepreneurship programs in the country." He preened for a bit before continuing. "I think we should all give Drs. Gatewood and Desiderius a hand for their part in making this project a big success."

Solicited applause rang out through the auditorium. I blushed from embarrassment this time and glanced at M. She'd slouched down in her chair, pulling closer to use my body as a shield. She really hated this, and suddenly, I hated it for her. Shifting forward, I angled toward the rest of the crowd, hoping to provide a better shield for her. "Thank you, Gene, it's been a wonderful ride. Those students were every professor's dream. Everyone on the selection committee did a wonderful job as well."

"Quite right." Gene shifted the focus from us to the five professors who'd been part of the selection committee.

"You all right?" I twisted back toward M.

"Yes, thank you." Her relieved voice brought a hitch to my breath. That and how close she was to me right now. She seemed to notice it in that moment, too, but instead of jerking away from me, she slowly inched back into the middle of her seat. A flicker of longing showed in her eyes when she glanced back at the place she'd burrowed into.

Gene continued with his praise of other classes and a pep talk for the fall term. I barely listened to anything he said, now hyperaware of how close M was sitting to me. If I moved my thigh I might be able to brush up against hers, but I couldn't do that. Not yet. I needed to know she wanted the same thing.

When he finished up, people started piling into the aisles. Alexa and Javier funneled into our row. "We must bow at your feet, oh great ones of venture programs," Javier joked.

"Shut it," I shot back with a smile. "Back to Texas?"

"I thought I might hit Vermont with you. I'm already packed."

"She'll take me before she takes you, mister," Alexa taunted and pulled me into a hug. "You did a great job with that symposium, lady. You too, M."

M started forward in her chair, surprise showing on her face. "Thank you."

"You have a great break, Bri. Take lots of pictures. We'll have a slide show when you get back."

"Sounds good. Have a great time yourself. You too, Javier." I gave them a quick hug and waved as they headed toward the exit.

"Well done, you two." Gene replaced my friends at our row.

"Thank you, Gene. And thank you for your kind praise earlier. We appreciate it."

"This went better than even I anticipated, and you're both to be commended."

"Thank you, Dr. Goudy," M said softly.

"I hope you're up for the same next summer because I see this being a permanent symposium each year. You two were stars; we'll need your help again."

My eyes widened, not expecting him to try to sign us up a year in advance of the class. "Why don't we talk about it next term? Give us a little time to recover from the unexpected summer?"

"Of course, yes. See you in a few weeks. Thank you both, again."

"You're welcome," I supplied and watched him take leave. "Guess the program really surprised some folks."

"Seems so." M finally stood.

I backed out before her eyes could plead with me to move. "I'll walk with you." I had to. I wasn't ready to let her go just yet.

We started up the aisle and flowed out into the now deserted hallway. Our colleagues must have scrambled to get off campus as soon as possible. This break between summer session and fall term was always the longest, and no one liked to waste a second of it. I wouldn't be surprised if we were the only two souls left on north campus.

Because my office was farther away, we found ourselves heading up the staircase to hers. "When do you leave for Chicago?"

"Saturday. When are you on a plane?"

"Tomorrow. My parents are expecting me for a day before we go pick up Caleb."

She gave me a wistful glance as she unlocked the door to her office. It was hard to tell if she was wistful about the idea of visiting parents or missing me. I hoped it was the latter. I didn't have much time to contemplate it before she invited me inside. Since we'd always met in class or my office, this was the first time I was seeing hers. It was a lot less cluttered with plain walls, no pictures, and tons of books. A sliver of color peeked out in between two books. A framed oil painting of all types of flowers in a blue vase represented the only color in the room.

She began putting her laptop into her bag. "I hope you have a nice time."

"I'm going to miss sharing class with you."

"It was fun," she confirmed without hesitation then grabbed her wallet out of her desk drawer and added it to the bag. Only her sunglasses were left to pack away.

"I'm going to miss you." My heart rate slowed to almost flat line as she stopped packing and gave me her full attention. Those reddish brown eyes stared intently at me. I wanted to reach out and touch her cheek again then run my fingers through the stylish strands of chestnut hair. I bet it was soft, really soft, especially at her nape where it was shorn shorter than the rest. I longed to rub the silky patch of skin just behind her ear. I wasn't sure how long I could keep these urges to myself. In fact, just the thought to restrain them had the opposite effect, and I found myself tilting forward to grip the back of a chair, sucking in a deep breath.

"Are you okay?" She stepped toward me, concern marking her expression.

"Yes, fine." I straightened up, feeling lightheaded and flushed.

"You don't look fine. You look like you need to sit down." She pulled out the chair I'd been gripping and gestured to sit.

"No, I don't." My mouth went dry. I was going to say it. I knew I was, and I knew I couldn't stop myself. "I'm wildly attracted to you, M. I don't mean to shock you, but I can't continue to act like you don't affect me. I felt I should give voice to it, but it doesn't have to change our friendship."

She'd started backing up the moment I opened my big mouth. Now she was slammed against the far wall, glancing at the door to either make sure it was closed or calculate how long it would take her to escape.

I held up a placating hand. "I've scared you. I'm sorry."

"No."

Back to single word responses. *Splendid.* At least she'd relaxed a bit, but she hadn't moved out of her corner. If I'd thought it would go differently, I was kidding myself. "I'll just go."

"No." She took one step toward me, and my heart went from no beats to a pace that could bring me to my knees. She wasn't dropping my gaze either. Could it be?

"I haven't scared you?" She shook her head in response. "You don't want me to go?" Another shake of her head. I swallowed roughly before continuing. "Are you attracted to me, too?" This time her head didn't confirm or deny my question. The gaze, though, didn't falter. I thought my heart might explode. *She's attracted to me. She is!*

"I'm not..." she hesitated.

Oh crap, she isn't.

After a long moment, she finished, "Normal."

"Don't say that, M." I started toward her, but she brought a hand up to tell me to stop.

"You're beautiful and wonderful, Briony. I want nothing more than to act on this attraction." Her voice was tight and raw, not the voice of someone who was ready to press me against the desk and rip off my clothes. Drawing a shaky breath, she continued, "That boy...it wasn't just once. It was two years. He threatened to kill me, which after the first few times I would have welcomed, but then he said he'd hurt SueElla if I told, so I just let him do that to me. For two years. It was painful every time. Do you have any idea how long two years is for a twelve-year-old?"

"Oh, God," I whispered. Tears pooled in my eyes and a lump the size of a small boulder formed in my throat. She'd been twelve, and it had lasted forever.

"I'm not like normal people who can act on their feelings. I've lived with that most of my life, and it never really bothered me." She shook her head and turned away. "But then I met you, and you make me want things I can't have."

"But you can," I encouraged. My heart felt exhausted from the sudden starts and stops of this exchange.

"No, I can't. I can't be touched. Do you get that?" She turned back with blazing eyes. "I hate it. I hate that my skin burns when someone touches me. I hate that I can't put my hands on someone without it hurting or feeling like I'm going to harm them. I won't do that to you."

"You won't harm me, M," I rushed to assure her. My whole body trembled from the hurt she'd been caused and the fact that it had robbed her of human contact.

Tears pooled and spilled onto her cheeks. "I can't imagine having sex without it being a violent act. I've tried to deal with it, gone to therapists, but after years, I'm no closer to being normal. The only useful advice cost me my self-respect, but I forced myself to participate. It never worked, and I won't do that anymore."

I didn't want to think about what a therapist would suggest for someone who'd been repeatedly sexually abused as a child and left without love for most of her life. She'd lost her self-respect, which meant it was an attempt at sex under controlled conditions. Probably a sex surrogate or sex with restraints. I detested that for her. No one should have to miss out on the physical expression of love, especially for someone who needed to feel loved as much as she did.

"I wish I could take away your pain. You've lived with it for too long." I inched closer, trying not to scare her. "Is your reaction as bad when it's someone you're attracted to?"

She scoffed ruefully. "Are you asking if I can stand to be touched by someone I'd like to touch?" She looked away and shook her head. "I've never had the opportunity."

Did that mean she'd never tried or that she'd never been attracted to anyone before? Both suppositions were heart wrenching. "We could try. Go at whatever pace makes you feel comfortable?" I asked with more hope than I'd had in years.

"Don't you see how screwed up I am?" She raked a hand through her hair. The path of her fingers made mine itch to follow. "I can't act on my feelings. I can't even express my feelings."

"There are a lot of ways to express feelings, M."

"But you deserve the normal way, Briony. You had it before. It was part of your life for so long."

I waved my hands to deny this concern. "I'm not looking for a replica relationship."

"But you should have someone who can give you more." Her eyes implored me to let up. "You deserve someone who can give you everything. I can't be that person. I wish I could."

I hadn't felt this much hurt in my heart since the police knocked on my door three and a half years ago. I knew what she was saying, and I couldn't fight it. "You're certain?"

"I'm sorry. I wish I could be different for you."

I wanted to assure her that I didn't need her to be different, but she hadn't meant it that way. I nodded, reluctantly accepting her decision. "I'll see you in three weeks. We still have to go bike riding." Her eyes widened at my certain declaration. "We're friends. I'm not giving that up." The grateful look on her face helped soothe my heartache.

Chapter 26

Three weeks off from work usually relaxes someone. Instead, the vacation had been a tumultuous time, moving from fun to tolerable to distressing. I loved being with Caleb again, catching up with old friends from Vermont, and visiting my parents. Even seeing Meg's parents and sisters was easy and enjoyable this time. But the entire trip had the sad undercurrent of missing M, wishing I could erase her past and hoping that we could become closer friends.

Our last day in Vermont was spent at Megan's parents' house. Her sisters, their husbands and kids joined us for the afternoon as well. Caleb was living it up with his cousins, and I was getting in my last bit of family time before we got on a plane later.

"Hey, lil' sis." Megan's oldest sister, Sadie, dropped into the chair next to me on the porch. She'd always called me this, mostly as a show of support for her sister's sexuality. Her other sister, Danica, had taken a while to come around to the idea of Megan being gay. Not out of any prejudice, but because they'd been especially close growing up and Megan had told Sadie first. Danica hadn't taken that very well, but she'd eventually come around and had always accepted me with open arms.

"Hi, Sadie. How are you still standing with five kids? Do I need to make a reservation for you at the state mental institute?" I joked, looking up at the face that would have become Meg's. Sadie looked the most like her sister, five years older with Meg's hair if she would have fussed with it as much. I'd always found it difficult to look at her these past few years. Now, I just marveled at her beauty.

"Wanna take a few back with you? Caleb would love it."

"Pack 'em up. I could get more stuff done around the house, rent them out to neighbors, a veritable goldmine."

She smacked my shoulder, laughing loudly, which drew a crowd. Danica, her mother, Allison, and my mom wandered over to join us. I was thankful that my mom and Allison had kept up their friendship. I'd hoped that Meg's death wouldn't act as the excuse not to stay as close as they'd become during our marriage.

"What are you girls getting into over here?" Allison mock demanded.

I smiled and stood to give her my chair, and Sadie did the same for my mom. "Sadie's giving away her kids. I told her there's a big market for them in Virginia."

"Take mine, too." Danica dramatically swiped her brow as she took up the post next to mine on the porch railing. She had a smaller passel at only three, but they were all boys and, my, were they rambunctious.

"You're supposed to be thanking your lucky stars for the little angels," Allison commented. "Of course, I had three girls, much more civil, you know."

"We were dolls," Sadie declared. "Or Meg and I were; you were a hellion." She pointed accusingly at Danica. "Middle child!"

"Oldest know-it-all!" her sister bit back, drawing a round of laughter from us.

"You and Bri had it right, Susan," she told my mom. "One kid, just enough to make you feel the wonders of motherhood but not enough to burn down the house."

"Tell me you don't have matches in your home?" my mom joked. She'd given me her sarcastic sense of humor but not her button nose or hazel eyes. My dad had dark brown eyes that mixed with my mom's hazels and gave my brown eyes a heavy gold tint. I'd also gotten his sharp nose but Mom's refined cheekbones. Depending on the day, I was a dead ringer for either one of them.

"Oh, no, I've learned my lesson," Sadie assured. "So, Bri, as much as I hate to admit it, Virginia seems like it's worked out for you." Everyone nodded in enthusiastic agreement. "I was worried there for a bit, but you finally seem settled."

"Happy," Danica inserted. "Are you seeing anyone?"

I shot a wary look at Allison, but rather than the sad expression I expected, she looked hopeful. "No."

"Oh, hon." Allison reached out to hold my hand. "You gave my precious girl the best years of her life. She would want you to find someone else. She wouldn't want you wasting your wonderful love."

"Ally," I whispered. She pulled on my hand to slide me off the rail and wrap me up in an embrace. Soon the whole lot of them were hugging me.

"Yeah, get out there again, toots," Sadie ordered. "You're not getting any younger."

"Which makes you ancient," Danica taunted her older sister.

My mom kept an arm around me as we settled back into our seats. She'd been telling me these same things for years now, slowly encouraging me to move on with my life. No one wanted to see her child grieving and have that grief keep her from living. Now that I'd made the break from it, I could see how much concern I'd caused for these people who loved me.

"Thanks for the blessing," I said to Allison and turned to Sadie, "and the encouragement."

"We'll expect to meet her when you do find someone," Allison insisted. "We're a tight knit group, aren't we, Susan?"

"You bet," my mom agreed, squeezing me against her. "We all want what's best for you, sunshine."

I'd believed it every time she'd told me over the past three and a half years, but this time I agreed with it. I wanted what was best for me, too.

Chapter 27

It wasn't like I couldn't stay away, I just didn't want to. The classroom was packed as usual. I watched M enthrall her students through the glass in the door. I couldn't decide which M I liked best: the shy, thoughtful woman who chose her words carefully and her friends even more carefully, or the brilliant, enthusiastic instructor who wanted nothing more than to share her passion for learning with her students. Of course, the fact that she was equal parts both was all part of her allure.

The bell sounded and I slipped inside after the first wave of kids through the door. Students surrounded her again, some waving add forms with the hope that someone would be stupid enough to have dropped her class after only one lecture.

She hadn't cut her hair. Throughout the summer, she'd kept up the routine of trimming to keep her three inch strands at three inches. The extra growth looked just as lovely as the shorter version. Too lovely. I was supposed to have used the vacation to gain control of this attraction, but instead I'd only gotten in deeper. This wouldn't be easy, but I wasn't going to give up her friendship because I couldn't stop wishing we could have more. I figured by the end of fall term, four months of hanging out as just friends might do the trick.

"Hey, Prof," Avery greeted as he stepped down from M's perch. I was starting to think he should be reclassified as a stalker rather than a student for all the classes he showed up in. "Did you stop by Selesia's headquarters yet?"

"Not yet. I was just checking in with your professor to see when I could do a walk through."

"You're welcome anytime. Professor D says we should have our first product out by January. The team's going berserk. We're gonna kick some major ass over those other teams."

"It's no longer a competition, Avery. You've already been awarded the start-up capital. Competition would be futile."

"Don't take away my fun, Prof. We want to make you both proud."

"We're already proud." M's voice came at us from behind Avery. He was both tall and wide enough to completely eclipse her. A swarm of students funneled out from behind him, having completed their pestering of the professor.

"Aww," Avery crooned, shifting to the side to speak with both of us. "I'm feeling a group hug coming on." His wide wingspan spread out in an attempt to draw us into a hug.

"Step away now, Av," I warned in a lighthearted tone.

"Not wanting to start any rumors, huh? I see how it is." He winked, and I couldn't help but laugh. While exasperating, Avery was one of the best students I'd ever had.

Turning back from watching his departure, I smiled at M. A moment passed where I was frozen with a gust of giddiness. "Hi," I managed.

"Hey." Her voice sounded even, but her eyes couldn't keep my gaze.

"How was Chicago?"

"Good, thank you. The fundraiser went well. Did you have a nice time in Vermont?"

"It was a good trip. Caleb was eager to get home by the end, though. Now, it's the daily drama of fifth grade."

She blasted me with a smile designed to make my mouth go dry. "Hank's had some fascinating tales as well. Sounds like their teacher is pretty unique."

"I'll say. Should be an interesting year." I watched her head back up to get her bag. "I came by to see if you'd mind if I went by Selesia and Dynasthai next week? I'm a little curious to see how everyone's doing."

"Please do. I'd like to drop in on the three you're coaching as well."

"Maybe we should combine trips?" This was the telling point. Would she hesitate to continue our friendship?

In response, she pulled her phone from her bag and tapped on the screen. "Thursday afternoon?"

"That works." I watched as she stepped down toward me, nothing reluctant in her gait, which meant she was okay with staying friends. "Do you have plans on Saturday? Hank's spending the day with us. I wanted to take the boys rollerblading. Any interest?"

Her eyes flared. "Sure. That sounds fun."

"Great. See you Saturday morning then." I turned and fled before I started babbling about how much more attracted I'd become in the weeks of separation.

On Saturday, my doorbell rang at the precise meeting time. M stood on my doorstep, striking as ever in long shorts and a fitted v-neck t-shirt. The urge to take her in my arms and kiss her rose as quickly as a geyser. "Good morning, M."

"Morning." Her shy smile almost did me in.

"M!" the boys screeched, vaulting toward the front door. I turned and blocked their path to her so that Caleb wouldn't hug her as was his custom with some of my friends. Hank had clearly been trained not to hug her.

"Let's let her get inside without wrestling her to the ground, huh, kids?" I joked. "Do you have your gear?"

"Yeppers," Caleb said for both of them.

"Is it invisible?" I teased because they didn't have the stuff in their hands.

"Nooo!" They laughed.

"Well, are we going or what?" I gestured for them to scoot back up to Caleb's room to get their pads and helmets.

"You have a nice home, Briony." M turned in place to take in my living room, kitchen, and dining room. She went toward the mantel and carefully studied each of the photos.

"Thanks. We like it." I saw her reach out to touch the one of Caleb and me in a canoe, but her hand pulled back before she'd reached it. "Both kids need to rent skates. Hank never had any, and Caleb grew two inches in Vermont."

"Something in the water?" she kidded.

"A few more years and he'll be taller than me."

"I've yet to meet a thirteen-year-old shorter than me."

I laughed at the incongruity. Her presence was so much larger than her petite frame showed, especially in class. Yet I was three inches taller and sometimes felt small in her presence. "I stop talking to them when they get taller than me." She laughed this time, and I thought my heart would burst out of my chest.

"Ready, Mom," Caleb announced, his cute face suddenly very near my shoulder.

"Move out, little monkeys," I ordered to their delight. Monkey sounds followed us out to M's car where we piled in and headed off to the sporting goods store.

It didn't take long to get the boys fitted for rental blades, then we were headed back to the parking lot to get over to the park. On our way out the side entrance, we got caught behind a large gathering of people. They were staring upward and our eyes automatically followed. A fifty-foot rock wall took up an entire section of the rugged outdoors part of the store. The boys looked reverently at it while M turned a concerned gaze on me.

"Still want to give this a try, boys?" I heard myself ask. My heart pounded an irregular pattern as I contemplated what I felt I needed to do.

"Really, Mom?" Caleb looked at me like I'd just spoken in an alien tongue.

"Mommy and I loved it, kiddo. That means you should be a natural. If you and Hank want to try, I'm going with you."

"Me, too." M stepped up beside me, awe in her expression. "Since you're so good at sounding like monkeys, I'd like to see if you can climb like them, too," she prompted, and the kids sprinted ahead to get in line.

"You don't have to go, but I need to do this." I knew she'd never gone rock climbing, and for some, it was a bit daunting.

"I know. I want to be there when you do." Her determined gaze fortified my resolve to put this final step behind me.

Once we got into the climbing harnesses, we clipped onto the line. The men and women working the wall gave simple and clear instructions, but I was already marking my ascent. As if by silent agreement, the boys and M let me go ahead of them. My palm grew wet as I gripped the first hold. Perspiration broke out over my whole body. I could see Megan on our last climb together. Effortless, graceful, and unflappable as she climbed slightly ahead and to my left. I'd never climbed without her.

"It's okay, Mom," Caleb interrupted my flashback.

"It will be, Caleb," I told him in a determined voice.

M gave me an encouraging smile as I took my first hold and pulled up. Planting my foot on another hold, I reached for the second with my left hand. By the third reach, the effortlessness was back. So was the enjoyment. It wasn't the same as being outdoors and finding holds on a rock face but still a lot of fun. I scaled the wall in no time and was back on the ground in even less.

"Whoa, cool," Hank praised. "See, I told you it looked fun."

"You did good, Mom." Caleb hugged me fiercely.

"Did well," both M and I corrected him before we looked at each other and laughed.

"Let's get you guys up there," I encouraged, pointing out the first holds for the kids before turning to M. "Do you need help?" I easily slipped back into the helpful role I'd always taken with our adventure tour clients.

"I think I've got it. I had an excellent demonstration, after all." She smiled broadly and took one of the holds to pull herself slowly up the wall.

I followed closely behind the boys in case they got into a bind looking for the right hold. As we reached the top collectively, I felt the last of the heaviness in my heart vanish. This had turned out to be a far better day than I could have imagined. And I'd imagined a pretty good one.

Chapter 28

While making my way up the marble staircase in M's apartment building, it did occur to me that I should have called first. That I should have at least buzzed her apartment rather than stepping inside behind another visitor. But I was a hopeless idiot who wasn't thinking clearly. Hadn't been for the past two weeks. Being around her was getting so difficult and yet so wonderful at the same time.

Shaking out my limbs, I steeled myself to knock on her door. I could do this. I had to. Three raps on the solid oak and my heartbeat went from normal rhythm to rapid fire. When the door opened and M stood before me in comfortable exercise pants and a clingy workout shirt, I lost all thought.

"Briony?" She stared at me with wide eyes. Thankfully, she could remember my name because I was having a hard time piecing together who I was. "What are you doing here?"

It was her smile that kept me from forming an answer. Those dusky red lips pulled wide, accentuating her cheekbones and enlivening her already stunning face. Wet strands of hair darkened its usually sun lightened shade. And she had on glasses. Thin, elegant, plastic frames in a maroon color that brought out the red shading of her eyes and hair. I'd known her for months, and I never realized she wore glasses.

"Are you okay? Here, come inside." She stepped back to let me in.

"Sorry I didn't call first," I managed with a scratchy throat.

"That's okay. You're always welcome here."

Her easy response made me want to jump for joy. "Thanks."

"What brings you by?" She pulled a duffle off a chair in the living room and gestured for me to sit. She must have just returned from Jessie's gym and taken a shower. Wow, she looked good all freshly scrubbed, but then again, she looked good in anything she wore, especially when the clothes hugged her figure.

I flicked my glance away from her to stare at the chair, knowing I couldn't sit. I had to be standing when I said this. Much easier to turn and run if need be. "I wanted to tell you something."

"Okay?" She frowned, obviously concerned that I'd lost my mind. Most people didn't make a trip halfway across town to tell a friend something. There were such things as phones for that.

Deep breath in, let it out slowly. I faced her squarely and locked eyes. "I'm falling for you. I've tried to stop, but apparently I can't help myself." Generally, when you tell the right person you love her, there's giddiness and immediate reciprocation. This time, I saw fear and amazement.

"But..." Her dropped jaw managed to form one word.

"I know what I said before about being friends, and I love being your friend. I always want to be your friend."

"Me, too," she agreed immediately.

"I also heard what you said and understand what it means."

She shook her head, confused. "Then how do you think we could ever...be together?"

"I guess what I'm trying to say is that I'll take whatever you can give me. If it means we have to work up to touching after a year, kissing after a couple of years, then apparently I'm in because my heart and mind can't stop the fall." I hoped it wouldn't take that long, but I'd been celibate for nearly four years. What was one or two more? It was more important to let her know that I would wait for her. If that meant I was pathetic, I was willing to live with the label because I knew how rare these feelings were. Once in a lifetime was lucky; twice was as close to a miracle as one could get.

She turned away, a huge breath expanding her slim frame. "What if I can't ever have you touch me or touch you back?"

"Let me make this clear first. I want to touch you, I want to kiss you, I want to make love with you, and I want you to do all that back to me. I want that very much." I walked around to face her. "But if you can't, well, then you can't."

"That wouldn't be right."

"M?" I waited until her chin lifted and she reestablished eye contact. "You said you were attracted to me. You said you wished you could act on it." Her unwavering gaze told me it was still true. "Could you...would you try? No rush and no pressure. I'm willing to wait as long as you're still interested." I held my breath, hoping that she'd be open to this.

"I can try," she whispered. "For you."

"For us," I corrected firmly because she had to know this would be for both of us. My pulse thundered at her willingness to trust what we already had together. "If you try and you still can't, then we'll know, and we'll deal with it then."

She shook her head, worry flickering in her eyes. "But that's not a relationship."

"No one can tell us what's right in a relationship. Sure, it might be a little different, but I don't care about that."

"You deserve—"

"I deserve the person I want," I cut her off before she set her mind differently. "And so do you."

"You really think this could work?" She looked so unsure of herself. The radiant smile she sometimes graced me with had disappeared behind the fear of what I imagined to be a jumble of unfamiliar feelings.

"Maybe you didn't hear me before. I'm falling for you, M. Of that, I'm certain." I gave her my own version of a radiant smile, trying to quell any uncertainty on her part.

"You're amazing." She matched my smile and let her gaze slide over me. The movement felt as good as a caress.

"And I'm patient, beautiful. So, at your pace. No rush."

"You're the one who's beautiful." This time the shy smile had a glint of slyness to it. "And brave."

"You're my inspiration."

Her hand lifted slowly, crossing into the space between us. My heart stopped and nerves wrung my stomach into a tight twist. "Let me try." Her voice displayed the same effort that her hesitant reach was showing. "Could you just...stand..."

Her unfinished request formed in my mind. It would make sense for someone who had trouble with touch. "I won't move."

Another grateful glance kicked my pulse into high gear. Her pace, I'd said that. I might have to repeatedly remind myself, but I meant it. Those fingertips, the ones I imagined were soft and insistent, darted forward toward my cheek. She wanted to touch me the same way I'd touched her in our classroom when I'd called her beautiful. An inch from their target, they stopped as an ocean of emotions swayed through her eyes. She let her hand drop back to her side with a frustrated sigh.

Just as I was about to whisper acceptance, I felt a pressure on my forearm through my shirt. I looked down and found those fingertips sliding across the length of my arm. Never had an innocent touch set me off before. I started trembling, unable to believe how good this felt. How much I'd wanted her hand on me, like I'd been missing her touch for years.

Her eyes were trained on the slow progress of her fingers. She seemed as mesmerized as I was by this chaste exploration. When the fingers tracked up past my elbow, she added her thumb, and I felt the whole of her hand circle my bicep and trail upward. She glanced up at me with wide eyes.

"Okay?" I asked her surprised expression.

She nodded once as her mouth stretched into a smile. Trepidation entered her gaze as she again focused on my cheek. She released my arm and brought those fingers back up. This time, she let them press against my cheek before her hand snapped back. I sucked in a breath, forcing myself not to follow the hand. With a determined stare, she reached forward again to graze across my cheekbone. When she started over, those soft fingertips were more insistent, trailing all the way over to tuck a strand of hair behind my ear before turning and brushing her knuckles against my cheek again.

"Does it hurt?" I managed with a raw throat.

Slowly, she brought her hand away, eyes popped wide. "No, I can't believe it." She turned away to hide her tears.

I reacted to the tears, stepping toward her. She retreated like someone had yanked her back. Her body went rigid. The look of fear returned before sorrow replaced it. "I'm sorry. Please believe me, Briony. It's just a knee-jerk reaction."

"It's okay. I told you I wouldn't move, but I did. It's my fault." As much as I believed everything I was saying, I couldn't help but feel a lash of rejection. "We both need to trust what we say. It may take some effort, but we'll both try, right?"

"Right," she agreed readily, relief helping to ease the tension in her frame.

"This was the best surprise visit I've ever paid anyone." It had gone even better than I'd hoped. "Thank you for being open to this."

"Thank you for being brave and patient." Her gentle way of telling me that was enough for today. "I want," she started in a soft but sure voice, stopping me before I pulled open the door, "all the same things you do."

"Your pace, M. Like I said, I'm happy to wait as long as you need." I gave her my most dazzling smile and opened the door before I found myself unable to leave. Who said different wasn't better?

Chapter 29

Finished with classes for the day, I hoped to persuade M away from office hours for an early afternoon together before I had to pick up Caleb from school. My smile appeared on its own as I approached her classroom, happy that I didn't need to make up an excuse to stop by her classroom anymore. The bell rang just as I was opening the door. M glanced over and stumbled on her parting words. I bit down on a wide smile as I edged against the wall next to the door. It was so satisfying to see that I got to her as much as she affected me.

"Professor," she greeted professionally. We hadn't made our three-week relationship public knowledge yet. I was ready to shout out from the center of north campus, but M's normally withdrawn nature kept me from sharing the news.

After receiving a nod from me, she turned back to her students. "Remember, we've got the Jucundus tour lined up for next week. One warning, the place is a little zany, lots of humor and practical jokes. So if the CEO, Willa Lacey, tells you she only lets the computer programmers out of the office once a week for fresh air before locking them in their dungeon, don't report her to the Department of Labor. She's kidding. I happen to know it's twice a week." The class erupted in laughter as she finished with, "See you next time."

The students shuffled their laptops and books together and headed toward the exit. Three of them cornered me about a class assignment for tomorrow's lecture, so I missed out on one of my favorite sights: watching M enthusiastically participate in discussions with her students. When my cluster finally finished with me, I looked over and caught M staring, a wicked smile on those provocative lips. She walked over with a confident strut. I loved watching her move like this. The only time my heart still ached was when I'd catch her pulling into herself, becoming invisible when she was among people she didn't know. I liked this M much better.

"Hey," she greeted in a low tone that finished in a whisper.

"Hey, yourself," I came back in the same tone. "You look beautiful."

She blushed at my compliment as was her charming nature. A new charcoal suit hugged her perfectly, but it was the lavender blouse I liked the most. She didn't wear much color, but I'd been noticing more colorful wardrobe pieces of late. I liked to think it was my influence on her comfort level.

When she was only a step away, she stopped, completely at ease in my personal space now. One of her hands came up and pressed against the wall next to my head. She locked eyes with me and said, "You *are* beautiful, and you look stunning."

My chest expanded. She could make me giddy with words alone. Months ago I wouldn't have imagined that my heart could feel so full in a relationship built on words and trust only. "I'm done with my classes. I was hoping you wanted to come out and play."

She laughed, her breath touching my face. I closed my eyes at the sensation. "Only if your invitation includes food first. I forgot to eat today."

"Ah, so that's your diet plan. I was wondering how you stayed so tiny." I let my eyes wander down her slender frame with just enough curves to keep her from being twiggy thin. I imagined how it might feel pressed up against me and could almost sense it. For now, that was enough. Actually, if she continued to make me feel as elated as I now constantly felt, I'd be fine for years just imagining how she might feel.

"You've no room to talk, slim," she scoffed. "I was on my way over to the cafeteria this morning, but you distracted me. So don't give me any guff about not eating."

"I did?" My eyes snapped back from their leisurely stroll down her body.

"I saw you talking to Quinn over by the arena and completely forgot why I was standing in the middle the pathway."

"Oh, really?" I teased flirtatiously.

"Yeah, really," she said seriously. Her other hand came up and cupped my face. I sucked in another breath, my skin tingling in the wake of her fingers. When it moved down to stroke fingertips lightly along my neck, I thought I might scream from the simple joy. I clenched my hands against my thighs to fight my natural urge to touch her back. She must have felt the twitch because her eyes came back up from watching her fingers. "Okay?"

"Yes," I confirmed immediately. "You just make me feel so good."

A pleased smile erupted on her face. "Good." She didn't need to say anything else. Her smile told me enough, but the soft response said that making me feel good made her feel good.

Her hand moved onto my shoulder, squeezing through my cashmere sweater as it slid slowly down my arm. When she reached the sweater's cuff, she hesitated only a second before her hand drifted over my fist. She looked up at me as she rubbed back and forth over my knuckles. The determined glint in her eyes prompted me to unclench my fist. Her fingers immediately rewarded me by threading through mine. My breathing grew ragged when her hand slid across my palm. She gripped it gently and slowly brought our linked hands up. I was getting good at reading her expressions, but this one I hadn't seen before.

"Will you touch me? Please, help me try?"

"Oh, M," I whispered. "I'll do whatever you want."

She released my hand just as it hovered next to her face. I looked at her questioningly, thinking she would have brought my hand to her face. "I don't want to control this," she said.

I nodded, and like I'd done on that day in our classroom, I reached out slowly until my fingers grazed her cheek. She jerked back for an instant before pushing into my fingers with a determined move. "Does it burn?" I asked, remembering how she'd described it before.

"No," she responded instantly and, guessing from her tone, falsely.

"I think it does, so I'm going to pull away now." We'd been successful thus far in our unconventional relationship because of communication. If I'd simply taken my hand away, she might feel rejected.

"Please, Briony, it'll get better." Her eyes glistened with the start of tears.

"Honey, there's no hurry. You make me happy with a glance. Knowing I can distract you just by standing somewhere or slipping into your class thrills me." I slowly pulled my hand back and hers came up to squeeze my wrist urgently, two of her fingers reaching to curl around the bare skin there.

"You're too good to me."

"Not possible," I replied honestly, still feeling her pliant cheek on my fingertips. "So, lunch then a bike ride? I've got to pick up Caleb after his music lesson at school. We're constructing a volcano or something equally fifth grade science class later tonight."

"Lunch and a bike ride sounds great." She released my wrist and pushed off the wall to step back. "Were you just saying hello to Quinn earlier?"

"Actually," I started, watching her hustle back up to her desk and grab her bag. The sleek line of her back, rear, and legs sidetracked me for a moment. "She was inviting us to dinner."

M twirled back toward me. "Us?"

"Us," I confirmed. "They know about us."

Her eyes blinked three times. "When did you tell them?"

"Apparently, you told Willa." I delighted in her shocked look. "She mentioned to Quinn that you seemed a little different at the gym last week, and Quinn pieced it together. Of course, it might've helped that I asked Quinn about you back in July."

"Did you now?" A flirtatious smile took over her expression. Months ago it probably would have been fear that met my declaration.

"Well, you and Willa looked kind of close when I spotted you at the gym once, so I asked Quinn about it. She saw right through my not so subtle question." We shared a laugh. "Dinner? It would just be Willa and Quinn. You don't have to, but you have dinner with Willa, right?"

She looked away and took a deep breath. "You want this?"

"Only if you do."

"Okay, dinner, but maybe not tomorrow. Or next week. Let me work up to it." Her teeth scraped the corner of her lower lip before a kidding smile appeared. She moved toward me again with that panther gait, and my heartbeat matched the rhythm of her steps. When she reached me, she didn't hesitate with her hand this time. It came up to press against my back and lead me out the door. I didn't miss the intended message. She was trying, faster and with more effort than I could have hoped for.

Chapter 30

Looking around the restaurant, I thought about the last time I'd been here. Really bad date, probably the worst of the bad setups. The only other time I'd been to this restaurant had been with Jessie, a good date, but not quite right. I glanced across the table at my date this evening. Absolutely perfect.

"How's the pasta?" M asked.

"Very good. Want some?" I nudged my almost empty plate toward her, knowing her answer before the grin appeared.

"No thanks." M hardly ate anything, no way she'd eat part of a dinner that she hadn't ordered. "You were going to tell me about your dissertation presentation."

"No, you were going to tell me about yours." I grinned back at her, loving how even her diversion tactics made her more attractive. Actually, loving a lot about her but knowing it wasn't the right time to say it.

"Lots of pleading, weeping, and finally, bribery," she listed with such a serious face I almost bought it.

"How'd you choose University of Chicago?"

She glanced away, eyes flicking to each of the nearby patrons. I was getting better at figuring out what topics would give her pause, but I hadn't guessed this one would. Regret snuck in, but I knew our relationship couldn't move forward if there were off-limits topics. Not the kind of relationship we had. "It's a good school," she started before her eyes returned to mine. "But mostly, I was eligible for more scholarships at state schools as a ward of the state. I was accepted elsewhere, but federal financial aid had its limits."

Oh, crap, I hadn't thought of that. I watched her expression, but she didn't seem to be saddened by what she'd shared. This was only the third conversation we'd had about her childhood after foster care. Her years in the juvenile detention center hadn't been good, sometimes violent in fact, but compared to the horror she faced in foster care, it was far better. Her only saving grace during that time had been her social worker. Against regulations, but probably due to the guilt she'd felt over placing M in that foster home, she'd sign her out of the center every other Saturday for the day. She'd drop her off in town where M would spend part of her day volunteering at the school for the deaf and the rest at a dojo where she'd bartered for jujitsu lessons in exchange for cleaning the dojo. As wonderful a break as those Saturdays must have been, I honestly didn't know if I would have survived without going insane. I'd already admired her strength before I knew any of the details, now I was constantly astounded.

As I was contemplating a response, I felt a soft touch on the hand I had resting on the table. Looking down, I saw two of M's fingers rubbing a circle on the back of my hand. I glanced up at her with a smile.

"It's okay," she said softly. She was telling me that I shouldn't feel bad about the fact that my college prep years had been worlds better than hers. "Like I said, it was a good school. So was U of I for undergrad. They would have been in my top ten even if I hadn't been limited in my choices."

"I agree, two very good schools." I lost a little focus when she pulled her hand back. Her touches were always too brief. "You must have had terrific SAT scores."

Color tinted her cheeks as she glanced away again. Her eyes widened, and she sat up straighter, that protective shield I'd come to recognize dropped into place.

Before I could turn to see what brought it on, I heard, "Oh, hey, Briony, is that you?"

Cringing, I twisted my head and watched disaster date, Rachel, approach with none other than immature date, Erin. "Hello, Rachel. How are you, Erin?"

Rachel slid an arm around Erin's shoulders and drew her in with a mock accusing stare. "You two know each other?"

"Jessie introduced us," Erin told her, either outright lying or forgetting that it was Caroline who introduced us.

Rachel grinned at Erin before turning a smirk my way. "That's right, you had a thing with Jessie, didn't you? But then again, who didn't, right?" She laughed at what she thought was a joke. I wanted to slap the smirk off her face. Neither she nor Erin had been with Jessie, as they were so eager to share with me, so what the hell did she have to feel smug about?

Her phone rang, interrupting my surely rude response. She unclipped the phone from its handy and oh, so attractive belt holster. "Go," she said by way of greeting.

Unreal! She'd actually gotten more obnoxious. Erin didn't seem to mind, though, so maybe they were made for each other. Although, she wasn't bashful about checking out my date.

"We gotta go, baby," Rachel told her as she flipped the phone closed and clicked it onto her belt. "Kat and Kim are waiting for us outside the theater. Erin likes Tarantino as much as me," she boasted, and I refrained from telling her that she shouldn't be thrilled that Erin liked a film director as much as she liked Rachel, but only because I doubted she'd understand grammatical humor. It was then that she noticed M and muttered, "Hope you like kids." Her head nodded in my direction to indicate what she thought of as my handicap.

M blinked twice before leveling her gaze at Rachel. "Got six of 'em myself."

I couldn't hold in the burst of laughter at M's dry delivery and the blank stares we received. I knew it was rude to laugh at them, but oh, how sweet it was to finally find a woman who was a perfect fit after suffering through the dates with these two.

Rachel's glare turned scornful. "Enjoy the rug rats." She grabbed Erin's hand to drag her from the restaurant. But before disappearing past the hostess stand, Erin turned back and made a "call me" gesture with her hand and fingers.

Gaawwd! I shook my head and scoffed before focusing on M, hoping she wouldn't be too upset by the odd interruption. I found her biting her lip, trying hard to keep in a full blown smile.

"Did that woman just ask you to call her while she was in the middle of another date?"

I opened my mouth but nothing came out. I was as astounded by Erin's behavior as M seemed to be. By both of them, actually. I tossed my hands up. "I believe I told you that my friends didn't have a clue about me when they decided to fix me up. Those two were exhibits one and three."

"Wow, I guess I should consider myself lucky that you were still available after quality dates like them."

"I'm the one who's lucky," I admitted more seriously than I'd originally intended. It was meant as a play on her usual return of compliments, but as I was saying it, I knew how true it was.

"Me, too." She held my gaze for a moment longer before signaling for the check. "Want to take a walk or do you need to get back to relieve the sitter?"

I loved that she wanted to continue the date even more than I loved her understanding about my situation with Caleb. Since this was relatively new and we were still feeling our way through this unusual relationship, I didn't think it was right to tell Caleb just yet. "Let's walk for a bit."

We headed outside after only a minor squabble over whose turn it was to pay for dinner. She won by distracting me with a tug on my arm to get me moving out the door. That touch could make me agree to anything, even if it was my turn to pay.

Outside, we strolled through the historic district, peeking into storefronts and enjoying the balmy fall evening. After a few blocks, we took a seat on a bench near Court Square. I got comfortable, bringing a knee up so I could face her. Her elbow propped up on the backrest then her hand came down to grip my shoulder, fingers drawing lazy patterns through my blouse.

I fought a shiver at the hypnotizing feeling. "About those women," I started because I wanted to clear the air.

"Briony." She gripped my shoulder, her tone telling me I didn't have to say anything.

"No, I want you to know. That afternoon we ran into each other in the coffee shop," I waited for her to nod at the memory, "that was actually the best of the six setups, and I didn't enjoy anything about it."

A soft smile stretched her lips wide. "I should say I'm sorry to hear that."

A matching smile tugged at my mouth. "I'm glad you won't. And the 'thing' with Jessie—"

The hand gripping my shoulder popped off and waved as she turned away. She definitely didn't want to hear this. I didn't need to read her mind to know that.

Still, I had to get this out. She deserved to know the truth. "We dated for almost two months. Dated, that's it. Jessie broke it off before it progressed to the next level because she knew I wasn't ready for anything more. I was never more relieved in my life."

Her eyes snapped back to mine, widening at the revelation. Guess even she'd heard about Jessie's reputation prior to dating me. "Okay." She nodded, looking away briefly before refocusing on my eyes. The hand came back to touch my cheek then slid feathery fingertips down along the column of my neck.

I bit back the groan that threatened to escape. "Feels nice."

She smiled and reached out with her other hand to grasp my wrist. Her eyes flicked to where she gripped me then back up to my eyes. I could read her expression as clearly as if she'd spoken her request. We'd tried this reciprocation every time we'd gotten together since that day in her classroom. On the first four attempts, she'd lied to me like she had the first time. But on the fifth, I knew she hadn't felt any pain from my touch. That had been a week ago. I still waited for her to instigate my touching her and would until her touch became automatic, but I was fine with that arrangement.

I raised my hand up to cup her face. She smiled as soon as our skin touched. Not able to resist, I slid my fingers into her hair. "I knew it would be really soft. Did I mention the other day how much I liked your haircut? It always looks nice, but I didn't want you to think that I'm a lousy girlfriend who doesn't notice or forgets to compliment you when you change your hair."

That lethal smile flared, and her head ducked down to hide the blush. I realized it was the first time I'd called her my girlfriend and both of us apparently liked the sound of it. "Thanks, but I cut it a lot, so I'm officially letting you off the hook for future comments."

"I noticed, every three weeks or so—wait, did you say you cut it or you get it cut?" My fingers tightened on her scalp when I realized what she'd said. The haircut was precise, no mistakes. Surely, she couldn't be that proficient.

"You're the first person to touch my hair in twenty-five years."

Or maybe she could be. I wondered if I'd ever get over the urge to cry whenever she told me something about her past. She didn't want or need that, though, so I did the next best thing. "It looks beautiful, M. It always looks beautiful, and I'm impressed that you can do it yourself. I should make you my barber."

"I wouldn't know where to begin with a style like yours, and I wouldn't want you to come after me with scissors if I screwed up." She smiled and reached up to grasp my hand, pulling it down with a gentle squeeze.

"Fine, but I want to watch you cut your hair sometime. I can't believe you don't mess up on the back."

For a moment, what looked like panic skipped across her face. Her head turned as if to break away from the topic with a physical movement. "Well...anyway."

Yet another time when I'd inadvertently stumbled on a subject or request that made her uncomfortable. I'd have to think about why this one had, but it only added to her intrigue. "So, your SAT scores? They were good, weren't they?"

She laughed, the panic and discomfort completely abandoned at my intentional diversion. "Enough to get in."

Probably a perfect score, I thought upon hearing her modest response. As I watched her cheeks turn pink, I realized I guessed right. "Holy cow, you aced it, didn't you? Probably the GMAT, too?

Jesus, woman, what are you doing with a moron like me? A perfect score? Unreal."

She shook her head and exhaled a sharp breath. "You're the one who's smart...and beautiful." Her hand reached for mine again, giving it a brief squeeze. "And perfect."

Yep, good date. Absolutely the best. Worth suffering through all those lousy ones.

Chapter 31

A few weeks after Quinn had issued the invitation, M and I found ourselves sitting around Willa and Quinn's dining room table. I was fairly certain the delay in getting our schedules linked up had been a relief for M, but I found myself enjoying both the food and the company. Other than the dinner I'd shared with them when I was seeing Jessie, I'd never spent time with the twosome alone. I could see why M got along with Willa so well and how Quinn and Jessie were best friends.

"This was delicious," M offered to Quinn. She'd bravely stepped out of her shell all night long. I couldn't be prouder of her.

"I'm glad you liked it, and I'm happy you came over tonight."

"She was a little worried you wouldn't," Willa offered in a stage whisper, setting off a smile from her friend.

"You two are always having fun when I'm not around. I wanted in on the fun," Quinn insisted, reaching around her partner's shoulders for a squeeze.

"M keeps me from only talking to the dogs when you're on your road trips, Quinnie. You should be thanking her for my sanity."

"Thank you, M," Quinn deadpanned.

The front doorbell rang while we were laughing. Quinn excused herself, mentioning that she was expecting her assistant coach to drop off the playbook. To our surprise, she returned with Jessie and Lauren in tow. I felt M go rigid in her seat beside me.

"Hi, everyone." Lauren's characteristic joy glowed. "We were headed out to a movie and thought we'd stop by to see if Quinn and Will wanted to come along."

"Hi, Bri, M, good to see you both." Jessie beamed at me. If everyone wasn't focusing on her, I thought she might wink at me in an obvious manner. "Laur, I don't think you've met M Desiderius. M, this is my partner, Lauren Aleric."

Lauren's eyes blinked in surprise and a sly smile spread across her beautiful face. She gave me an eyebrow flutter before returning her gaze to my date. "Nice to meet you, M."

"And you," M managed softly.

"Join us for dessert?" Quinn offered.

Just then, I felt a pressure on my thigh and looked down to find M gripping me almost like a lifeline. This was the first time she'd touched anything other than my face, neck, or arms. As much as I wanted to enjoy the sensation, I knew this meant that M had started to panic.

Willa must have noticed her friend's unease because she responded before they could. "We don't want you to miss your movie."

Jessie studied us for a moment, probably guessing why Willa was politely suggesting they leave. "Yeah, you're dying to see this thing, Blue." She wrapped an arm around Lauren's waist and dropped a kiss on her cheek.

"Like you aren't? She's just embarrassed to admit that she loves romantic comedies, aren't ya, toughie?" Lauren cuffed her shoulder. "We can see it anytime, though. I'd like the chance to get to know you, M, seems like I'm the only one who doesn't."

The hand tightened before M met her gaze. "That would be nice, Lauren."

Bravery comes in all forms, and my girlfriend had an abundance. Her hand pulled back as Jessie and Lauren settled around the table. The next hour was one of the nicest I'd spent in a long time. Definitely better than the time I'd been there and they'd ambushed me with a blind date.

"Did you have fun tonight, honey," I asked while stepping out of the car in her parking garage after returning from dinner.

"I always have fun when I'm with you," she replied sweetly, coming around to meet me.

I pressed back against the car, taking a moment to compose myself. Sometimes she could floor me with her tenderness.

"Are you okay, Bri?"

"Very." I smiled, hoping she could tell how elated I was by everything she did and said.

"Coffee?" She gestured to the elevators.

Since Caleb was at a birthday party, I nodded and headed toward the elevators with her. We stepped inside, and she hit the third floor button then settled in as close to me as she could without actually touching. Before we'd gone up a floor, the most amazing feeling pinned me in place. The softest touch slid across my palm until it molded into a perfect fit. M's hand pressed against mine as her fingers curled around to grasp the back of my hand. I nearly jumped with surprise. She was holding my hand, not just touching it but holding my hand.

After another floor, I waited for her to pull back because her touches never lasted as long as I wished. Instead, I felt the glorious sensation of her other hand curling around the inner crook of my elbow. There was no mistaking this gesture.

Our hands melted together, fingers alternately pressing to grasp more firmly, thumbs bravely rubbing along knuckles and at the base of wrists. I couldn't bring myself to make eye contact, fearing the reality of her action might force her to stop and return to our separateness.

The ding of the elevator brought with it a sense of dread. I'd been sending signals for it to slow down, get stuck, anything to keep this long anticipated moment from ending. The elevator paid me no heed. Too soon, we arrived on her floor.

As the doors slid open, I held my breath preparing for the ache that would surely follow when she dropped my hand. Her side brushed against me as she stepped forward out of the elevator. I loosened my fingers because I didn't want to experience the awkwardness of her fighting to release her hand. In response, she laced her fingers through mine.

She's not letting go! my heart sang when I felt the gentle tug of her hand. With a giant step, I was back at her side walking closer to her than I'd ever been allowed. It was a heady experience gliding down the hallway with our arms looped together, hands linked as one. I couldn't remember the last time holding hands with a woman had been so rewarding, had been enough to delight me, excite me, sate me. That there might be something more intimate between two people never entered my mind.

We slowed as we reached her apartment door. She pulled out her keys and, with a noticeable tremor, unlocked her door to bring us inside. Two steps in, she stopped and turned back as the door closed behind me. I got the impression she'd been reacting to what she wanted this whole time. Now, her mind was taking over. She made eye contact for the first time since reaching for my hand. Her eyes lowered to my mouth and a flush tainted her cheeks.

Nerves released from a tight bundle and bounced around my stomach, making me feel like a human pinball machine. My heart pounded with ferociousness when her eyes purposefully went back to study my lips. I tried to keep my gaze level, not betraying how much I wanted to kiss her. To let her know that I'd be happy to stand here all night holding her hand.

After a long while, M gave a self-conscious, nearly inaudible laugh. Her head dropped in a defeated motion and shook slightly. My hope faded as she struggled with herself again. Seeing her lose faith in herself was heart wrenching.

When she raised her head again, she stepped forward, filling the space between us. She squeezed my hand, reached for the other, and brought them both up to cup her face. I let my fingers gently tighten on her jaw, loving the feel of holding her face in both hands. The fingers of one hand slid down to trace the side of her delectable neck. I was so entranced by the feel of her skin that I almost missed her whispered request.

"Kiss me."

My eyes snapped back to hers, heart pounding loudly. "Oh, M, are you sure?"

"I've never been kissed, Briony. I want to share that with you." She raised her hand to lace fingers into my hair, resting her palm on the side of my neck. Her other hand pressed against the door beside my head, bringing our bodies only inches apart. "Show me how good it can be."

I swallowed roughly. As much as I wanted this, the added pressure of giving someone her first kiss made me nervous. I tilted my head forward, keeping her stare, trying to send messages of desire and assurance. When I had to, I dropped my gaze to the inviting curve of her lips. I could feel her pulse speed up under my fingers on her neck.

Because I couldn't wait any longer, I closed the final distance and found heaven with the first brush of our lips. Her head pitched backward in my hands. I kept still, waiting, knowing she'd come back to me. She released a shaky breath that blew across my chin before tilting her face back up. This time, my lips pressed fully onto hers in a gentle kiss that she accepted eagerly. My abdomen felt a blast of fire as soon as she stopped just accepting and started kissing me back. Our lips moved across each other's mouths, and I had to consciously keep from trying to deepen the kiss. Her lips were supple and persistent and nourishing and addictive.

At the first tentative nudge of her tongue, I moaned loudly, the sound echoing through her silent apartment. Her tongue retreated at the sound, but her mouth continued to explore mine with an expertise that belied her inexperience. When her tongue came back, it pushed forward until it found its mate inside my mouth. I let her lead, meeting every new discovery with approval. After it seemed like she would accept it, I took over and reached into her mouth. A small sound left her throat, and while I hoped it was a pleasurable moan, I had to make sure it wasn't too much to handle. I eased up on the kiss softly until its natural end. Pulling back, my eyes fluttered open to see hers blinking in a startled manner as breaths pumped through her frame. Her first kiss. Judging by her stunned but jubilant recovery, I figured it went okay. Not that my reaction was any different. Had the door not been right behind me, I would have stumbled backward in a daze.

My fingers slid under her chin, coaxing her to look up into my eyes. She trembled slightly, and I tried to transfer my emotions to her though my touch. I wanted to assure her startled eyes that I didn't expect anything else. That what she'd given me was more than I'd ever fantasized about. "Goodnight?" I asked in a trouble-free tone.

M smiled gratefully then reached for my hand, the one she'd held in the elevator, and squeezed. She didn't have to say anything. The astounded look in her eyes told me that she'd been as overjoyed as I had by our first kiss.

I turned around, ready to open the door when I experienced another undeniable urge. Since they'd not failed me with her so far, I went for it. "Oh, M?" I turned back to face her. "The fall's over. I'm in." I watched as interest furrowed her brow. "I love you. I thought it was time you heard that."

Her expressive brown eyes glistened, but thankfully, she wasn't panicking. In fact, she looked so amazed I wanted to burst into tears for all the years she'd gone without knowing what it felt like to be loved.

"And I loved that kiss." My still tingling lips stretched into an elated smile. "If I have to wait thirty-nine more years for another, it'll be worth it. Goodnight, beautiful."

The stunned expression I left in her doorway would be enough to keep me warm as many nights as it took until she was ready.

Chapter 32

"Mom?"

"Hmm?"

"You're humming."

I turned back from unloading the groceries and found Caleb staring at me with wide eyes. We'd been getting ready to make dinner together, and now he looked flabbergasted. "I am? Am I making your ears bleed, kiddo?" I snatched him against me, rubbing my thumbs along his ears.

He giggled and squirmed out of my grasp. "No, but you haven't hummed while making dinner since...since Mommy died."

"Oh, sweetie," I whispered. I hadn't realized I'd been humming and certainly wasn't aware that I hadn't done it in years.

"No, it's good, Mom. It means you're really happy." He stared up at me with his earnest gold-brown eyes. "I'm not a little kid anymore. I know when Holly kidsits at night that sometimes you're out on a date, right?"

My heart tightened at his declaration that he wasn't a little kid anymore. Still a half year out from eleven, his gangly limbs were getting longer every time I turned around. "Would that be okay with you?"

"Yeah, Mom. I told you." He rested his hands on his hips in a very Peter Pan way. "But now you're humming and you don't even know it."

I cocked my head and pursed my lips. "You said that already."

"You don't hum for nothing."

"Really, and what do I hum for, huh, wise guy?"

"Love," he said it simply and without any resentfulness. "Is it, Mom?"

I took a deep breath and looked my grownup boy right in the eye. "Yes, son, it is."

"Yippee!" The little boy returned with glee. "When can I meet her? Can she come to dinner sometime? Is she nice? Does she like kids? Is she tall like Mommy? Maybe you can bring her to my soccer game this weekend? Does she like sports? Is she as smart as you? Can she pitch better than you? 'Cause Hank and I need more batting practice before baseball starts next year. Does she have a dog?"

The rapid-fire interrogation would have continued if I hadn't grabbed hold of his shoulders. "What's wrong with my pitching?" I teased.

"Moawmm!" he drew out, fists pounding back onto his hips.

"Seriously, what's wrong with my pitching?" I demanded.

"You almost beamed me last year," he said matter-of-factly. "Twice."

"Yeah, but I was trying to beam you. You'll notice that Hank stayed unharmed." I couldn't keep my expression serious.

He nudged me with a broad grin. "C'mon, Mom."

I took a deep breath, preparing to tackle his questions in order. "You've already met her. She can come to dinner anytime. She's very nice. She loves kids. She's not very tall. I'll ask her about coming to one of your soccer games but maybe not this weekend. She likes sports. She's smarter than I am. I've never seen her pitch, but no one's taking over my pitching duties. And no, no dog, and you're not getting one, either, bucko."

"I don't see why I can't get a dog. Everyone else has a do—" Realization dawned on him. "I met her? Who is it?"

"M." I waited for a response before I said anything else.

"M?!" he yelped. "Hank's M?"

"That M, yes." I smiled at how he classified her. In the past two months, we'd gone to the movies with the boys once, but I'd found it nearly impossible not to show affection. We both decided that I'd need to tell Caleb before we tried another outing together. "Is that okay, Caleb? You have fun with her, and she really likes you. She's become very important to me."

"This is so great!" He started hopping a happy bounce. "Hank's not gonna believe this. Can she come over for dinner sometime?"

"I'm sure she'd love that."

No sooner had the words left my mouth than he raced to the phone. I assumed he was calling his best friend, who adored M as much as he adored his own grandmother. He pressed two buttons and waited to be connected via the TTY relay service. When he spoke, my heart jumped into my throat. "Hi, M, this is Caleb."

I lurched toward him, stunned by his action. He never called anyone other than his friends without asking permission.

"No, Mom's fine, she's right here. So, um, do you want to come over for dinner tonight?" He showed me all his teeth in a big grin. "Yeah, she knows. Mom, tell M you want her to come to dinner." He held up the phone but danced out of my grasp, giggling.

"Please come to dinner if you're free, M," I called out, knowing I'd never catch his wiggly little form when he was determined to play keep away.

"You'll come? And do you want to come see me and Hank play soccer on Saturday?" He waited for a response before signing off and daring me with a gleeful stare.

"You kind of put her on the spot, kiddo," I chastised gently.

"I know, sorry. But you probably wouldn't bring her over till Christmas otherwise." That dare persisted. "I'm not little anymore, Mom. She makes you hum. I like when you hum."

"I like it, too." More than I could express.

Fifteen minutes later, an astonished but delighted M showed up on my doorstep. We'd barely had time to smile at each other before Caleb loudly crashed down the stairs and grabbed her around the waist, hugging tightly. The sight would have made me burst into tears at his obvious happiness if I hadn't known what this hug would do to M. She'd flinched at first then stood rigidly, her eyes shocked but softening when she caught my surprise.

"Thanks for making my mom hum." Caleb's soft voice brought my hand to my heart. M sucked in a breath and raised her hands up to pat his back. He released her and started in on the excited jabber. "It's taco night, do you like tacos? We were going to make spaghetti, but I thought you might like tacos better. I do."

"So do I," she confirmed with a warm smile then turned it on me.

"I still have to grate the cheese, so you and Mom can say hi." He turned a sly grin my way. "I won't look, just don't make all those gross smoochy noises."

Laughter burst from me at his unsolicited permission. I winked at a stunned M before turning back to my beautiful son. "I'm now going to make gross smoochy noises all over you." He squealed and slipped out of the reach of my hands, darting off toward the kitchen. When I turned back to M, she hadn't recovered much. "Hey," I greeted in the tone I reserved just for her.

"I make you hum?" she asked, partly bewildered, mostly delighted.

"You definitely make me hum," I responded seductively.

She grinned and reached to touch my face. This was becoming her standard greeting now, and I loved it. After the briefest hesitation, she leaned forward and brushed her lips against mine. A soft hello kiss, something she'd never initiated before. "Caleb said I could kiss you."

"Yes, he did." Now I was the stunned one. "We had a little talk."

"You must have." She turned and flicked the door shut behind us. When she reached for my hand, I nearly fell into her from the headiness of this surprising evening. "He seems okay."

"He's more than okay. He's ready to brag to Hank. If you wanted to tell him yourself, I might be able to hold Caleb off for a day."

She brushed her free hand through the air. "I told Lucille last weekend. I'll give her a call on my way home tonight. If she wants to say something to him first, she'll have the chance."

"What did she say?" I couldn't contain my curiosity, thrilled that she'd told Lucille about us. That was a huge step for her. I knew how highly she valued Lucille's opinion.

"That she'd figured it out when she saw how I reacted to seeing you in her living room that day." She smiled and shook her head. "I've never said anything in all the years I've known her, but somehow she knew."

"It's hard to fool women of that generation."

"Something I learned with Kathryn," she confirmed with a nostalgic smile.

"You guys done smooching yet?" Caleb called out from the kitchen.

"Caleb!" I admonished gently. His boldness was getting a little obnoxious, but I knew it was mostly born of excitement. Once it settled down, he'd start to remember his manners.

"What? I'm starving. C'mon, it's taco night!"

I turned back with an apologetic smile. Getting used to a ten-year-old might take a while for M.

She grinned and tugged on my hand. "Yeah, it's taco night."

Taco night with my son and my new love, nothing could be better.

* * *

Caroline's last phone call had a threatening undertone. Unlike the last time she'd summoned me to the café for lunch, this time she meant business. Apparently, Lauren had mentioned the dessert we'd shared at Quinn's, and Caroline was feeling a little miffed that I hadn't yet introduced her to my girlfriend. I'd held off her attempts at fixing me up by telling her that I was working on a potential relationship. She'd been fine with that for a while, but now she was insistent. M was due in my office any minute for our lunch date, and I crossed my fingers that she'd agree.

The knock on my door didn't sound like the one I was expecting. The fact that it opened immediately afterward also told me it wasn't my girlfriend. My two closest friends on the staff burst inside.

"Howdy, Bri," Javier offered first.

Alexa shoved him out of the way. It was often hard to imagine these two were respected professors in their fields. "Hello, friend of mine. Lunch?"

"Got plans," I managed casually. "How 'bout tomorrow?"

"Mm-hmm," Javier mused, raising his eyebrows at Alexa. "Told ya."

"Told her what?" I half rose out of my chair, wondering why they were acting so suspiciously.

"You're in luuuvvv," he sang. "Does she have a cute brother?"

Alexa elbowed him, turning a studious gaze on me. "Does she have a cute heterosexual brother?"

I knew I looked like I was doing an impression of a fish, but I couldn't help it. I didn't think I'd been acting any differently at work. M and I met up a few times a week on campus, but we'd met up all summer, too. Nothing suspicious there.

"Oh, stop with the shock, sister," Javier chastised. "Caleb let me in on your little love affair at the last practice." He was the assistant coach on my son's soccer team. He'd gotten the job two years ago when he'd been dating a guy with a son. He'd gotten hooked on coaching—the boyfriend, not so much. "Didn't tell me who, though."

"I figured that one out," Alexa declared proudly.

"With the help of a photo, genius," he taunted back.

Sometimes their code talk was even more complicated than my son's with his friends. "What?"

"We were headed to my office yesterday and spotted a photo of Caleb and Hank in their uniforms through an open door. Guess whose office it was?" Javier taunted with a huge grin.

Alexa smacked his shoulder. "It's the only one she has in her office, so it obviously means a lot to her."

I pushed out an amused breath. Caleb had picked out the frame and wrapped the gift for M himself. He decided that she needed a picture of her two favorite kids—his and Hank's egos at work—to brighten her workspace. I knew he was just a big ol' ham who liked having his picture taken. My heart melted when I stopped by her office last week and saw it displayed front and center on her bookcase. "It does, and she means a lot to me," I confirmed happily.

"She's your lunch date?" Alexa coaxed.

"Yep. She'll be here any minute." In response, they both rubbed their hands together with a plotting look about them. "Be good. Better yet, be gone."

They tried to look affronted but their mock anger was interrupted by the sight of M appearing in my doorway. What made my heart jump, other than her appearance, was that she clearly fought the urge to try to disappear within herself when she was surprised by the people in my office.

"Hello, M," Javier greeted furtively. Both Alexa and I grabbed his arms and yanked him back from crowding her. "What? I was just saying hi."

"Ignore him," Alexa advised. "He's on his fourth pot of coffee today. How are you? Here for your lunch date?"

The startled expression M wore turned a shade of pink as it moved into shocked. "Hi," she offered then looked questioningly at me.

"They were just leaving, right, guys?" I pleaded.

My colleagues recognized my tone, or perhaps they could sense the alarm in M's stance. "Yep, the coffee's burning a hole in my empty stomach." Javier patted his solid abdomen then slid an arm around his best friend's shoulders. "Let's roll, sexy lunch honey."

"Watch it! That's sexual harassment. You're both witnesses. I can sue and finally get my roof fixed just in time for winter."

"You could sue, but my worth won't be enough to roof your birdhouse." Yep, respected professors in their fields. A marvel, isn't it?

Alexa pushed Javier toward the door. He and M switched places so she could get inside. "She's a good one," Alexa commented on her way by with a nod of her head in my direction.

"Yes, she is," M agreed quietly as they both waved and headed down the hallway. She shut the door behind them and turned with yet another version of an amazed expression. I was starting to think she'd never experienced anything good in her life because she was constantly amazed by simple kindness. "Hey, you."

"Hey, yourself." I stood to greet her.

That soft hand darted out to slide knuckles against my cheek as she stepped closer. This time, her body brushed a light bump against mine. After only an infinitesimal straightening that pulled her back a fraction, she set her gaze and slowly rested her front against me.

The first time I felt her body press against mine during a goodnight kiss nearly caused an out of body experience. I was still getting used to how amazing this felt and how much she obviously trusted me to get this close. In the past, the press of breasts, hips, and legs against mine might have escalated to feelings of lust, but with M, I felt perfectly satisfied by even the simplest touch or look or kiss.

"God, M, I really love you, you know?"

A shudder shot through the frame leaning against me before her arms came up and hugged me fully. Our tenth in this nearly three-month relationship. Yes, I was still counting; I'm sickeningly in love, sue me.

"I do. Thank you," she whispered.

Not the response of someone awkwardly speechless from an unwanted declaration of love. No, she was actually thanking me for loving her. She hadn't said it back to me yet, but I guessed with the lack of love in her life, those words might be a little difficult to manage. As further proof, I'd overheard Hank innocently tell her he loved her on our last get-together. Her eyes had widened and softened all at once. She smiled then told him that he was the best, but she didn't say the words I knew she felt for him. Without consciously thinking about it, I knew I'd be fine with her just accepting my declarations, especially since she didn't seem to have a problem believing them anymore. Her responses were always varied, from a gentle touch, to a soft kiss, to these wonderful hugs. That was enough for me. That and her expressive brown eyes that told me without words how she felt.

"Ready for lunch?" My lips grazed her ear.

"Where to?"

"Well," I hesitated, which made her pull back to look at me. "A couple of my friends own a café and want us to stop by, if you don't mind. They would like to meet the woman who's made me nauseatingly happy. Their words, not mine."

She was managing the panic again. "Just how many friends do you have?"

"In addition to the four we had dinner with and the two loonies who just left, there's Sam and Caroline, who own the café, Isabel and Kayin, who are very low key, and Des and Skye, who require large amounts of alcohol to endure sometimes. Don't worry, though, it'll just be Caroline and Sam today."

She gulped visibly. "I think I can handle that."

"Thank you, honey. They'll be on their best behavior, I promise."

"It's not like I'm meeting your parents or anything," she joked to ease her apprehension.

"Yeah, about that," I started tentatively and watched her retreat two steps when she recognized my tone. My stomach twisted as I contemplated how to word this request. "I hope you don't have any plans for the winter break. My parents are kind of insisting I bring you along." I reached out and grasped her shoulders. "Don't panic yet, beautiful."

"No, 'course not. I've got five weeks for that," she responded.

As much as I enjoyed the sarcasm, I liked even better that she hadn't given a second thought to the fact that we'd still be together by Christmas. Without her needing to tell me, I knew she was in this for the long haul like I was.

Chapter 33

Even though it made me feel a little guilty, I always enjoyed the dates M and I shared by ourselves. Being able to stroke her fingers or arm or neck without having Caleb giggling or nudging me was a treat. Ten-year-olds were not good dating accessories. I loved that she was happy to include him once or twice a week, but I cherished our alone time all the more. Tonight, we were headed out to dinner and possibly the play we'd been talking about for weeks.

A familiar scent from our favorite restaurant wafted over me when M opened her apartment door. She must have decided on something different for tonight. "Hi." She smiled broadly for a moment before what looked like tentativeness tightened the expression.

"Hey there." I cocked my head, puzzled by her unexpected insecurity, but tilted toward her for a hello kiss. Like every kiss, whether a brief hello or lengthy parting, she seemed to savor the sensation. I had the feeling she wouldn't ever take kissing for granted.

"I ordered in," she told me after pulling away. "You don't mind, do you?"

I glanced around her apartment, noting the low lighting, classical music, and candles on the table. If I didn't know better, I'd think she was trying to seduce me. As exhilarating as that thought was, I stamped out all flare ups of lust because I'd made a decision at the start of our relationship. If, well, hopefully when, she was ready for sexual intimacy, she'd have to be the one driving down that road. I wouldn't push her, ever. "Not at all," I assured. "Smells delicious."

She looked relieved, but it didn't last through dinner. The constant flush on her face reminded me of that time in my office when I kept noticing her blush. I sat tight, waiting her out. I knew she'd let me in when she was ready.

After dinner, she faced me on the couch, spine ramrod straight, eyes looking everywhere but at me. "I have something I need to tell you."

I felt my heart rate kick up, fearful that her discomfort wasn't a simple matter of embarrassment. Rather, that she'd made a decision about our relationship not working for her. "You can tell me anything." *But please don't let it be that we're over.*

"I don't do it anymore. I never wanted to do it. It's not part of my life, but I don't want to be dishonest with you either." The words were rushed, desperate.

I reached for her hand, cradling it in both of mine. This didn't sound like a breakup speech. "Just say it, whatever it is."

"I went to a therapist for help with...you know."

Touch, intimacy, yes, I knew. She'd mentioned the therapist to me before. I'd been overjoyed that she'd spoken with a professional about her trauma, if for no other reason than she had to talk about it to take back her power.

"She recommended I try something so that I could be like everyone else." Her eyes flicked to mine to test my expression before refocusing on the bookcases. "A specific...well, certain way to have sex."

I trained my features not to show surprise. She'd alluded to something like this when I'd first told her I was attracted to her. So, she'd had sex. I'd had sex with a few women I'd been involved with before meeting Megan. I should just shut down the ache in my chest at the thought of her with someone else. It wasn't fair to her.

"I mean, I didn't, I wasn't, well, fully involved." Her hesitant starts and stops brought the aching I felt into perspective. I needed to stop with the jealousy and focus on how difficult all of this must have been for her. "There's this club in DC."

Ah, the club that Jessie mentioned.

"It's for a particular lifestyle." Her eyes cut to mine. "Dominance-submission."

Gulp. Way out of my league, even as open and experimental as I'd been.

"The therapist said that I'd need a partner I could control and keep from touching me. Then I could participate to whatever degree made me comfortable." Her breathing increased with the rapid acceleration of my heart. "But that never happened. Even when they were completely bound, I never felt comfortable. I used toys rather than touch them, and they never touched me. I barely had anything to do with their pleasure. I was just there."

Even battering past all the images I conjured of M in that club, not once did I picture her doing anything other than being an extension of an apparatus. Technically, any intimate act was sex; I'd always believed that. But this, what she was saying, how she described it, this wasn't sex. Not for M. She'd been more of a cursory participant, almost like a scientist working on an experiment. One that had failed miserably for her.

I disliked the shame in her voice. Given the trauma she'd gone through as a child, this type of club made perfect sense. She would have ultimate control over anything she experienced without the fear of being touched. I didn't like that she'd been so desperate to feel like everyone else that she'd forced herself to go and that she hadn't enjoyed it. She deserved so much more.

When she finished by telling me a few other details, like how she'd always stayed dressed and worn a mask and gloves, I wanted to cry for her. I'd never had the hang ups about sex that most people did. It couldn't be perverse if the people involved were consenting adults. Whatever got someone off didn't have anything to do with me unless I was in that relationship. I wouldn't judge someone based on what made them feel good. I certainly wasn't going to judge M, especially since it never made her feel good.

"I don't need it. I never did," she ended urgently. "The therapist insisted that it would help, but it never did." Her eyes flicked back to mine before glancing at the door. She stood abruptly, obviously expecting me to storm out of her life and probably never come back.

"M?" I stood, getting her attention back from plotting my escape route. "I love you."

Tears pooled and trickled onto her cheeks. She didn't try to hide it from me this time. "You're not disgusted?"

"Nothing from your past touches you or us. Even if you told me you still needed it, we'd deal with it together." And I meant that. I'd try going to that club with her, if that would make her comfortable. She needed to know that I'd be willing to try anything with her. "Nothing you've done will ever disgust me." I stepped closer, reaching a hand out to her. "We've been doing great so far, haven't we?"

"Yes." She grasped my hand, holding on for a full minute before she stepped into my arms. Her body trembled as it settled against me. She let me hold her until her tremor stopped and for some time longer.

* * *

"You're all so great to do this for me again. Thank you." I headed over to stash the microphone in the audio-visual cabinet.

My friends stood from their seats on stage, having come through for me yet again. This was the third time they'd shared their start-up stories and answered questions for my entrepreneurial students. The speaking engagement had grown so popular I now had to book the auditorium to accommodate all of the graduate business students who wanted to attend.

"We're happy to do it, Bri," Jessie proclaimed for the group. Like after the first time she'd spoken to my class, I wanted to hug her for helping me out.

"Except Des, who wasn't even awake for most of it," Caroline joked.

"Hey, I work construction hours, sister. You don't even roll into your café until nine. By then, I've already been on a job site for two hours."

"Aww, Des is cranky 'cause it's past her bedtime," Sam shot back. She also didn't have to get in to open her bookstore until nine.

"You haven't seen cranky, yet, bookie." Des's threat made us all laugh. As exasperating as some of these women could be, I was so thankful to count them as my friends.

"Jessie!"

I turned toward the doors, surprised to see Caleb and M entering the auditorium. She'd offered to stay with him tonight because my usual sitter, Holly, had gotten the flu. I'd thought I'd have to postpone the speaking engagement when M volunteered to help out. In Vermont, I would have called one of his grandparents or aunts, but since moving to Virginia, I'd trusted only Holly among the sitters I'd tried. If she wasn't available, then that was my tough luck. But without having to ask, M had stepped in, making me wonder how I'd made it as a single mom so long without help. Now that I had M to rely on, life seemed so much better in every way.

"Hiya, CeeGy." Jessie caught Caleb as he tore down the aisle and jumped into his buddy's arms. She swung him from a perch on her hip to dangling upside down in seconds. Cackles of laughter erupted from him and got everyone else giggling, too. "You gonna say hi to your mom, maybe?"

His now ruddy face tilted toward me as he gripped Jessie's shins for support. "Hiya, Mom." He giggled again when Jessie flipped him up then slung him onto her back.

"Hey, kiddo, this is a surprise." I glanced back at M, who stood rooted to the ground just inside the doorway. She must not have expected everyone to still be here.

"M helped me finish my homework, so we thought we'd surprise you at work and take you out to ice cream." He probably thought he was getting away with manipulating ice cream into the deal. Not that I minded since I figured it was M who'd come up with the idea to surprise me.

"So you're M?" Des boomed out across the auditorium, shooting a knowing grin at me.

I groaned inwardly. This was not what M had in mind for her surprise tonight. I didn't need to be any closer to see her tremor. She hadn't met Des, Skye, or Kayin yet, and I was afraid some of my stories might have made her hope that she'd never have to meet them.

Des started toward the stairs, but Jessie stepped into her path, shifting Caleb from her shoulders to the ground in front of her. He high-fived Des and Skye then turned to greet everyone else, which gave me enough time to hustle down the stairs and up the aisle.

As I got closer, M's tremor subsided and a peaceful smile came over her face. My heart, which had been squeezed with tightness over how she might handle dealing with most of my friends all at once, now expanded with love at the happiness I could so clearly see in her expression. "Hi," I whispered and, because I couldn't help it, leaned in for a brief kiss.

Her mouth stretched into a smile as soon as I pulled back. "Sorry, we thought you'd be alone and packing up by now."

"I'm glad you're here. It's a great surprise. Thank you." I touched her cheek and turned back to my friends. "Des, Skye, Kayin, I don't think you've met my girlfriend, M. And M, you remember Lauren, Caroline, and Sam."

Her hand came up to rest against my back as she greeted them. "Yes, it's good to see you again, and nice to meet the rest of Briony's friends. I've heard a lot of wonderful things about you."

"Hey, M." Jessie strode toward us, the pack following close behind. Before they could completely surround us, Jessie turned and pulled Caleb close, effectively creating a barrier between us and them. I really wanted to hug her for that.

"Hi, Jessie." M flashed a grin at her.

"Jeez, Jess, do you know everyone?" Kayin joked.

"Yes," she deadpanned, reaching her hand out to Lauren who edged in next to her. "You've got a trial to prepare for, Blue. We'd better skedaddle. And Des, weren't you whining about having to get to work early?"

"I'm liking the idea of ice cream right now."

I didn't know Des well enough to know if she was kidding. Feeling M's hand shift from my back to clutch my waist told me the idea of Des joining us terrified her. I couldn't blame her since the idea terrified me as well.

"You weren't invited," Jessie told her blandly and casually clamped a hand on Caleb's shoulder to keep him from issuing the invitation that I knew would fly out of his mouth. Damn, Jessie was good with him.

"Don't tell me—" Des's statement was cut off by a shot to the ribs from her partner.

"You've got an early day, baby," Skye told her, looking up at the wall created by Jessie and Lauren.

"Fine," Des said in a bothered fashion.

"Thank you all again. You were a major hit, as always," I reiterated.

Sam and Caroline grabbed me into a group hug with Skye. Des cuffed my shoulder, and Kayin waved in parting. Lauren and Jessie each hugged me then turned to M. Jessie spoke her farewell, but Lauren moved toward her. M tightened her grasp on my hip and took an unconscious step behind me. The movement caused Jessie to wrap her arms around Lauren to keep her in place. Lauren cut her a sharp glance before apparently reading the signals correctly.

"See ya, Jessie. Bye, Ms. Lauren." Caleb hugged them both before they sauntered out of the auditorium. "Ice cream now?" His eager face brought a laugh from us.

"Run up backstage and find the lights to bring them down, will you?" I spurred him into motion then turned to face M, delighted by her appearance tonight and her courage among the large gathering. She'd been dreading meeting all of them, but she managed it so well. I no longer worried how she'd handle meeting my family in a couple of weeks over our break.

"Hey, you," she greeted again, her smile much more confident. "We couldn't stay away."

"I'm so glad. I know the feeling." I cupped her face in my hands. My body brushed up against hers as I pulled her in for a private kiss, the one I'd wanted to give her the second she walked through the door this evening.

She moaned into my mouth and reached around me to crush us together. Her soft lips caressed first my upper lip then my lower before coaxing them wider to allow her tongue entrance. It stroked over mine, shooting flames through me as I strained not to rub up against her. She felt so good, and I was having a harder time of late reining in the desperate need I felt every time I got my hands on her. But just kissing her brought on a satisfaction I never thought I'd achieve. I could be happy with this for as long as she needed.

"Eww, smooching," Caleb called out from the stage, having found the light switches already.

We broke apart. My laughter helped ease the crimson on M's cheeks. This had become a common occurrence whenever Caleb joined us. I knew he was secretly pleased that his mom was so happy. Not to mention how thrilled he was that I'd chosen a woman he already cared about.

"Ice cream!" M prompted and we watched as my son leapt off the stage hopping excitedly toward us. She turned her grin on me, and I felt a balloon of emotion swell inside. I wondered if she realized that with her simple gesture tonight, bringing Caleb to surprise his mom after her long workday, she'd just locked in her role in our little family.

Chapter 34

A week before we were supposed to leave for Vermont on winter break, M rang my doorbell for our date. I'd been expecting her to back out of the trip every time we'd seen each other for the past two weeks because it was so clear how nervous and uncomfortable it made her. Perhaps tonight would be the night.

"Hey, beautiful," I greeted her smiling face.

"Hey, yourself." She leaned in for a kiss, setting off a tumbling routine inside my stomach. Too quickly, she ended it with a look over my shoulder, expecting Caleb to come barreling down the hall.

"He's sleeping over at Hank's tonight. They're headed out with Lucille's son to the Redskin's game tomorrow afternoon."

Her eyes flashed, a sexy smile slinking across her face. She was trying to give my heart a workout without any exercise. "We're all alone?"

"What shall we do?" I asked with a mischievous lilt.

"I'm sure we'll figure something out." Her tone was seductive, husky, something I'd only heard glimpses of thus far.

On jellied knees, I turned and pulled her with me toward the kitchen. "Hope you're hungry, Mona."

She huffed an amused breath. "All the way out to the M-O names now, can't be many more to guess." I was going to retort that it'd be months before we'd get through all the names starting with M, but she distracted me by sidling over to brush against me. "Dinner in, huh?"

"We can hit a movie later or drinks somewhere. I think a new play just opened at the Paramount."

"Dinner, then we'll figure it out." She grabbed the salad and brought it over to the table. "Aren't you exhausted? You had one more class than I did this term, and I'm still grading finals."

I nodded with a soft laugh. "Pretty tired, yeah. I'm looking forward to the break, even though going home takes some energy, too."

"Are you sure about this?" She'd been asking this question ever since I first brought up the trip.

"Honey, you don't have to go if you don't want to. I love you no matter what. They want to meet the woman I love, but they can wait." I locked eyes with her to make sure she knew I meant it, then joked, "Not too long, though. You don't want Sadie getting on a plane. She'll bring at least three of her five kids just to torture you."

She laughed at the threat. "I can't believe Megan's family wants to meet me."

"They're part of my life, not only because they're Caleb's grandparents and aunts, but because they've always treated me like their daughter. They want the same opportunity to know you that my parents will have."

She nodded nervously, digging into dinner as a diversion from what must be a scary topic for someone whose family consisted of one person who died too early in her life. We ate in silence for a while, table manners and the daunting notion of meeting the family of the woman she was involved with keeping us quiet.

After dinner, we loaded the dishes into the dishwater and headed into the living room. I changed the music in the stereo and sat next to her on the couch. This was nice, sharing an evening together. I'd missed this the most about my marriage. Everyone always thinks they'd miss the sex or having someone to help make decisions or get through the difficulties in life or a companion to go places with. I missed the simple intimacy of sharing thoughts and opinions. With or without touch, it never mattered.

M shifted a bit until her shoulder nestled in against me. With a slight turn, her thigh touched the length of mine. I became hyperaware of how each little touch could make my skin dance. "Thanks for making me dinner, Bri."

"You're welcome." I smiled at her formality. "Did you want to go out?"

"Not really, unless you want to." She wrapped a hand around my arm.

"You look beat."

"I am, but this is too good to cut short right now." Her smile was irresistible this time. Especially when it turned sly and came closer. Her lips pressed against my throat and nipped lightly up to my jaw. The heavenly pressure started a shiver that didn't seem to want to stop. Only recently had I found out that my neck was her fetish. Well, fetish wasn't quite right, but like me with her legs, she never failed to touch it and often her lips would find their way to my neck. I hadn't told her that it was an instant trigger spot for me. I didn't want to pressure her by telling her that every time she brushed her lips or fingers along the column, I'd be on fire, ready to jump her if that's what I thought she'd want.

When she shifted again and brought her torso against mine, I couldn't suppress the moan. Her mouth hesitated on its journey to my lips before I tilted to kiss her. One moment she was on the attack, the next I was. Tasting her, just a hint of the dinner's flavor still lingering, satisfied me completely. When her tongue darted along my lower lip, I moaned again before it plunged inside. The constant back and forth of aggression and yielding was always my ideal. Most relationships required one or the other. With M, both emotionally and physically, she seemed to like the give and take as much as I did.

The hand curled around my arm slid onto my stomach. Our kiss deepened as her touch set off a blaze so hot I wasn't sure if I'd be able to douse the desire this time. It roamed gently then skimmed upward, a thumb brushing against the swell of my breast. After a few seconds, her palm and fingers slid up to close over my breast. I groaned loudly, arching into her hand, not fully realizing just how much I needed this.

"Okay?" She pulled back to glance at me. Our code word for: "Do you need me to stop?" Usually, I was the one asking.

"Yes. Are you?" I thought her eyes showed the same desire I felt, but this was a huge leap for us.

"I want this. Before we leave. Before I meet your family."

My heart pounded so hard I thought it was trying to make a break for it. What I'd thought was a further exploration of touch had just turned into a precursor for sex. As much as I wanted to make love with her, I needed her to know that timing alone wasn't the right reason to take the next step. "I want whatever you want, M. But meeting my family shouldn't be part of this decision. Caleb's staying with his grandparents, and we've got a two-room suite, so no one's going to know about our sleeping arrangements. There's no pressure."

"I want you, Briony," she stated without trepidation. "You're gorgeous and so damn sexy. I just want to be like anyone else in a normal relationship."

Normal was an important word and concept to her. I'd never liked the word myself, but I understood that her definition was different from mine. I'd hoped for the chance to be sexually intimate with her, but she'd already given me so much without it. "I love you, and you're incredibly sexy, too. So much it hurts not to touch you sometimes. If you're sure, you set the pace. Anytime you want to stop, we stop."

Her eyes showed equal parts gratitude and desire. Fire blazed so hot inside me I thought I might singe her fingers. She stood and reached to pull me up with her. Unsteadiness shook my legs as I felt the weight of responsibility for being someone's first, for hopefully erasing the memories that plagued her. I should be the self-assured one. Instead, she was guiding me to my bedroom with what I hoped wasn't the false confidence I'd seen her display in front of her colleagues and my friends.

"May we turn on a light?" Anxiety marked her question as we entered my room. "I don't want it to be dark."

I squeezed her hand and pulled her with me to turn on the bedside lamp. A soft glow spread around us. I recognized some of that false bravery in her even without the word choice she'd used. "Is there anything else you don't want? You can tell me whenever something makes you uncomfortable, but if there's something I need to know now?"

She shook her head, looking away for a moment. "Just don't...hold me down."

"Honey." I tilted over to reestablish eye contact. My insides tightened at her request. "We love each other, and we're about to make love. Nothing about this is going to be like what you've known. I trust that about you. I need you to trust that about me. At any time, you can tell me to stop what I'm doing or stop completely. Please, tell me you get that?"

She slid her arms around my waist and gripped tightly, releasing a shaky breath. "You're amazing, Briony. I'm so fortunate to have found you."

"I feel the same way, M." And I'd put words in her mouth before, but I felt more sure of her love than if she told me every day.

She tilted up to kiss me, reigniting the flame of passion I'd felt back on the couch. Her hands slid to my hips and underneath my turtleneck, pressing against my abdomen as they moved upward to take the garment with them. I raised my arms to help her shed my shirt. Her eyes slowly moved from mine down to my mouth and onto my neck before finally landing on my bra. She let out another shaky breath at the sight of the pink lace. My nipples hardened under her gaze, and I mimicked her unsteady exhale.

Pants now unbuttoned, they practically flew to the floor as excited about this as I was. "Sit," she requested with a voice that sounded like it came from a dry mouth. She knelt before me and reached to unzip my boots and take them and my pooled pants off. Now in only my underwear and she fully clothed, I couldn't remember feeling more vulnerable in my life.

Hungry brown eyes quelled some of the nerves as she pressed me back against the bed, following to kneel over me. Fingers pressed against my lips then traced down my neck and into the groove between my breasts. Gooseflesh rose in their wake, and my body squirmed under the examination.

I reached up and gripped a button on her shirt, an unspoken question in my eyes. She nodded before returning to record every ridge and plane and valley of the skin on my torso. In no time I'd stripped away her shirt only to be tantalized further by the silky stretch cami that lay underneath. Cranberry in color, I was so happy to see that she wore color close to her skin. She bent upright to pull the shirt from her shoulders in haste before slanting back to continue with her exploration. My fingers unhooked her slacks and pushed them over her hips. She didn't seem to want to help me, but my insistent groan got her to briefly pause and go up to her knees, pushing her slacks off those incredible legs. I barely got my fill of her chic hipster undies before she pushed up onto her fists above me.

Holding steady for an interminable length of time, she nearly made me beg before she lowered her body to mine. "God!" The sudden burst of breath carried her exclamation, and it rebounded inside my head. Her face, which had tilted up at the shout, dropped back to kiss me with the passion of her exclamation.

I wrapped my hands around her waist and let my fingers search under the cami while her lips worked a spell on my own. Her warm, smooth skin acted as a magnet for my fingertips. I wasn't sure I'd ever be able to pry my hands away from her. Especially not when her mouth caressed mine with a proficiency that could make me sit up and beg. And her hands, meandering with purpose now, left no spot untouched on my upper body.

Teeth grazed my bottom lip, nipping softly. Coupled with a delightful squeeze of my breast, I went a little wild, clutching her to me and rolling us over. She stared at me, eyes wide with surprise but nothing in them told me to stop. Leaning up on my elbows, I looked down the length of her, spending a little extra time on her fantastic legs, relishing the feel of her stretched out beneath me. When I could tear my eyes away from the provocative flare of her hips and toned legs, I concentrated on the small breasts just inches from my own. An overpowering need to get to them forced my hand under the clingy silk and up to grasp the treasure I knew awaited me there. As soon as the firm flesh filled my hand, I felt her body still. I glanced up and watched as the light in her eyes dulled.

"M? Stay with me." I requested, fearing she'd just checked out.

"I am," she replied immediately. Then, with what seemed like a programmed movement, she brought her hands up to my breasts.

I bit back the hiss of pleasure, not wanting to let her sidetrack me. Releasing her breast, I hoped to jolt her into abandoning her automatic responses to either our position or my actions. "You look like you want to escape. I need you to stay with me, be here with me for this. If you want me to stop, tell me. It's okay."

She turned her head away on the pillow, clenching her eyes shut. When she finally spoke, her voice was hoarse, assuring me that she'd snapped out of whatever trancelike state she'd entered when I'd touched her breast. "That's not fair to you."

"Honey, having you here is like a dream." I nudged her chin over to look at me. "We don't have to do anything else. Just don't slip away inside your mind. Be here with me. Please try."

M nodded, focusing on me with cautious eyes. "Maybe if we just..."

She hesitated so long I had to prompt, "What? Please tell me. You can ask me for anything."

"I don't want to be cruel to you." She looked away to mask the frustration. I drew my fingertip down her nose to get her focus back. "Maybe if we just slept, I might be able to..."

"Sleeping sounds wonderful, M. Whatever you want," I assured her when she couldn't finish what she thought she might be able to do. Rolling to the side, I tried to ignore the throbbing ache from unfulfilled desire. I'd meant what I said about being happy to have her here with me, in bed, out of bed, just so long as she was nearby. I let out a deep breath to calm my racing heart and turned to face her. "Do you want—"

Her hand slipped into mine, cutting off my question of whether or not she wanted to be in my arms. She tilted toward me and wrapped her other hand around my arm. "You're so beautiful." Her lips brushed against mine in a soft kiss.

I wanted to gather her in my arms, but this had to go at her pace. The fact that she was settling in to sleep with both hands on me gave me everything I needed. "This is beautiful, M."

Falling asleep with the woman I love. Yes, beautiful was the right word.

Chapter 35

Sometime later, I awoke to pitch darkness. I rarely woke at night unless Caleb was sick or had a nightmare. Only Caleb wasn't here, and neither was M. Before the dread set in, I heard the faucet turn on in my bathroom.

"M?" I called through the door after a quiet knock.

"Come in."

She was rinsing her face when I opened the door. I tried not to focus on the curve of her ass as she leaned over the sink because I was being good, but it wasn't easy. And let's not discuss her sleekly muscled legs. *Be good. Killer legs. Be good!*

"Sorry, did I wake you?" she asked after patting her face dry.

"Couldn't sleep, honey?"

"Bathroom break. Then I forgot I hadn't washed my face or brushed my teeth before we went to bed. I never really thought about the logistics of..."

"Sleeping with the person you love?" I finished for her with a gentle smile.

A becoming shade of crimson crested along her cheekbones. "Yeah," she confirmed, setting my heartbeat into a gallop. "Hope you don't mind, but I swiped a new toothbrush out of your drawer."

"You're welcome to anything." I grabbed my own and stood at the other sink.

In the mirror's reflection, she watched me brush my teeth. Her hand darted out to graze my shoulder. Those slender fingers glided over my skin until one hooked under my bra strap. "You can't be comfortable," she guessed.

I waited for her fingers to make the move toward the bra clasp, but they merely slid across my shoulder blades to brush against my nape. It probably didn't occur to her that she could take off my clothes even if we weren't about to have sex. She had no frame of reference for intimacy. If it took years, I'd make sure that we changed that about her.

"I'll put on a t-shirt. Are you warm enough?" I stroked her bare arm, trying to keep my eyes from staring at the beaded nipples making themselves obvious under her cami. I could be good, if I focused on something else. What had we been talking about? Oh, yes. I tugged gently on her arm to bring us both into my walk-in closet. Rummaging through my shirt drawer, I picked out two long sleeved shirts and held one out for her.

"I'm fine, thanks." She turned to give me privacy, but I pulled her back.

"It's okay to watch me change for bed." I loved the shy smile she gave me. It told me she wanted to be there, but she hadn't known she could be. "In fact, it's okay to help." I flaunted a sure grin meant to ease some of her seriousness. "Relax, honey, I can manage on my on. For now."

I reached around and unhooked my bra, letting it slip down my arms. Her eyes flared before blinking twice then closing slowly. If it weren't for the ragged breath she let out, I might have felt a little insecure. But the suddenly unsteady woman in front of me said I had nothing to worry about. My first time half naked in front of a woman in nearly four years, and she couldn't look without needing a moment to regain composure. Yeah, that'll do.

Once the collar of my shirt had cleared my head, I saw that she'd opened her eyes again. The color returned to her cheeks, not in embarrassment but the flush of excitement. "Shall we try to get back to sleep?" I asked, knowing it was still a few hours until morning. As exhausted as she'd seemed, I doubted the three hours we'd had would be enough.

"Okay." She hesitated before stepping backward then changed her mind and stepped toward me. Her hands grasped my hips, and she tilted up to capture my lips. "You're the most beautiful woman I've ever known. Thank you for tonight."

"Wow," I whispered the exclamation. "You're awful good at that." I kissed her again, just enough to rev up my heart but not enough to unleash my lust for her.

Twirling her around, I pushed to get us moving back to bed. We slid under the covers and scooted closer together. She turned on her side again and reached for my hand. "Let me hold you?" I formed a question out of my request.

It was too dark to make out her features, but I could tell she wanted to. After reaching both arms out and a few awkward adjustments where she attempted to hold me to her on her side, she sighed. "I don't know how..."

"Here." I stretched my arm out on top of her pillow, swallowing the lump in my throat. She'd never experienced this simple closeness before. "Slide over, put your head on my shoulder and wrap your arm around my waist." She followed my instructions and tentatively added some of her body weight. "That feels nice. You good?"

"Yeah."

"Goodnight, M."

"Goodnight, sweet."

I didn't know whose gasp was sharper. It was the first time she'd used an endearment with me. I wanted to jump out of bed and dance around the room. Instead, I gripped her tightly against me with a sense of peace that I hadn't known in years. But the problem with getting everything you wanted was that you couldn't get to sleep with your focus so divided. Add to that, her hand under the hem of my shirt, and I might be awake until dawn. Her warm breath dusted across my throat, and the weight of one breast tantalized with every one of her breaths. When her hand started to move, I thought I might have a seizure from the mix of sensations.

After ten torturous minutes, her lips pressed softly on my neck then moved across my clavicle. That teasing hand grew bolder, skimming higher until fingertips swiped the swell of my breast.

They traced the curve before moving up to grasp my breast. When her fingers flicked my sensitive nipple, an explosion of breath escaped me. It wouldn't do to spontaneously climax, not when I was supposed to be the experienced partner. But damn, she was making it difficult to contain myself.

Her mouth found mine in the darkness, and I was temporarily distracted from how good her hand felt. She finished the kiss with a nip and shifted to lean more of her weight on top of me. "The light?"

My heart felt like someone was taking running leaps and bouncing off all of its chambers. She was ready. If her unabashed kiss hadn't told me, then her confident tone did. I nodded, knowing she'd feel my answer even if she couldn't see it. A second later, one of the bedside lamps clicked on and the muted light didn't cause the glare it usually did. Not with the sight of her beautiful face over mine.

"Hey," she spoke softly. "I shouldn't have let you put on this shirt."

I smiled at the suggestive tone. "You're here to help me take it off."

She grinned and brought both hands to the hem. Together we pulled it up and over my head. Her eyes landed back on my breasts before a hand followed. For someone not used to touching, she was unbelievably good at knowing exactly what amount of pressure, which were the most sensitive spots, and how much my nipples could take.

"So, so good, M, feels amazing. I love what you're doing."

Her brown eyes widened momentarily before an appreciative smile overtook her face. I didn't know if I'd said something that she really liked or—talking, that must be it. She probably hadn't imagined that communication added to the sexual experience. I lost that thought when her mouth kissed downward and closed over a nipple, tongue flicking softly at first then with relentless precision.

"M, please, touch me. I need your touch."

She pulled back and curled her fingers under my panties. I lifted my hips to help her strip them off. Her lips parted as her eyes raked down my body, starting at my face and ending at my toes. "Stunning," she whispered reverently. "Spread your legs." Her eyes snapped to mine with a look of panic. "If you want, I mean."

I tried to make sense of the panic, but nothing came to mind. She'd asked me for something she wanted; then she'd backtracked. Oh, that's it. She hadn't really asked me; she thought she'd ordered me.

"Honey," I reached for her hand. "You can tell me what you want or what you want me to do at any time. I'm open to almost anything, and I'm never going to think what you ask for is wrong. If I don't want to do it, I'll tell you why. You can phrase it however you like. I'm always going to take it as a request not a command, okay?" She nodded, blinking back her emotions. "I need to know that I can do the same with you."

"You can."

Because she seemed to have stalled a bit, I encouraged, "Tell me again what you want."

She leaned back in to kiss me, all tension draining from her body. "I want to touch you. I want to feel you moving under me when I do. Part your legs."

Quick learner, I liked that so much. She slipped her palm between my thighs to help me give her what she wanted. I should be embarrassed by how excited she'd find me. Yet the only thing I could focus on was how full my heart felt.

She rose up over me, hovering for a moment before settling between my legs. Her head lifted up from watching where she'd placed her hips against mine. "Hey," she blurted in that soft tone I'd grown to crave hearing. Somehow the shy greeting seemed perfect in that moment.

"Hey, yourself." I lifted up to kiss her because she was too close not to and because I had to feel her mouth on me again.

Her hands started to roam. I brought mine up to stroke her back and onto her bare shoulders. She slid one hand down my side and onto my hip. Curling her fingers under my thigh, she brought my leg up so that I was completely open to her. She looked into my eyes as her hand drifted over.

"Yes!" I cried out when her fingers finally reached home. Tracing lightly at first then delving in through my folds.

"Wet, hot," she gasped when her hand began to love me. Swirling, then stroking, our hips meeting and retreating as her head dropped her mouth to mine at first before moving over my chin and onto my throat.

My head tilted backward to give her better access. Sucking and licking, her mouth and tongue pleasured the hottest spots on my neck, both satisfying and torturing me with the need for more. "Inside, M, I need you inside me."

Her eyes came back as her fingers swiped against the entrance of my sex. We both groaned as she shoved two fingers into me, inch by slow inch. When she slid all the way inside, I raised my legs and locked my heels around her waist. Her strokes were slow at first; then she sped up somehow knowing exactly what I needed. Testing how fast and hard she could drive into me, she found a rhythm that left us both panting ragged breaths. "Come, Bri, come for me."

That wasn't a request, not that I could fight it. I arched toward her, my breasts brushing hers, my mouth finding her neck and taking some of the soft skin between my teeth before the whirl of tingles turned into an explosive orgasm. "Yes, M, all for you!" I shouted, pitching up under her. Contractions squeezed her fingers, imprinting their shape inside me.

"You're beautiful," she spoke hoarsely after my spasming body had relented to periodic shudders. "Flushed here." Her free hand touched my sternum. "And here." It trailed up to my neck. "I have to taste you." She disappeared from my hazy view.

My equally cloudy brain didn't realize what she was saying until her mouth closed over my still throbbing clit. "Oh God! Wait, wait," I screeched at the surprise attack.

Her lips pulled back immediately. Brown eyes looked worried for a moment before she realized I wasn't upset. She used that husky voice that sent shivers through me. "Again, Briony. I want to feel you come in my mouth."

I struggled up onto trembling elbows to get a better look at the incredible sight of my lover staring at me from between my thighs. She flexed the fingers still inside me, causing a loud groan before I collapsed back against the bed. "Your turn next," I warned her, not bothering to look at the satisfied grin I was sure she now wore.

She brought her mouth back to nibble lightly along my labia then latch onto my clit. Sucking, licking, and flicking while she began a slow pump of her fingers again. It had been too many years to count since I'd orgasmed twice in one lovemaking session, but I could feel it starting again. Her mouth pulled off with a loud smack, and I whimpered at the loss only to feel a cool stream of air hit my over sensitized clit. My hips jerked erratically as the cool reprieve gave way to the insistent suctioning of her mouth again. "Yes, yes, yes!" I cried at the crest of another glorious wave of pulsations.

She slowly kissed her way back up my body, stopping at my breasts a little longer than the rest. She didn't slip out of me until my body stopped shivering. "Perfect. You're absolutely perfect."

"I am?" I questioned incredulously, giving her a lethargic smile to go with my completely sated, strung out body. "You're the perfect one, love." I kissed the mouth that had just spirited my body into orbit.

Tilting my hips, I rolled her to my side, extending the kiss until the sensation came back into my extremities. I moved my hand over her abdomen and hooked my fingers under her camisole. "Time for this to come off."

Her eyes dilated with desire not fear, nodding in encouragement. I pushed the cami up until her breasts were uncovered. Dark rose nipples, more red than pink, stood at attention on small, firm breasts, perfectly sized for her petite frame. I'd never been with someone shorter and smaller than me. Deceptively delicate, but I'd felt the power in her frame when she'd brought me off twice and loved me with her whole body. Elegant muscle definition marked every slope and curve of her torso, matching the overall tone of her arms and legs. I wanted to feel those muscles jump under my fingertips and caress them with my tongue. I wanted to know every inch of her body.

"Okay?" I checked in with her because her eyes flicked away after I'd gotten the cami off. She nodded again. "You're beautiful, M. Gorgeous, sexy, amazing."

Her hands grabbed mine and brought them to her underwear, a signal I happily complied with. Seeing her completely bare, gloriously naked, I nearly choked on the beauty of this moment. My body rolled onto hers, a thigh nudging between hers. I watched her eyes carefully because, as uninhibited as she'd been while making love to me, this was entirely different.

"You feel almost as good over me as you did under me." She shared in that barely recognizable husky voice.

"We can do this with you on top. Or sitting up or standing or any way you want. Anything you want." I just wanted her, whichever way she was most comfortable.

"No, like this. I need to know it can be good like this. I need you to make it good like this." She clutched the backs of my arms to keep me from moving off of her. "We'll try the other positions tomorrow. Or next week. Or next month." A shy smile squeezed my heart more than the words had.

"Or next year, or next decade and every decade after that," I finished, letting her know I wanted her forever. Her eyes sparkled and she took in a shuddering breath at my promise. "We'll make it good together, M."

She slid her hand down to tangle with mine then brought it to her breast. I took over because I couldn't stop myself from touching her. Her breast filled my hand, the spiking nipple tickling my palm. She gasped when my fingers flicked across the erect nub. Gently, because she needed to know that making love could be gentle before we worked on what she liked best. If she was anything like me—and so far she hadn't disappointed—she'd want soft and sweet one day, vigorous and fiery the next.

I leaned down and licked her nipple once then again. Her body stiffened but not in fear. Closing my lips over her areola, I pulled the nipple into my mouth and lashed my tongue mercilessly. She bucked underneath me, nearly dislodging my lips.

"You like this?" The cords in her neck strained with her head nod. "Say it."

Brown eyes blinked at me in surprise. If I hadn't been wearing a wicked smile, I might have frightened her. "So much, Bri. I like everything you do to me."

My lips pressed wet marks down her body, still too tense for my liking. But unlike when we'd stopped earlier tonight, this tension had nothing to do with not being able to experience this properly. She was tense from fear of the unexpected. Her body had already surprised her; I could see that in her eyes.

Placing my shoulders between her thighs, I studied the swollen, glistening lips of her sex. Downy soft hair, a shade darker than the sun lightened strands on her head covered her mound in a neat trim. I reached forward with my tongue first, wanting just a taste. Savory, part sweet, part tangy, pure heaven. The jerk of her hips brought on a smile before I kissed her fully and let my tongue lick the length of her.

"God!" she exhaled again. Her hands flew to my head to have something to hold on to when her body kept sending her different signals. I assumed she'd climaxed before, but by the erratic jerks and lunges as I explored then sucked her clit into my mouth, I started thinking she may never have experienced an orgasm before. For someone with her sexual history, it wouldn't be that wild a possibility.

"Okay, M?"

"Yes, I just, it feels, yes," she managed roughly.

I replaced my mouth with my hand and climbed up over her, keeping up a constant touch but needing to be near her when she exploded. "Can you handle more?" Her brow furrowed followed by a harsh blink. "I want to be inside you." When the immediate acceptance I'd hoped for didn't happen, I instructed, "Tell me no." I wanted her to know that she could stop anything before it happened or as it was happening.

"Yes," she whispered with a steady gaze.

That wasn't the word I expected. "Inside?" I clarified.

Her hands slid down the length of my back to grab my butt. "Everywhere you want to be, Briony. I want that from you and with you."

"I love you," I whispered, suddenly choked up. Her mouth met mine to seal the promise we'd just made. I wanted her so much, but mostly I wanted her to want this as much as I did.

My fingers, having kept up a light rub along her slick creases, moved lower. Poised at her opening, I popped off her mouth to watch her eyes while I entered her. Her teeth bit into her lower lip as soon as I penetrated her, but she kept my gaze. The tight channel clutched my fingers as they slid deeper inside. Slick warmth drew me in, the sensation familiar but also unique as was everything with this woman. Once buried to the hilt, I held them steady until she got used to being filled and let up on her tension.

"I'm kinda fond of that lip, honey. Don't bruise it," I teased gently before leaning down to coax her lips into a kiss. Soft nips at first, a method to distract from all the thoughts racing around her brain. The technique worked as I felt her mouth demanding more until it started to devour my own.

When her hips started rocking to invite friction, I took the cue, pulling almost all the way out then thrusting back inside. A slow rhythm at first until her hands started pressing more insistently on my rear, helping to drive us at the pace she wanted. My hips combined with my thumb and fingers to take her higher and higher. I stopped kissing her to watch the sway of emotions in her eyes.

"It's...can't...want," she stammered, head tilted back against the pillow, muscles straining in her neck and shoulders. A light sheen of perspiration broke out over her body.

Seeing her on the cusp and hearing her try to voice what she was feeling confirmed that she'd never experienced this before. "You're there, honey. Let it happen. Come," I directed, thinking she might not understand that she didn't have to hold in the sensations she was feeling.

"Briony!" she shouted as she heaved up against me, sliding her hands up to grip my back. Her sheath squeezed divinely at my thrusting fingers. The pulsations of her climax lasted over a minute, her body shaking and twitching throughout.

I stilled my thrusts and pulled out slowly to let her work down from her peak, all the while kissing lightly along her neck and onto to her breasts. Eventually, the shaking turned to sporadic tremors. I looked down at her, stunned from her climax, and my heart began a new joyful rhythm that I couldn't remember ever experiencing. M had done this for me, healed every hurt I'd ever known, made me happier than I could remember being in many years.

Her breathing slowed to short exhales as her body finally stopped trembling. She gazed at me with those expressive eyes. They made me feel like I was experiencing every emotion running through her. I'd never been this connected with anyone, like our souls were talking to each other.

It was a while before she spoke, and it wasn't anything I would have guessed she'd say. "Mabel." Her voice was so soft I almost didn't hear her. "Old fashioned, I told you."

I drew in a shaky breath, tears pooling in my eyes. Old fashioned, fitting, lovely. As perfect as the woman in my arms. "Mabel," I tested in a reverent whisper. "I love your name, Mabel. I love you, M."

"And you have my heart, Briony."

Now, that was the best way I could ever imagine for her to finally tell me she loved me. Worth the wait. Just like she'd been. Twice blessed in my life, and I planned to share that fortune with this woman.

Chapter 36

Checking my watch, I realized it had been nearly an hour since we'd last touched. I glanced about the family room then into the kitchen. Kids, the tiny ones, and one lazy husband lounged in front of the television. Megan's mother and mine were chatting over coffee in the kitchen. Megan's sisters were negotiating a détente between two of the kids over a much prized Christmas gift. Our dads, one of the husbands, my son, his cousins, and my girlfriend were nowhere to be found.

Since arriving at Megan's parent's house for Christmas dinner, M had stayed close by. After dinner, though, she'd rounded up the kids for the first of their snowball fights. Every fifteen minutes or so, she'd wander back to me. A simple touch, sometimes a word or two, but basically she'd used me as her touchstone all evening. The terrified look she'd shown as we'd been getting dressed at the hotel had been replaced by cautious delight. I'd wanted to wrap her in my arms and never let go, but she'd bravely faced yesterday's festivities with my parents on Christmas Eve and done so well in meeting Megan's family today. With every return to me this evening, her brown eyes grew more and more amazed. She was learning what family meant today, and I loved every person here for it.

I wandered out into the living room and checked the front window. Found her. Steve, Sadie's husband, was monopolizing her attention despite the two kids trying to get her to join their King of the Hill game. Stepping out onto the porch, I sucked in a deep breath as her eyes immediately found mine. The crisp winter air didn't shock my system as much as her glance could.

My dad joined their conversation as soon as Caleb and his cousin moved back to the mountain of shoveled snow where kids were sliding from the top and taking out anyone else trying to climb up. I knew the smile I wore had the potency of moonshine, but I couldn't help it. The men in my family had become very protective of M. One or the other had kept her in their sights at all times. Caleb knew her fairly well, but I'd only told my parents that she was shy and easily overwhelmed.

When she excused herself to head over to me, her smile looked just as wide as mine. She'd been so fearless with this trip. Especially when I thought about how terrified I'd been while meeting Megan's family the first time, and I didn't have all the social anxieties that M did. In a few seconds she'd touch me again. My skin tingled in anticipation.

"She's a tiny little number, isn't she?" Sadie said from right beside me.

I jumped at the sound, breaking eye contact with M. "Jeez, Sadie, give me a heart attack, why don't ya?" I glared up at her five foot ten inch frame, an inch taller than her younger sisters.

"You're so out of it, lil' sis." A hand dragged me over to the chairs on the front porch. "She's distracting, I'll give you that."

I glanced back at M, who'd stopped walking toward me as soon as Sadie appeared at my side. She'd been especially cautious around Megan's sisters. I couldn't blame her. They were intimidating without the added issue of being the sisters of my late spouse. Caleb rushed up to her and tugged on her hand toward the hill. I cringed for her. I knew she was getting used to Caleb's touches, but she wasn't at the point where she could freely accept contact from anyone but me.

"Is she a pied piper? Hypnotist perhaps?" Danica plopped onto the armrest of my chair. Her eyes were trained on the hill where M had taken charge of the seven kids with but a few words and now had them building snowmen peacefully. "Although with my kids, it's probably more like a snake charmer."

"You should see her with her students," I bragged.

"I've never seen my boys do anything without fighting." Danica shook her head in wonder.

"You guys like her, right?" My stomach twisted with nerves as I awaited their verdict. I hoped that my choice would be acceptable to Megan's sisters. I knew that Meg would approve, actually felt it in my heart, but her sisters were harsher critics.

"Like her?" Danica frowned.

Sadie turned with a serious look and my stomach coiled more painfully. Their usual open expressions and warmth had cooled considerably. "Assure me that she's a lesbian, lil' sis. If not, I'm gonna have to kick her ass for the crush I'm now convinced my husband has on her."

Danica burst out laughing, but I could only manage an audible sigh of relief. I caught Sadie's husband striding toward M again, starting up yet another enthusiastic conversation. He'd always been a great guy, but I'd never been able to get him to talk very much. He preferred to lie low at the family affairs, let his wife do the socializing while he controlled the kids. I figured it was the opposite whenever they visited his family.

"He's finally got someone to talk to about architecture." I knew that his profession was his greatest passion outside his family.

"You'll notice she didn't answer my question," Sadie spoke to Danica like I wasn't there.

I let out a chuckle. "You don't need to worry, Sadie."

"That's not really what I was asking and you know it."

"Yep, details, please." Danica winked.

"Not a chance." I stood firm despite knowing the sisters openly talked about their sex lives to each other. I'd never joined in and cringed any time I saw the three of them huddled together on this porch. I'd told Megan that I never wanted to know how much she shared with her sisters about us specifically. Way too embarrassing.

"You might as well. I'm guessing you don't want us asking M." Danica raised her brow, the sinister intent obvious.

"You will not!" I practically barked at them.

"Ooh, feisty thing, isn't she?" Sadie teased.

"Always was, or so Meg used to say," Danica agreed. "The way she spoke, I was ready to leave my husband for you."

"You guys!" The heat that consumed my face fought off the chill of the winter night.

"She's blushing. A modest sex goddess." Sadie was relentless.

"Cut it out!"

"All right, take it easy. Meg gave us an instructional manual anyway. Almost all of it she learned from you. Some really creative stuff."

"My sex life hasn't been the same since." Danica nodded her head sagely.

I felt like crawling into a small space. "You guys suck." I hoped the finality in my tone would end this topic.

"Apparently, you used to suck on—"

"Stop it, now, Sadie." It usually took two warnings with them before they backed off.

"Fine, fine," she relented.

"My kids want to go back with her." Danica watched as her boys, Caleb, and three of Sadie's kids stood around M in rapture while she showed them how to juggle snowballs. She could juggle, too? Every day I found out something new about her. I had a feeling that I'd still be learning things about her even after ten years together. For a professor who loved to learn, that quality made her the perfect match for me.

"Mine want to keep her locked in their bedrooms. My husband talks more to her than he does to me. Mom and Dad are ready to build an addition to their house to keep her nearby as ready child care. The only way I'm not spending my life insanely jealous of her is if you tell me she's lousy in bed," one-track-mind Sadie persisted.

I bit down on the immediate denial, knowing they were just trying to get a rise out of me. I hoped the blush from just thinking about what M and I had done in bed over the past week didn't tip my hand. Yes indeed, the perfect match.

"No comment?" Danica persisted. "If you didn't look sickeningly happy and embarrassed right now, we might be able to give Sadie a little peace. Too bad, sis. Bri's new love is good at everything, I guess."

"You like her, right?" I asked again.

"We like her," Sadie confirmed, throwing an arm around me.

"We're happy for you." Danica squeezed my other shoulder.

"You guys are the best."

"Second only to you," Danica said.

"In bed," Sadie piped up like she was completing the fortune she'd pulled from a fortune cookie.

"I'm leaving now." I got up to their cackles of laughter. As intimidating as their chat sessions had been when Meg was involved, I much preferred my role as the one who was talked about rather than having to feed their voracious appetite for gossip.

"Hiya, Mom." Caleb appeared at my side once I'd stepped off the porch.

"Having fun, handsome?"

He nodded, his wind burned cheeks bobbing up and down in the dusk. "I love M." The admission slipped out easily and wasn't entirely a surprise even though it was the first time he'd told me. My heart couldn't help but swell at how sweet my son was.

"I'm glad, big guy. I do, too."

"I know. It's okay, right? That I love her?" His eyes flicked away for a moment. "Mommy wouldn't be sad, would she?"

My hand flew to my heart at his guilty tone. I bent to look him in the eyes. "Not even a little, Caleb. She'd want us to be happy. We can love someone else, and it won't ever take away from how much we loved Mommy."

"That's good. I like loving M." He turned and searched her out in the crowd. "It's okay that she doesn't say it back. I know she loves me, too. Hank says she doesn't say it."

Surprise rocked my head back. "You told her you loved her?" I wished I'd been there to hear it and help M manage her reaction.

"After dinner. She was so quiet, like maybe she wasn't having any fun." He nodded with a grin. "She hugged me, and I know she doesn't hug people very much either." His grin turned sly. "I think we should ask her to marry us."

"Do you now?" I managed through my shock. It was quite a lot to go from realizing he loved her to wanting her permanently in our lives.

"Yep. Then she could live with us, and we could love her all the time. I don't think she's had much."

"Who made you so smart?" I ruffled my hand through his hair and pulled him against me. "I'm glad you love her, kiddo. I want her to live with us, too. But we're not going to rush her, okay? Forever can be scary to some people. It takes them a little longer to get there. So, let's give her some time."

"Mm'guess," he agreed. "You'll tell me when we can ask her, though, right?"

"I'll tell you when I'm going to ask her. Deal?"

"Maybe she'll ask you." His hopeful little face was heartbreaking. I almost wanted to agree, but I knew it was unlikely that she'd be proposing any time soon, if ever. As uninhibited as she'd become around me, I wasn't certain that asking for someone to share a life together would even occur to her. First, I'd have to convince her that sharing a life was possible.

"We're going to let her take whatever time she wants. No pressure, no guilt, no expressing wishes that she lived with us, no asking for her to stay with us just because you want it. Am I clear, bucko?" I had to make sure he understood that even a hint of permanence before she was ready might prompt her to pull back or away completely.

"Yeah," he offered with a sigh. "I'm still going to tell her I love her, though."

"Good plan. I love you, Caleb. I'm so proud of you."

"Thanks, Mom." He hugged me quickly and ran back to his cousins.

I headed around the corner of the house toward my rental. If I was going to stay outside, I'd need a parka. When I resurfaced from the car, a hand caressed my back. That was the touch I'd been missing for an hour. "Hey, M."

"Hey, sweet." She pressed up against me as soon as I turned to face her.

The feel of her body against mine ignited a memory flash of last night's lovemaking session. She hadn't been kidding about trying all possible positions. She was more imaginative than I was. Last night had been up against the hotel room door, and I was certain it wasn't solid enough to muffle our sounds of ecstasy. My heart started pounding as the heat of desire surged through my body, rendering the need for the parka useless.

"How you holding up, beautiful?"

She smiled softly, resting her head against mine. "Everyone's so nice to me." That amazed tone returned. "I really like Megan's family."

"And they really like you. So do Mom and Dad, but I told you that last night."

"This is all so..."

"Overwhelming, intimidating, frightening?" I offered, gripping the back of her neck to get her to look at me. "No one's crowding you, are they?"

"No, it's okay." The immediate denial spoke volumes, as did her arms coming around to hug me tightly. She hadn't wanted me to tell anyone not to touch her, probably because she thought I'd have to tell them why. All day, I'd watched her suffer through a few hugs and other affectionate touches, hoping she wasn't in agony. I figured the constant return to touch me helped calm some of the burn she might feel from the unwelcome ones.

"One more hour. I promise." I planted my lips on her cheek.

She turned into my kiss and cranked up my heartbeat with her soft lips and tongue. When she pulled back, she was breathing as heavily as I was. "I've missed kissing you today."

"So have I. It's been way too long since we left the hotel this morning." Where we'd barely managed to leave the room without ripping off the clothes that we'd just put on. But we knew that Caleb was waiting on us before he could open the rest of his presents at my parents' house, so we managed to behave ourselves. A full day of festivities later, I wanted nothing more than to wrap myself around her and never let go, preferably in private.

She glanced away to check if we were still alone. Her eyes came back to mine with a hesitant look. "Caleb and I spoke earlier."

"He loves you," I supplied for her.

Her eyes widened. "He told you?"

"I knew it before he said anything, but I'm glad he told you. Are you okay with it?"

She nodded with a soft smile. "I adore him. He's a wonderful little boy."

"Yes, he is, but you seem amazed that he loves you." I tightened my arms around her when she shrugged and broke eye contact. "Before we got on a plane, I did a little search on the Internet and found out what Mabel means. Do you know?"

Her eyes snapped back to mine with the change of topic. A blush crept onto her face, letting me know her answer.

"Tell me, M, tell me what your name means."

It was a whisper, but she finally admitted, "Lovable."

"Yes, it does, Mabel. And it's about time you knew how appropriate it is for you."

"For the first time since Kathryn died, you've made me believe it." The blush remained, but I knew that Kathryn had told her, probably often, why she'd picked her name. I wished she was still alive so I could hug that terrific woman for protecting and loving M the way every child deserved.

"You're definitely lovable, M."

"You're the one who's lovable, Briony."

My chest expanded with so many emotions I couldn't pinpoint one more than any other. "That works out well for us, then, doesn't it? We're in love. I've got a son who loves us both. My family wants you to stay in Vermont permanently, which means they love you. I couldn't ask for a better Christmas gift."

"It's been my best ever, but I only want to be in one place permanently." She closed her eyes, expelling a long breath before bringing a hand up to pat my chest, right over my heart.

"Only if I can be in your heart permanently," I responded when I found my voice.

Making sure to lock eyes with me, she spoke in that husky smooth voice, "You already are."

I was pretty sure I'd never lose the smile she just put on my face. Maybe it wouldn't take as long as I thought to convince her of forever.

M's Epilogue

Ten months later

Have you decided on anything, ma'am?" the tentative salesperson asked.

I probably should have been friendlier when I came in or when she asked me what I was looking for or if I wanted to try them on. Briony always warned me that I could come across as intimidating. Deceptively intimidating, she'd told me once. The deceptive part, she said, was due to my short stature.

"No one expects a shrimp to be intimidating," she'd said as I'd pinned her onto her back on my bed. I'd made her pay for that comment. She'd called me other names that night, too. Two hours of not letting her use her hands while I could do anything to her gave her plenty of time to come up with other names. But I knew she liked being taller than me. I never gave it much thought, but I was glad it made her so happy.

"Perhaps I could tell you a little about each?" the saleswoman persisted.

"No," I replied then thought of Briony and added, "Thank you."

"Nothing catches your eye then?"

"I," I started, but the words tumbling around in my brain couldn't seem to make it out. Why did I always get like this? Talking in front of my classes, that was a breeze, but having a conversation with a stranger made it so I couldn't form enough words to make a sentence. "If I could..." What? What was I trying to say to this poor woman who just wanted to do her job? Well, and make a commission. She didn't wake up this morning and think, *Gee I hope I get to the store and have to help the most socially inept person I've ever met in my life.*

And what the hell was I thinking? Driving two hours into Washington so I wouldn't have to worry about anyone I know seeing me make an ass out of myself. Not to mention the asinine idea floating in my head that made me drive this far from my home on a rare day off from work. I had papers to grade, a mid-term to write, and two businesses to look in on.

But I was here, looking at these beautiful creations, thinking...I don't know what. That somehow, my life, which had been such a mess until a year ago, could be normal or as close to normal as someone like me could ever get. And these things, if I could just pick one, would make that possible.

As much as I'd noticed little differences in myself around Briony when I first met her, it wasn't until she'd called me beautiful that it hit me. She might actually like me; she might actually think of me as something other than a freak of nature. Until I recognized how hard my heart beat in her presence, I'd only ever felt the warmth of usefulness to Lucille and the respect of my students. That had always been enough. I'd never cared that my colleagues thought I was odd because I wouldn't socialize with them. I didn't care that many of them, my boss included, were afraid of me. Nor did I care that I only had one real friend. None of that mattered. I worked hard. I loved my work. I helped Lucille whenever she needed. I listened to Hank and let him know that he was important. Life was the best I'd ever known, even if I was only a shell of a human. Until I met Briony and she teased me about my name. Until she treated me like I was normal. Until she thought of me as beautiful and I felt my heart beat for the first time in my life.

That was why I was here. Why I'd driven 126 miles on a Saturday morning. Why I'd stopped pacing along the sidewalk and pushed through the door. Why I'd accepted the help of the salesperson.

"Just browsing or are you getting close to making a commitment with your boyfriend and wanted to get a head start on ring shopping?"

My eyes flipped up from the array of engagement rings to the salesperson's face. *Terrific.* Should I explain that the ring wasn't for me? Should I share that I wanted to propose to my girlfriend? Should I tell her anything at all? I wished Briony was here. She'd know what to do. She could talk to anyone, anywhere, anytime. I rarely had to say anything to strangers when she was around. But she couldn't be here because this would be a surprise. I wanted it to be a surprise, if I could do it.

With one last glance at the rings, I said, "Thank you for your help. They're lovely, but I'm just looking." I nodded once and turned toward the exit. Maybe I'd try another store next week or next month.

After only two steps toward the door, it opened and I heard a familiar voice. "I almost didn't come in."

Looking up from the ground, I took in the sight of the voice's owner. Willa, my only friend, until I met Briony, that is. *Even more terrific.* I'd driven 126 miles to a jewelry shop that specialized in engagement and wedding rings specifically to avoid running into anyone I knew, much less the one friend I'd had before Briony opened my world. Truly, what were the odds of that happening?

As if reading my mind, Willa offered, "My plane got diverted to National along with several other flights, so the airport is out of rentals. I was on my way to the place up the street and saw you heading out without a purchase. Didn't find one you liked?"

My eyes darted to the door. I knew it was five steps away, thirty-eight steps to my car, 126 miles home, seventeen steps to the building's staircase and sixty-two steps up to my apartment. Two hours and fifteen minutes tops. I could start walking now, taking those steps back to safety, back to only a semblance of a normal life, but a hell of a lot better than I'd ever imagined for myself. Fuller than I'd ever dreamed possible. And I could do it without a word to Willa. She'd never hold it against me. She'd call me next week to hang out, even if I walked out without saying anything to her now. But I wasn't that person anymore. I had learned that over the last year. Briony's faith had changed me.

Still I didn't know what to say to my friend. She knew why I was here. With a quick flick of her eyes through the window, she'd guessed instantly. No judgment, no condescension, and best of all, no warning that I had no right to be thinking about this.

"Would you give us a moment, please?" she asked the salesperson who'd started packing away the tray. The woman smiled, obviously thrilled to be dealing with a normal human who understood the subtleties of interaction among the species. "M?" Willa stepped closer to me, nowhere near the limits of my expanded personal bubble, but still closer than I let anyone other than Briony and Caleb get to me. "I came inside because I thought you might be considering not going through with this. I wanted to give you a few extra moments to rethink that if you needed them."

I felt pressure build behind my eyes. I knew tears would start to well if I didn't gain control. I looked behind her, counting the steps again. I did need those extra moments. I did. I came here for a reason. I owed it to the woman who'd saved my life by showing me what life was really like. I nodded once, not bothering to reestablish eye contact.

She came a little closer. "You're thinking you have no right to be here."

Yes.

"The question's not on your part," she guessed.

Exactly.

"You think she might stop, maybe not in five years or ten years, but sometime, she'll stop."

God, yes.

"Because no one could ever love you for the rest of your life."

I bit back a groan. How did she know this? We didn't have these kinds of conversations. Willa, in particular, never had these kinds of conversations. It was why we were friends.

"I was like a robot before I met Quinn," she admitted softly. "No feelings at all. I wasn't looking for a relationship. My job didn't pay me much, and if I started my business, it would be three years before I'd make a dime. What the hell could I offer? When I met Quinn, she was a pro basketball player. She's beautiful, fans adored her, she's funny and clever. She honestly had her pick of anyone she came across. I certainly didn't look like any of the gorgeous women who threw themselves at her. All I kept asking myself was, what did she see in me?"

You're generous, even without the money you now have and offer freely; you're generous with your time and attention. You're smart, gentle, respectful, nonjudgmental. You're kind. You're a good friend. I wished my brain would allow these words to come out of my mouth. How could she not see these things?

"Then I realized that I loved the person I became when I was with her," she continued. "Loved, not just liked. Quinn did that for me. And I no longer feared that she might not stay as long as I could. I'd risk everything for one more day with her."

An involuntary breath left my lungs. "Yes," I heard myself whisper. I loved how Briony made me feel about everything, including myself. How one touch or one look or one smile from her would temper my nerves. She brought me calm, something I hadn't known since I was nine years old. And when she was near, I never had to be on alert. She made me feel like life wasn't something I had to struggle through. It was something to enjoy.

"I'm going to do something that will scare the crap out of you, my friend. Get ready," she warned.

Please, don't touch me! I screamed inside my head but remained where I was, resigned to accept the unwelcome touch if it came. *This is Willa. She won't hurt you.* The thought calmed my elevating heart rate.

She reached past me and pulled one of the mirrors over. "Look in the mirror for a sec."

I shook my head, not just because I avoided mirrors in general, but because the only person I felt comfortable watching me look in a mirror was Briony.

"Please? I want you to see something about yourself." She waited for me to relent. "Good. Now, I'm going to say one thing, and I want you to keep looking...Briony."

I felt the smile start in my heart before it bloomed outward, reaching my face. I knew Willa wasn't calling out to her because I would have known if Briony was nearby. At first, it was her lovely scent—mountain crisp air with a hint of evergreen and roaring whitewater—that helped me identify Briony's nearness. Now I could feel her presence, even in a crowded room.

"See?" She watched me look at my reflection. "Just her name brings out that beautiful smile. You're in the right place, M." She walked around me to examine the tray of rings, mercifully letting me stop looking at myself. "I wanted to give you a little encouragement, but I'll let you shop on your own." She started for the door.

"Did you...How did you choose...?" My brain went into super speed mode again, and I couldn't piece all the words into the right order.

She looked away, studying something on the street before turning back. "Didn't have to. Quinn beat me to it." She laughed at my best stunned face. "Briony might do the same, so you better make a decision."

"No." Briony wouldn't. She'd wait for me. Like with every first in our relationship. Our first touch, our first kiss, our first hug, our first time making love. She'd wait for me because she would never, ever rush me. She seemed content to wait for me for everything, but I didn't want that for her anymore. She loved me, and I loved her, even if I was too much of a freak to tell her. I'd never loved anyone like that. Never. I'd known unconditional love for nine years from Kathryn. Then nothing. Not until last year when I met Briony Gatewood, the love of my life. The woman who made a real life possible for me.

"All right." Willa held up her hands.

I could tell she didn't believe me. She didn't know Briony well, though. She thought that because Briony often spoke her mind that she'd ask me first. But I knew that wouldn't happen. As surely as I knew that, if I managed to propose, Briony would be okay with not having a ceremony. That she'd agree the best step for us would be to buy a house together rather than me moving into hers. It would make things easier to combine our lives and introduce Caleb into a new living situation. She'd want our house to be an original, one we could restore to its 19th century splendor. She would insist on that because she knew I loved period architecture but would never insist on it. She would do the insisting for me, everything else she'd leave up to my comfort level. God, I loved her.

I'd worried that conducting our class together again this past summer and practically living together while Caleb was away at camp might smother me. Instead, I loved waking up with her, starting our day together, and really loved walking through the door after work and hearing her call out a sweet greeting, obviously thrilled that I was back for the night. I loved how the little things that I considered selfish on my part, she considered romantic gestures. All summer, I'd bring her coffee in bed to coax her into sharing breakfast with me before I ran off to my first class. She thought it was sweet when really I just wanted to spend time with her before I had to get to work an hour earlier than she did. Or how much she adored when I'd heat up a towel in the dryer while she was taking a bath after a long day, just so I had the excuse to dry her off when she was done. Best of all were the simple moments like movie nights when I could run my fingers through her hair or caress her neck any time I wanted. No, being together every day hadn't been a hardship at all.

The clincher, though, the reason I was here on this Saturday morning, happened last weekend. I'd been terrified that if Briony ever saw my potential for violence that she'd leave me. I'd probably leave me. But she'd watched me incapacitate an inebriated man who'd grabbed at her outside a restaurant last weekend. She'd watched how quickly and efficiently I'd pulled his arms off her shoulders and swung him around to brace his arm in such a painful way that he'd dropped to his knees. I'd threatened him in a low voice that I no longer recognized. Instead of being horrified, she'd placed her hand on my shoulder and spoke soothing words until I let him go. Her arms came around me, whispers of thanks and assurances of love filled the air around us. She hadn't been afraid of me or thought of me as a freak. She hadn't wanted to end things because I could become a person she didn't recognize. She still loved me. So, here I was, taking a chance at forever because, even though she didn't know everything about me, she loved everything about me. I felt that instinctively. As much as I loved everything about her, and I couldn't manage my life without her anymore.

"Traditional is nice." Willa brought me back from my musings. She was glancing down at the rings.

"Not right, though," I joined her. It was probably why I couldn't decide. Then it hit me. "Yellow sapphire, to compliment her eyes."

"Very nice." She stared at me a little longer, knowing the limitations of my comfort level. "If I leave you to it, can I catch a ride home with you? I promise no more of this crazy talk out of me."

"Sure," I agreed, relieved that she understood that I had to do this alone. I tossed her my keys and pointed toward where I'd parked the car. She took her leave without another word. Willa had always been the perfect friend for me.

I turned back to the salesperson. "May I see your yellow sapphire stones, please?"

"Of course," she seemed pleased by my transformation. She took away the traditional diamond rings and resurfaced with six loose sapphires and seven rings with similar type stones.

I saw it instantly. The right one. But I inspected each, saving it for last. Yes, perfect. A thin, platinum band for her long, delicate finger. Two carats, nothing too garish because Briony wouldn't like that. Roundish, but I was sure the cut had a proper name. I could picture it on Briony's finger. Picture it there for decades to come. She'd be happy with a simple wedding band. I knew that because of the pictures I'd seen. She'd worn a gold one before. I wanted something different. I wanted her to have everything that she couldn't have before when she'd married so young. Something singularly beautiful. She deserved beauty everywhere because she brought so much of it with her.

"That's the one. If it's not a size six, I'll need it resized." I handed the ring over to the salesperson. I couldn't wait to wear whichever matching band Briony picked, to make it clear to everyone that I was the most fortunate person in the world because I finally belonged with and to someone as amazing as Briony. "How many letters can be on the inscription?"

The saleswoman looked at me strangely. She didn't understand why I would have what she thought was my own engagement ring inscribed, but it wasn't up to me to make her understand. "Depends on the font, but usually forty or so."

Like with the steps, I knew already how many letters I wanted. I just needed to know the limit. "Here's what I'd like inscribed." I handed over the piece of paper.

I love you, Briony. Always, Mabel.

A breath escaped before she looked back at me. I could tell she thought it was unoriginal, but only because she didn't know me. I would finally say it. Briony had waited more than a year, seemingly content to have me tell her in other ways. But when I proposed, I planned to say the words I hadn't said since I was nine. I'd tell her I loved her, then because the words were so hard for me, she'd at least have them with her always.

"I'll pick it up next weekend." I handed over my credit card.

This encounter would probably be one of those that the saleswoman would recount for people in the future. Freakiest, but fastest high priced sale she'd ever made. I didn't like that she'd remember me. Almost enough to make me go to a different store, but I didn't think I could go through it again.

As soon as I had the ring in hand, I'd go about planning how to ask my love if she'd share her life with me. It would have to be special, something as unique and spectacular as Briony. Something that would make her feel as amazing as she always made me feel.

* * *

Red tinged the horizon as the sun began a slow decent. I was stretched out on a chaise lounge on the balcony of our suite overlooking the Atlantic Ocean. Virginia Beach, it was my first time here, and for a short weekend trip, absolutely perfect. I felt the calm of the color wash over me as I settled into my chair.

"Everything all right, M?" Briony said from the chair beside me. "You had fun today, didn't you?"

I tilted to look into the golden brown eyes of the woman I loved. The calm I felt just looking at her overpowered any serenity I could get from a lovely sunset. We'd spent the day sea kayaking, something she loved doing, something I'd never tried. It was fun, but I knew I'd feel the burn of the unused muscles on Monday when we returned to work. "I believe I've told you that I always have fun when I'm with you, Bri."

A beautiful smile erupted on her face. I loved that I could put that smile there, that I was the cause of such happiness for her. It was a new sensation for me and I craved it. "Same here, honey. I'm so glad you suggested this getaway. It's just what I needed."

With four classes this semester, I'd known that her schedule was starting to bring her down. I didn't like seeing her so overworked. I planned to pamper her for the next two months until she could get a more manageable schedule in January.

"You've been kinda quiet all day. Anything you want to share with me?"

I loved that she knew me so well. That she knew I was holding onto something, but that I might not want to spill it yet or ever. She always allowed me this luxury. It was one of the reasons I knew she was perfect for me. Yet her question sparked a thumping heartbeat and extended breathing. I'd suggested this weekend away for a reason. This was the moment. Romantic, spectacular, and with Briony, as always, breathtaking. I just had to open my mouth.

"Are you over-thinking last night, honey?" she asked.

Heat touched my face. *Last night.* I'd asked her for something neither of us thought I'd ask for, but I needed her to know that I trusted her completely. She'd never suggested I couldn't trust her, but I knew with someone as insightful as Briony that she might harbor that slight doubt in the back of her mind. She'd forgive it, and had been for a year, but I didn't want that for her anymore. "Last night was..." I searched for the perfect words to describe how safe and loved she'd made me feel when we finally defeated what had always been my nightmare.

Fear surfaced in her eyes. I could tell she was aching to say something, but she would let me talk. She was brave enough to listen to me tell her that I'd hated it and didn't want that ever again. That what I'd asked for now reminded me of the horror I'd gone through, but this time she'd been in the starring role.

I reached out to stroke her soft cheek and down to her throat. I loved her neck, loved burying my face there, brushing my lips against it, taking her skin lightly between my teeth, running my tongue over the spot that never failed to bring out that husky moan. I lived for that sound. "You were wonderful. It was exactly what I wanted, what I knew you'd do for me."

Her breath of relief brushed across my cheek as she popped off her lounge and slipped onto mine. "You were wonderful, too, you know."

"You weren't shocked?" I asked, just a hint of humor because I already knew her answer.

"I saw those scarves and just about passed out, beautiful." She snuggled in closer to me. "I didn't think you'd ever want that, but I'm so glad you asked. I've loved when you've tried it with me. It makes me feel almost liberated."

The exact opposite of what I thought bondage would be. The exact opposite of my own experiences as a child when I was held down. It was why I'd asked for it. Until last night, I still felt there was one obstacle left in the sharing of our bodies. We didn't need to strive for something uncommon when it came to lovemaking, but she hadn't lied when she'd told me that she was open to almost anything. I loved being adventurous with her, but when it came to bondage or limiting movement, that particular activity had always been one-sided with us. She'd let me restrain her, but I hadn't let her reciprocate, not that she'd ever asked. The act calls for complete trust, and she'd given it to me. So, last night, I decided it was time to give it to her. "I'm glad you didn't pass out, sweet. We wouldn't have had as much fun."

"If it wasn't last night, what's got you so quiet today?" She shifted to swing her legs over my lap. The feel of her in my arms, with her wrapped around me, it was the closest I could get to heaven.

"I was thinking about the first sunset we shared together. Do you remember?"

Her eyes sparkled. "Yes, do you?" That teasing tone made me smile. I wasn't the one who brought up sentimental topics.

"You were on a date—"

"Which you rescued me from."

"And you cajoled me into an entire day together." I squeezed her tighter against me.

"Don't start with me." The tone was firm, but the smile gave away her mischief. "You wanted to go. You could have said you were busy."

"I wasn't. I saw you with that woman, and my quiet Saturday turned into a quest to spend more time with you."

"You never told me that."

"I'm full of surprises."

"Don't I know it?" Her eyebrows fluttered, making the heat return to my cheeks.

"We spent the day together and you picked a restaurant where we could watch the sunset from the patio."

"It was beautiful. Not as beautiful as you, but still pretty beautiful."

I made sure to lock eyes with her. "Nothing's as beautiful as you, Briony."

"Sometimes you floor me, you know?"

"Now you know how I always feel around you."

She sucked in a breath as moisture prickled her eyes. Quickly, she leaned in and kissed me, her soft lips pressing then pulling on my own. I loved kissing her. She was the only person I've ever kissed and somehow I lucked into an expert. "What's got you all nostalgic?" Her hand pressed over my heart, and I knew she could feel my elevated heart rate.

"When I'm uncomfortable, I count." That just slipped out. I hadn't meant to say that. I'd never told anyone. Not even a therapist. I could tell by her startled expression that she didn't expect me to say that. It wasn't the answer to her question, but she wouldn't go back to that now that she had this.

"You count?" she prompted, tightening her arms around me.

"I didn't mean...I, that wasn't what—"

"Honey? Tell me, please?"

"It's a habit. It allows me to concentrate on something else when things are happening that I don't like or make me uncomfortable."

She nodded encouragingly but there was a fleeting look of pain that skittered across her face. "Do you still count?"

"I know how many steps from my office to my classrooms, from my apartment to my car, from the street to the park. I know how many seconds it takes to get through a line at the supermarket, to pick up my dry cleaning, to have a conversation with the dean or for an average office visit with my students. If I've done it, I know how long or how much of whatever it is that I'm doing. I count almost everything and with everyone."

"Does it bother you?"

"Sometimes."

"Can you stop it?"

"Most times, yes. If it's really nerve racking, then no. It took 9,932 seconds from the moment we stepped through Willa's door last Sunday night until we left."

Her eyebrows rose. "You're still nervous there?"

"Yes, but I like being there with you. I'm starting to like it better than making you go alone. I'm glad you only go once a month, though."

"I like it, too. Is there anything I can do to help you?"

"That's just it." I took a breath. "I count with everyone. It never mattered how comfortable I was with them." I tightened my grip on her and looked directly at her beautiful golden eyes. "Until I met you. I didn't notice it at first because it was such a habit, but then I realized that even when you pressed me on things or asked me questions that no one else had asked I didn't count. You're the only person that makes me so comfortable I don't use that protective habit. If you're near, I need only look at you and I stop counting."

"Oh, Mabel, I'm so happy to hear you say that. I'm glad I can do that for you. You're my comfort, too, you know?"

"You're the best thing that's ever happened to me, Briony. I know we've only known each other for a year and a half, but I've never felt so comfortable with anyone before."

"Me, too." Her fingers came up to stroke my cheek.

"I missed you so much when you were in Vermont and I was in Chicago. I don't want to have to miss you like that again."

"Me, neither, honey. I should have changed my plans so I could at least see you for a few days in Chicago."

"Next year, we'll have to plan something else."

Her smile split her face as it always did whenever I brought up a future. It's why I knew she'd be open to my question. "Next year?"

"Yes." I leaned in and kissed her this time. I loved her taste, her smell, the feel of her wrapped around me. "I miss you when you leave my place at the end of a date or when I leave yours before Caleb wakes up."

"I've told you that if we have an honest conversation with Caleb, we could change that. You could spend the whole night. He knows that sex is between people who love each other. He knows how we feel about each other."

That was one of my favorite things about her. She knew I loved her without my having to say anything. She said it for me, sometimes in passing, sometimes teasing, sometimes when she wanted me to know just how much she loved me, but I'd promised myself. "And you know how I feel about you?"

She blinked once but smiled serenely. "Yes, you show me every time I see you. Every time you look at me or touch me. I know."

"And that's enough?"

A small frown appeared. "Of course, M, have I given you the impression that it isn't? I love you, and I feel your love when I look in your gorgeous brown eyes that tell me almost everything that you're thinking."

Smiling, I teased, "What am I thinking right now?"

"That you like having me practically sitting on top of you, that you thought I looked sexy paddling through the water today, that you can see the four grey hairs on my head but won't say anything about them, oh, and you can't live without me."

I laughed. There was so much I loved about this woman, but her wit ranked almost as high as her kindness. I also loved that she had a dark edge to that wit. It clashed so well with her compassion. "I love having you in my lap. You always look sexy to me. You're delusional about the grey hair, but when you finally get it, you'll look just as gorgeous as you do know. And no, I can't live without you, but more importantly, I don't want to live without you."

Her smile faded a bit as she registered my serious tone. Her hand pressed against my chest to take in how hard my heart was beating right now. She looked like she wanted to say something, but I wanted to get this out.

"This past year has been the best of my life. I feel like I must have gone through everything that happened to me when I was younger so that when I met you, when you gave me your love, I'd feel like I deserved it. You make me feel like nothing will ever hurt again. Like I belong, finally, and I'm so proud that you've chosen me." I brushed away one of the tears that had dropped onto her cheek. "I love you, Briony. Will you honor me as my wife?"

"Oh, God, M!" She breathed out, a small sound leaving her throat. "I love you so much."

I waited for more, but her face was now buried in my neck and small tremors ran through her body. I stroked her back, helping to soothe her. "Bri?" I asked when I felt her take a cleansing breath and push herself back. "Is that a—"

"Yes! Yes, M, I want nothing more than for us to be married."

"Thank you." I didn't have time to think about how stupid that sounded before her lips landed on mine, kissing with such abandon that I forgot everything else I wanted to say. She'd always had that effect on me.

"I'm so happy you asked. I wasn't sure how much longer I could hold off before the hints about a permanent future with you became anything but subtle." She grinned, a sheepish look making her all the more lovable.

"I've been thinking about it for a while now, but we'll have to talk to Caleb. I know some people don't think their kids should have a say, but I don't want to force myself into Caleb's life."

She laughed, a soft rhythm of sound that caressed me. "He wanted to ask you to marry us last Christmas."

"What?" I couldn't hide my shock.

"Kids are like that. He knew how much I loved you and he'd just told you that he loved you. He wanted you to live with us right then. He's going to be thrilled about this."

I let out a breath of relief. "That's wonderful." I reached down under my chair and pulled the ring box out I'd been hiding. "I got this for you, but if you don't like it, we can get one you like."

She stared wide-eyed at me before looking at the box. "You bought me a ring?"

"I wanted to give you a ring. Is that all right? If you'd rather not, we can just get wedding bands. I thought you could pick those out for us." I lifted the lid on the box so she could see the ring.

"It's beautiful, honey. I love it. I love you."

"I had it inscribed."

She carefully pulled it free and read the inscription. Tears sprang in her eyes again as she looked back at me. "I love you, too, Mabel. Always."

As with everything about her, those words told me that I'd never want for anything else ever again because of her.

Other Publications by Lynn Galli

VIRGINIA CLAN

Wasted Heart (Book 1) – Attorney Austy Nunziata moves across the country to try to snap out of the cycle of pining for her married best friend. Despite knowing how pointless her feelings are, five months in the new city hasn't seemed to help. When she meets FBI agent, Elise Bridie, that task becomes a lot easier.

Imagining Reality (Book 2) – Changing a reputation can be the hardest thing anyone can do, even among her own friends. But Jessie Ximena has been making great strides over the past year to do just that. Will anyone, even her good friends, give her the benefit of the doubt when it comes to finding a forever love?

Blessed Twice (Book 3) – Briony Gatewood has considered herself a married woman for fifteen years even though she's spent the last three as a widow. Her friends have offered to help her get over the loss of her spouse with a series of blind dates, but only a quiet, enigmatic colleague can make Briony think about falling in love again.

Finally (Book 4) – Willa Lacey didn't think acquiring five million in venture capital for her software startup would be easier than suppressing romantic feelings for a friend. Having never dealt with either situation, Willa finds herself torn between what she knows and what could be.

Forevermore (Book 5) - M Desiderius never thought she could have a normal life filled with love. She gets all that and more when she marries Briony, including an amazing foster daughter named Olivia. Every wish she'd never allowed herself to voice became real. When someone from Olivia's past threatens M's newfound family, can she carry on in the face of loss or will it push her back into a life of solitude?

OTHER ROMANCES

Uncommon Emotions – When someone spends her days ripping apart corporations, compartmentalization is key. Love doesn't factor in for Joslyn Simonini. Meeting Raven Malvolio ruins the harmony that Joslyn has always felt, introducing her to passion for the first time in her life.

Full Court Pressure – The pressure of being the first female basketball coach of a men's NCAA Division 1 team may pale in comparison to the pressure Graysen Viola feels in her unexpected love life.

About The Author

Despite having a job that requires public interaction, Lynn Galli prefers to avoid people while at work. Her off hours are split between writing and helping family and friends with tasks that often trigger lower back pain. She lives in the Pacific Northwest where she's learned to embrace overcast weather, coffee, and software programming. Writing is her cheapest and most effective form of therapy.

CPSIA information can be obtained at www.ICGtesting.com
Printed in the USA
BVOW08s0503100616

451197BV00001B/73/P